WILD STEAMY HOOK-UP

PIPER RAYNE

Cover Photo: Wander Aguilar

Cover Model: Travis S.

Cover Design: Mad Hat Covers

First Editor: Joy Editing

Second Editor: My Brother's Editor

Proofreader: Shawna Gavas, Behind The Writer

Wild Steamy Hook-Up

He's the quiet brooding guy who's owned my heart since I was sixteen but has refused to claim it.

I'm the naïve woman who believes that someday our time will come.

I just didn't realize that someday would include waking up in Vegas with a raging hangover and a ring on my finger.

If we believed in fate, maybe one of us would've trusted that something more powerful than ourselves interceded because our love is one of tangled vines. As twisted and frayed as they've become over the years, they've never broken.

An annulment seemed like the easy way out. We should've known it wouldn't be fate that intervened, but our Italian Mamas. They can deliver Oscar-worthy performances when heaping on the guilt.

We thought it'd be easy to pretend to be a happily married couple in front of our families for three months and then say we gave it our best shot and go our separate ways.

But nothing is easy when it comes to Dominic Mancini and me. Nothing

WILD
STEAMY
HOOK-UP

CHAPTER ONE

Dominic

The sound of thumping in my head continues and I roll over, throwing my hand over my face before it suddenly stops. I groan. Thank God. But then it starts up again, and though it takes me a minute, I realize it's not actually coming from my head.

I push up on my elbows, and though the sound might not be coming from inside my head, the throbbing sure as hell is. I look at the unfamiliar room, and it takes me a second to remember that I'm in Vegas for my cousin's bachelor party.

I push up off the bed and trudge to the door. When I swing it open, I find my youngest brother, Carm, in the hallway.

"Jesus, bro, I don't wanna see your dick. Although I am happy to know mine's bigger."

I glance down to find that I am indeed naked. Ducking

into the bathroom, I grab a towel and wrap it around my waist.

"Fuck off. What's going on?" My voice is rough, and I realize now that my mouth tastes like ass.

"You're late for bungee jumping. Everyone is waiting. Where'd you disappear to last night anyway? One minute you're sulking at the bar and the next you text us to say you're out."

I stare at him for a moment, trying to figure out the answer to his question. He uses the opportunity to slide to the side to look inside the room. I run a hand through my hair and down my face, blowing out a breath and trying to get myself together.

"What the fuck is that?" Carm points at my finger.

I lower my hand, staring at a silver ring around... shit... my *left* ring finger.

What the actual fuck?

"Holy shit!" Carm laughs hysterically.

I cough on the bile shooting up my throat.

Carm weaves to the side of me to look behind me at the bed and the woman who might be my... God, I can't even say the word. There's absolutely no way I got married last night, no matter what's on my hand.

I take my brother by the shoulders. "You can go."

He fights me, his head swiveling to try to catch another glimpse.

I don't know why I got *married* last night, but I do know *who* I hooked up with and Carm cannot find out unless I want a call from Mama. Everyone knows that out of my two brothers, he's the last one to trust with a secret. He doesn't mean any harm. He just can't help himself.

"What about bungee jumping?" he asks.

We're in Vegas for my cousin Luca's bachelor party,

which was supposed to be a fun weekend away—something I rarely allow myself. Instead it's turning into a colossal fuck up.

"Make up an excuse for me. And do not tell anyone what you saw. Just say you can't find me, or I'm puking, or—I don't really care. You're a good liar, do what you do best."

His feet halt on the carpet. "Low blow. I don't lie about stupid shit anymore, just ask Bella."

His pitiful tone, the one he's used his entire life when the truth hurts, says I've hit a sore spot. Usually I'd smooth over my comment, but today I've got more pressing shit to do than make sure Carm's ego stays intact. "Go."

"But what—"

"Bye." I click the door in place softly, though I want to slam it.

But the last thing I want is to wake the woman sleeping in my bed. I need a minute to sort this out and try to figure out what it means, what the repercussions are. I don't need to worry about our lack of a prenup because she's not the kind of woman who's after me for my money. Quite the opposite actually. Most of the time, I think she resents it.

I strip off the towel and pull on my boxers before sitting in the chair by the window.

What the hell have we done?

I weave my fingers through my hair and blow out a breath, looking at the bed.

Her long tan legs from half a summer spent in the Hamptons only brings back memories of last year. But last year hurt like a bitch. I had to say goodbye to her then, so why would I have willingly gotten together with her now?

Grabbing my phone, I pull up her alias, Marge, (just in case my brothers ever saw) and check what happened last night. Damn, I initiated the conversation.

Me: *Hope the dance competition is going well.*

Then the memory floods in like a tidal wave. The innocent text exchanges once I saw her dance studio was in town for a competition. Each of us mentioning where we were staying. Her asking me out for a drink and my stupid horny ass accepting. Going to her hotel bar, gambling at blackjack, drinking some more. Her studio won the competition and she was excited to celebrate, and I, of course, took any excuse to be with her.

I'm an idiot.

She stirs under the sheets, her dark wavy hair sprawled on the pillow. I examine her while her eyes are still closed and see the matching silver band on her left hand. Then I spot a few crumpled up papers on the floor near the edge of the bed. I must've taken them out of my jacket or pants last night when we returned.

When I open them, the reality of the situation comes crashing down on me like a crumbling building.

One of those papers is a marriage license, and the two names listed have me squeezing the bridge of my nose.

Dominic Anthony Mancini and Valentina Daniella Sommerland

I can't help the small smile that forms on my face when I think of how we all used to make fun of her name when she was younger. No one said her first name without also using her middle and her last—though it was Cavallo back then. To the grade school kids, using her whole name was fun, and it stuck all through high school.

Now, she's Valentina Daniella Mancini, though I don't hold my breath—she'd probably expect me to become

Dominic Anthony Cavallo. Doesn't matter that Cavallo isn't even legally her last name anymore.

Why the hell is my mind heading in a direction this situation is never gonna go?

As I'm wondering whether we'll qualify for an annulment, her eyes pop open. She smiles at me, her naked body sliding across the sheets. She's always been slow to wake up, though I only know that from the rare occasions she let me sleep in bed with her.

"Hey," I say.

"Hi." She wiggles up to rest her back on the headboard, making sure to keep the sheet over her.

"No need to be shy. I am your husband, after all." I raise my hand, the stream of light coming through the curtains making the silver band shine.

Her breath leaves her in one rush and her mouth hangs open. She snaps her head down to look at her perfectly manicured hand, with red polish that matches her toes and plucks the cheap wedding band we must've gotten along the way as though it's a piece of foil. But it's not foil. It's the real deal.

I pick up the marriage license from the side table and toss it on the bed next to her. "Do you want breakfast, Mrs. Mancini, or should we each call our attorneys first?"

No sense in pretending this situation is anything other than what it is—a mistake.

Her plump pink lips that have always turned me on dip, and she twists the sheet in her fingers.

Yeah, figured as much. Attorneys it is.

"I'll let you get dressed," I say, walking around the bed, and picking up my pants and shirt from last night. Anything goes in Vegas, no one will give me a second look.

"Dom," she sighs.

But I put up my hand, hurrying to get the hell out of here before I ask more questions like why, drunk or not, she'd agree to marry me. "No worries. Not sure how we got ourselves in this predicament, but I'll handle it."

I slide the ring off my finger and put it on the nightstand. Then I walk out the door, and this time, I do let it slam shut.

Valentina isn't meant to be mine. She's always belonged to someone else. This time, I'm determined to remember it.

CHAPTER TWO

Valentina

I pull back the sheet once the door shuts with Dom's departure. The ass didn't even let me get a word out before he assumed he knew what I was going to say.

He *always* assumes.

I pick up the paperwork he tossed beside me. How the heck did we end up married? When his text came through last night, I was still on a high from the kids at my studio winning the competition and figured one drink couldn't hurt. We drank, we danced, we gambled... and from there, everything goes fuzzy.

When I attempt to get out of bed, my head spins and I have to sit back down. After a few deep breaths, I push my hair out of my face and notice how silky it is. That means I must've showered when we got back here last night.

A hazy memory surfaces. I touch my lips and sure

enough, they're tender—Dom is a biter. I stand again, and this time my brain doesn't swim in my skull, so I head to the bathroom. I don't have to remember every detail of our night to see how much we enjoyed one another. Small nibbles mark the tops of my breasts and down my torso, evidence of Dom's attentions.

No man has ever enjoyed mapping out my body like him. And that's probably why I answered that text. Dom and I might not be a good fit long term, but in the bedroom? That's where we're a perfect fit.

Somehow, even with his easy dismissal of me and pissed off attitude, I crave him again. To have those big hands unlatch my bra only to hear the groan that escapes him as though it's the first time he's seen me nude.

I shake my head. My demented head, which refuses to accept that Dominic Mancini does not care about me. The only person in this world he cares about more than himself is his mama, just like any good Italian boy. And after that comes money.

Moving around the room, I pluck up my garments one by one. The small skirt I changed into when he said he'd meet me at the hotel. The skimpy panties I hoped he'd strip me out of. The push-up bra and tight shirt I wanted to entice him with.

Lastly, I snag the marriage license off the bed because I won't allow him to go all caveman and take charge of the divorce. When I stuff it in my clutch, a picture falls out and flutters to the floor.

I pick it up, all my energy depleting when I stare at the photograph. I fall back on the bed. We're both clearly glossy-eyed and sloppy. I can't believe they let us get married. Isn't there some sort of law against that? The wad of cash the officiant holds makes me think Dom paid him off, but who knows?

It's the two of us and I'm leaning against him with my arm around his middle smiling at the camera. Instead of his eyes being on the camera, he's looking down at me with an uncharacteristic warm smile on his face.

How come getting that man to smile makes me feel like Wonder Woman?

LATER THAT EVENING, I'm walking through the lobby of my hotel—which is two down the Strip from Dom's—thankful there's no way I'll bump into him again. Maybe we can get a divorce without having to interact.

Since the dance competition is over, most of the parents and kids from my studio have headed back to New York. I opted to stay an extra night, knowing how drained I am after nationals. I figured I'd have a spa day and spend the day relaxing. And thank God I thought ahead, because if there was ever a day I needed to relieve some tension, it's today.

After a day at the spa, the dull ache of my hangover is almost a distant memory. Nothing a shot of caffeine won't fix at this point. I debated not keeping my appointment but freaking out by myself in my hotel room did seem like a good idea. At least at the spa I stood a chance of finding some peace.

With a fresh glow to every inch of my skin, I feel confident that I've scrubbed Dom from my consciousness. Okay, that's a lie. But like I always tell Ryder, success and effort go hand-in-hand.

I smile politely at the gentleman serving customers at

the Starbucks. My plan is to kick this hangover then veg out in my hotel room until my flight tomorrow.

"Valentina Daniella Cavallo?"

Hearing that name raises the hairs on my neck. It means they're from my old neighborhood back in Brooklyn. The fact that the voice sounds eerily similar to my new husband's has dread forming in the pit of my stomach.

I glance over my shoulder and the dots connect. "Enzo Mancini?"

I really hope I feigned surprise well and he believes that I don't already know he's here for his cousin's bachelor party. Or that as of last night, I'm his new sister-in-law.

"I thought that was you, but then wondered what the chances were that both of us are in Vegas?" He hugs me briefly and kisses my cheeks. "Sorry, just got back from bungee jumping with the guys." He glances down at his roughed up athletic gear. "Our cousin, Luca—you remember the Biancos from Chicago?"

I nod.

"He's getting married, and they're having their bachelor and bachelorette parties here."

He's speaking, but all I can concentrate on are his similarities to Dom. Enzo goes on and on about how one of the guys with them today threw up as he was free-falling because they got a little crazy last night. He and his brother share the same nose and smile. Then again, Dom doesn't smile very often, so maybe I'm imagining it. Enzo was pretty serious back in the day too, whereas Carm was always the live wire.

"So you'll come then? Dom and Carm will both be there, and it's totally casual."

I'm flustered, so I step up in line. "I'm sorry, I must have zoned out. I'm just coming from a day at the spa. What were you saying?"

What I really want to ask is what Enzo's doing here at my hotel, rather than the one they're staying at.

"Dinner. Tonight. It's just a small group of us. It's our last night before we head home tomorrow. Join us."

I'm able to delay answering by ordering my coffee. If I join them, it'll ruin Dom's mood.

Before I can pay, a twenty slides across the counter to the cashier. "No, Enzo, I have it."

"My treat. It's been so long since we've seen each other. What have you been up to?"

The cashier takes his order—a caramel latte with skim milk. That doesn't really sound like Enzo, but who am I to judge?

"Not much. I was here for a dance competition."

"Oh, you're still dancing?"

He's polite enough to act as though he hasn't heard the rumors over the years when we both know that our predominantly Italian neighborhood in Brooklyn gossips enough to put Page Six in the *New York Times* to shame.

"No. I own a few dance studios in the city. My kids were performing," I say.

"Oh, that's awesome."

We stand by a pillar, and though I don't have to pry—since I know all about his life over the past two years—I ask because *he* doesn't know that. "And you? Keeping out of trouble?"

A grin with wattage that would match the Strip's electricity bill lights up his face. "I met someone." He nods toward the coffee place. "Hence, the caramel latte. I'm not even staying at this hotel."

He laughs, and I can't help but smile. Back in the day,

the Mancini boys were all so driven to succeed that I never thought I'd see the day when a woman nailed them down. They broke a lot of hearts without even knowing it. The fact that a woman scored Enzo says she's probably amazing.

"I'd love to meet her."

His hand touches my arm. "Tonight."

The barista calls out our drink orders. Being the gentleman his mother raised him to be, Enzo picks up both cups and hands me mine.

"It'll be fun," he says. "Are you here with someone?" I have no chance to answer. "Bring him along."

Don't worry, he'll be there.

"Nah, I'm by myself, but it's a family thing."

He tilts his head. "No such thing. You know that. Come on." He pulls out the one thing I've feared this entire time— his phone. "Let me grab your number and I'll text you the details."

"Um... well..."

"Come on. Did you hear about Carm? He's practically got the ball and chain around his ankle now too. You can't tell me you don't want to meet the woman who wants to spend all her time with Carm?" He laughs.

Carm... the one Mancini who always smiles.

"Okay, maybe just a quick dinner."

I don't know why I'm agreeing. Unfortunately, it's hard to fool yourself and I know exactly why I said yes. It's as simple as the fact that my relationship with Dominic Mancini has always been complicated and after a drought of almost nine months, I'm not ready to say goodbye just yet.

"Great. Give me your phone number."

I rattle off mine, then my phone dings in my bag.

He says, "That's mine. It's around seven tonight. Nothing dressy. I'll text you the details."

"Sounds good. Thanks for the invite."

As Enzo leans in to hug me goodbye, I wonder if I should give Dom a heads-up or not. Would he give me one? Probably not. Might as well play a little game of my own this time around.

CHAPTER THREE

Dominic

"You're such a pussy. Where were you this morning?" Luca jabs me in the arm with his fist.

"I'm the oldest. I can't spring back from a hangover as fast anymore." I sip my scotch on the rocks, hoping my younger cousin accepts my lame-ass excuse.

"Did you hear about my buddy puking?" He shakes his head as his fiancée, Lauren, comes over and slides her arm behind Luca's back. He pulls her closer but continues his conversation with me as though it's a natural occurrence. "He's still up in his room. We'll see if he can fly tomorrow."

She laughs and Luca kisses the top of her head, chuckling himself.

Never did I think I'd see my youngest cousin so at ease with a woman who's about to be a permanent fixture in his life.

"How was your bachelorette party last night?" I ask Lauren.

"Fun. How were the strippers last night?" She raises her eyebrows.

Luca throws his head back and laughs. "No lap dances."

That's the truth—unless something changed after I left. Something tells me that's not why Luca came to Vegas for his bachelor party.

"Yeah, but you had naked girls dancing for you." She pokes his stomach before stealing his beer and downing a sip.

"I would've gladly sat in a chair all night and watched you dance around a pole naked."

Her face tints pink because she knows it's true. Just like all my cousins and my brothers, Luca has fallen hard. I'm practically the last of the singles in my family.

My baby sister, Blanca, comes up next to me. "There you are."

"What's up?"

"You're the only other single person here. I need to get away from the kissy and huggy sweetness of it all. Can I get at least one fight? Show me their lives aren't all roses and sunshine." Blanca pushes between Luca and me to reach the bar. "No offense to you guys. You're the wedding couple, so you should be all unicorn and rainbows."

She orders her drink and I slide money to the bartender. She's my little sister and is still working her way up the corporate banking ladder.

"Thanks, big bro." She twirls her straw in her drink. "All of this wedding stuff must cost a fortune."

"Blanca." I shake my head, but when you're dirt poor just out of college, you obsess over how much everything costs. I've been there.

Luca laughs. "You only get married once." He and Lauren smile at one another.

"Here's hoping." Blanca laughs.

My gut twists as the realization of my predicament sets in with Luca's words. I'm now going to be a second marriage guy. If I meet a woman I want to marry one day, I'll have to tell her she's about to become my second wife. I know enough about women to know that she'll feel as if she's my second choice, and she might not be far off in her assumption.

Val is just something I've never worked out of my system. That's all she is. I thought I'd accomplished it after nine months of silence. Sure, I'd stalk her on social media, but other than a few personal pics of her and Ryder, it's all business on there.

"Especially for an Italian. Could you imagine what Zia or Ma would say about a divorce?" Blanca shakes her head.

She's unknowingly pissing me off. I can't imagine if Ma ever found out about my wedding. She'd be heading to church and praying every day for my immortal soul.

"Oh my God!" Blanca screeches and hits me in the stomach before pointing toward the door. "Look!"

The three of us turn and look in the direction she's pointing. My drink slides through my fingers and falls to the floor, where it smashes into a million pieces.

"Party foul," Luca says.

Flustered, I crouch to pick up the shards of glass. What the hell is Valentina doing here? She wouldn't come here to out us, would she?

"Who's that?" Lauren asks.

"Valentina Daniella Cavallo," Blanca answers.

"What kinda name is that?" Luca comments.

He doesn't remember, but he knew her once upon a

time. He'd just never imagine that the knockout brunette in front of him is the same girl who used to wear pigtail braids and sport skinned knees.

"Everyone always referred to her by all three of her given names. Even after she got married."

I drop a piece of the glass in my hand at the mention of Val getting married. When I glance up, a waitress is on her way over to help me. The four of us step away so she can wash the floor after I've picked up all the glass.

"She's married? Here I thought she'd be a good date for Dom." Lauren winks at me.

Little does she know I'm her husband, so technically speaking, Blanca's the only single one in the room.

"She's divorced," Blanca whispers.

Is that what I have to look forward to? My sister lowering her voice when she's asked about me?

"Got pregnant young and married the guy. Her whole dancing career ended. Her ex is Max Sommerland, from the morning show, *Wake-Up America*. He's not the main guy, but he's the segment guy. You know who I mean?"

My eyes keep straying to Val as Enzo hugs her and introduces her to Annie. Did she know we were here? Why would she come if she did?

"Oh, I love that guy. He's why I watch," Luca says.

"He's a douche. Always flirting with the women like they want him." Lauren rolls her eyes.

"No, you must be thinking of the wrong guy, babe," Luca says.

"I'm not..."

Luca and Lauren's arguing fades into the background when Val's searching eyes land on mine. The animosity I expected isn't there.

So... she knew I was here.

"Excuse—"

Carm comes up behind her and picks her up, circling around. She squeals and laughs at his antics. He's her type. Eccentric. Outgoing. Happy. It's the same reason Luca loves her asshole ex. He's a lot like Carm. The party guy.

"She and Dom always had a connection."

"What?" I whip my head in my sister's direction.

"Oh, come on. You beat up that guy who was picking on her in the third grade, and after that, it was only a matter of time."

"Were you even born then?"

She shrugs and puts up her hands. "The story has been told so many times, I feel like I was there. A young Dom saving his princess."

I roll my eyes at my sister's ridiculous fantasy.

Truth is, I was never Val's type. I just saved her from the ones who were. Until I didn't.

"I wonder why she's here," Blanca whispers.

"Yeah, and why's she in Vegas?" Might as well *try* to keep this marriage thing under wraps.

"Oh, her dance company was here competing. I saw it on Instagram. Maybe it's just a coincidence. I'm going to say hello." Blanca touches my arm before she walks toward Val.

"Go ahead, Dom. We can keep ourselves busy," Luca says, already turning his soon-to-be wife toward him and finding her lips.

"I'm going to find a seat."

Since dinner won't start for another twenty minutes, I sit down in the lounge beside the bar, pulling out my phone. My annoyingly loud family carries on with Val, who I haven't had the nerve to look at again for fear our eyes will lock and people will figure us out.

Carm falls into the seat next to me. "Always working. Did you see who's here? Small world."

"Yeah." I run my thumbs over my screen, responding to a work email.

"So, bro"—he clamps me on the shoulder—"I get huge props because I've yet to tell anyone, but I want deets. I see you took off the hardware." He eyes my empty ring finger.

Both rings from last night are tucked into my suitcase. Val was gone when I returned to the room and her ring was left behind, so I guess it's mine. "It was stupid, and I'll get it annulled."

"But who's the red-toenail-polish hottie?"

I should've guessed that he got a peek before I shoved him out the door.

"And what the hell is with you marrying someone after only a few hours? Classic me, but you? Hell no." Carm is chomping on a piece of gum, and the slapping of his jaw aggravates me.

"It was just some woman. No one important."

"No one important? You married her." Carm leans back in the seat, resting his ankle on his knee.

I glance up to see Bella escorting Val over here. "I was drunk. Beyond drunk. Obliterated."

Not really. Not enough that memories haven't come forward throughout the day. I'm not sure whose idea it was, but the memory of the two of us in the hotel room has surfaced through my hangover haze.

"Shit, man. I'd hate to be you and have to tell Mama." He cringes.

"I'm not telling Ma. And you're not either." I rub my temples, another headache setting in.

"So we're keeping this a secret for a long time?"

I turn my attention toward him. "For life."

He sags into his chair. "I don't have the stamina for that. Shit. I almost spilled to Enzo today. If I wasn't so scared about falling to my death and never seeing Bella naked again, I would've slipped. And I don't keep secrets from my woman. This is too much."

I sigh. The worst possible person found out about my untimely nuptials. My brothers should thank their lucky stars they have me in this family to keep their secrets. "Just keep your mouth shut and eventually you'll forget it even happened."

Bella and Val step up the stairs into the lounge area.

"Valentina," I say, rising to my feet.

She walks toward me with a smile as though nothing is amiss. My arm casually slides around her, my hand resting on her lower back as I kiss her cheek. She smells like she always does, and my dick reacts. She's his favorite flavor.

"Dominic," she says in a breathy voice.

I step away before I embarrass myself and motion for her to take the chair I was occupying. She accepts, and I take the one across from her, Bella sitting beside me. The slit of Val's dress shows off her long legs, and it takes everything in me not to stare at them. The only thing that would make the fact that Carm knows I got married worse is if he knew *who* I married.

"Bella was just telling me how well your business is going, Carm." Val crosses her legs and I somehow keep my attention on her face.

Carm laughs, raising his hand to flag down a waitress. "That's because I'm a killer salesperson."

"Well, you did sell her on yourself, so I'd say I agree." She smiles at him.

"Absolutely. She's way too good for me."

"At least we can agree on one thing," I murmur.

The waitress comes over and Carm orders for him and Bella. I order a scotch, then Val's favorite drink almost slips out of my mouth. Thankfully she interrupts before anyone notices.

"I can't believe two Mancini men are already off the market. What about you, Dom?" she asks with a smirk. "Still loving the bachelor life?"

"I work. Work is my life *and* my love."

"Spoken like my ex-husband." She raises her eyebrows.

It isn't her first time throwing my work into my face, and the fact that she's comparing me to her asshole ex grates on me. Her eyes hold mine for a second, testing me.

"Well, I guess when love knocks me over, work will take second place."

Yeah, I know that was a low blow. When the smirk falls off her face as if a swift wind blew it away, regret eats at my insides like termites.

"You never know who it could be. A fling even," Carm chimes in.

Val's vision shifts to him. She's wondering if he knows something, I'm sure. He does, but not enough to do damage. I've always kept Val's name out of my talks with my brothers.

Bella changes the subject, talking to Val. "What did you do today?"

Thank God. I'll have to apologize later for my comment.

"I had a spa day."

The waitress comes over and distributes our drinks, and I take a healthy sip of mine. *Tell me this dinner is going to start soon.*

"Oh, that sounds so nice. My feet are killing me from wandering around and shopping all day." She leans in and looks at Val's feet. "I love the color of your polish. Did you get a pedicure?"

I glance at Val's shoes, which show off her red nail polish, and another memory of massaging her feet last night accosts my brain. Is that how it all started? She was complaining about being on her feet all day.

"Carm!" Bella yells, and I look up to see her entire face is dripping wet.

Carm is staring at Val's feet.

Fuck.

His eyes shift from Val to me and back several times.

"Carmelo!" Bella yells again. "You just spit your drink all over me!"

Carm isn't made to keep a secret of this magnitude. I just know it's all about to blow up.

CHAPTER FOUR

Valentina

Dom hoists Carm up by his arm and pulls him out of his seat.

I grab all of our drink napkins and hand them to poor Bella.

"He didn't even apologize," she says, dabbing at her face. "That's not like him."

I know why he didn't apologize—he's having a coronary right now because somehow, he knows. I have no idea how he figured it out, but I'm sure he did.

I know one thing for certain—Dom wasn't open with his brother. He's always kept me hidden behind closed doors like a dirty little secret.

"I'm sure he has his reasons," I say, flagging down a waitress for more napkins.

"Is my makeup ruined?" Bella asks, still dabbing under

her eyes and her forehead. He did one helluva job spraying her.

"Not at all. You're still gorgeous."

She shakes her head. "I'm going to head to the bathroom. I'll be right back."

She heads out and I glance over my shoulder, not finding Dom or Carm. Enzo and Annie are still in the bar area, talking with Blanca.

Maybe coming here was a bad idea. What am I saying? I *knew* it was a bad idea when I accepted Enzo's invitation. But I felt slighted by Dom's departure this morning and I wanted payback.

I walk toward the exit. This was a stupid idea. There's no re-writing the past. Nothing will ever change with us. It's always going to be one thing or another. My ex, Ryder, his work.

The doors are in sight when someone grabs my elbow to stop me.

"Hold up," Dom says.

I stop, but I don't turn around.

He steps up to my back, and my breath hitches as his large presence hovers over me. "I'm sorry. I should have never said that." His voice is low and contrite. His fingertips have yet to leave my skin.

"I don't want to play games anymore."

"I've never once played a game with you," he says softly, his breath igniting shivers as it caresses me. "Why are you here?"

"I ran into Enzo and he asked me to come."

"Why did you?"

"Right now, I have no clue."

He slowly applies pressure to my elbow, directing me to turn around and face him. "Stay."

I stare at him for a moment and nod. "Okay."

"Thanks," he says and steps aside, waiting for me to head back in front of him. When I do, he places his hand on the small of my back.

To anyone else, it'd mean nothing. We're Italian, and Italians touch one another. But we're stuck in this growing cyclone whirling around and around, finding one another one minute and swearing off each other the next. We're not made for stable ground, but I crave it just the same.

AFTER A NIGHT of laughs and good food with the Mancinis, Dom put me in a taxi and sent me back to my hotel. I fell asleep dissecting everything he did or said. It was one of those nights that made me think we'd be great together. Until right before he closed the cab door and told me he'd handle the dissolution of our marriage when he got back to New York and would be in touch.

Now I'm sitting in the airport, praying we're not all on the same flight. My phone ringing distracts me.

"Hello," I answer.

"Hey," Lulu says.

"How are the kids?" I ask.

"I don't call you to talk about my kids unless they're pissing me off. So how was Vegas? Do anything crazy?"

"You know what they say, 'What happens in Vegas, stays in Vegas.'"

"Except you tell your best friend. I have three kids under the age of eight. Throw me a bone here."

I exhale. "I saw the Mancini brothers."

There's dead silence, and let me tell you, Lulu is rarely quiet. "All of them?"

What she's really asking is whether or not I saw Dom, while at the same time telling me that if I did, I'd better have kicked him in the balls for her. "Yes."

"How are Enzo and Carm?" she asks. "Blanca there too? Let's just talk about those Mancinis before my blood pressure gets any higher and they have to induce."

"Someone's in a mood."

"I told Vinny if he knocks me up one more time, I'm going to give him the vasectomy myself and there'll be no local."

I laugh.

"His ma told him that birth control is bad, but if we're so insistent, then it should be on me. She actually said that he should leave his options open."

"I thought Catholics were against divorce?' I joke with a chuckle.

"Only when they wanna be, I guess." A little voice comes up behind her and asks her something. "Daddy can do it." I hear more whining in the background. "I swear he's fully capable. Go and give him the pouty lip."

I laugh, a little jealous of the life my best friend has. Yeah, it's crazy, but Vinny loves her so much and their kids are adorable. Here I am with a fifteen-year-old who acts as though hugging me is the same as petting a wild lion. My little guy is grown and doesn't need me anymore.

"Now, where were we?" Lulu says, getting back on track. "Oh yeah, tell me you got some good sex in Vegas and share all the details. Because the only thing I got is Vinny nailing me Sunday morning in the bathroom while we pretended we were showering before my ma came over to grab us for church."

"Sorry to disappoint you."

"Bullshit. I know you." I hear some water running in the

background then the sound of a bell or an alarm of some kind. She's probably doing laundry or a million other things while talking to me.

I pick at a piece of imaginary lint on my T-shirt. "Why would I lie?"

"I'm thinking it's because you slept with Dominic Mancini. If that's the case, spare me the details." There's annoyance in her tone, and I haven't even been honest with her about what happened.

I squeeze the phone a little harder and confess my sins. "I did sleep with him, but I also married him."

Nothing has felt more freeing than releasing those words into the world.

"Haha. Funny."

"I'm serious," I say.

"*What?*" There's some commotion on her end of the phone, then she says, "I'm fine. Auntie Val is just playing a game and it's not a very funny one."

"I wanna play," one of the kids says.

"I'm not playing a game. At the moment, I'm Valentina Mancini." I shouldn't like the way that sounds, but how many times did I write that on my notebooks during high school?

"It does sound better than your maiden name, but you should've gone after Carm or Enzo."

I'm silent because she knows why that would never happen.

"But your eyes were always on Dom. Stupid, ego-driven, workaholic Dom."

"Lulu," I sigh.

"I know. I know. I'm sorry, I just can't believe it. What are you gonna do now that you're married? I'm assuming a lot of alcohol went into that decision. Then again, knowing the two of you, maybe not."

This is Lucia. I trust her with my biggest secrets, and this one is the biggest of them all. If word gets back to Ma about me being married again... I can't even imagine. A daughter with two divorces? The shame. The guilt. The despair.

"Give him a break. He really is a good guy." I cross my legs and check the sign with my boarding time because I want to get out of this place.

"I know Dom is a good guy. He just doesn't know where his priorities lay."

"He gave me space to make my decision."

I can't fault Dom. We'd promised one another a no-strings hook-up that was all about sex and not at all about feelings. We were doing so well until last summer in the Hamptons. Then my ex came knocking and asking for a second chance.

"Like a doofus," Lulu says.

"Doofus," a little voice mimics.

"That's not a word for you to say," she says.

"See? You're not being a very good role model."

"Please. Gia said fuck yesterday. We're not doing a stellar job, but they're alive and healthy."

This is why I love Lulu. While I tried to follow all the rules with Ryder, Lulu has a two-year-old who still uses a bottle and a three-year-old who sleeps with her every night and has yet to go to preschool because she can't get him potty-trained. I guess the best of friends are opposites.

"Well, she is her mama."

"I say she's Vinny." Lucia laughs. "Okay, I have to get back on the mom clock, but have a safe flight and call me when you get back because I want all the details."

"Needless to say, this stays between us."

"Well duh." One of her kids cries in the background. "Hey, Val?"

"Yeah?"

"Do you think that maybe..."

"No, Lulu, it's not a sign that we're meant to be together. It's just a sign that we need to cut the cord between us before one of us never recovers or we take down the whole world while trying to make something happen that shouldn't."

She sighs. Because she and Vinny found each other young, she believes you can actually find your soul mate when you're still a child. It's just not as easy as movies make it out to be, though I wish it were.

"See you soon."

"Love you," she says.

"Love you."

I click off and pull up Ryder's name to send him a text message.

Me: *I'm about to get on the plane. Dinner tonight? Sushi?*
Ryder: (*a thumbs up emoji*)

That about sums up our mother-and-son relationship these days. Not that I expect a fifteen-year-old to have a lot of conversation with his mother. When I was his age, all I thought about was boys. One in particular. Guess not much has changed.

CHAPTER FIVE

Dominic

I might be the only person who comes into work on Monday morning in a good mood. I'm usually happy to start a new work week, but today my mood is soured because my first line of business is calling a lawyer. A divorce attorney, to be exact. Whether they're any good is a mystery because I can't ask for a referral from someone. Which leaves my fate in the hands of Google.

I press the button on my phone that connects directly to my assistant's. "Ash, hold my calls."

"Sure thing, Mr. Mancini."

Ash is a professional. I could ask her for a referral, but I can't take the chance of this getting out.

I pick up the phone and dial the number on my computer screen. The ad looks professional and the reviews are mostly positive. A receptionist answers and puts me on hold before I can get a word in. I hang tight while listening to the music, leaning back in my chair. I grow impatient after a minute or so, and my gaze wanders to my office window, where I see my co-worker Nell approaching.

My eyes catch hers, and a small smirk tilts the corners of her lips. She takes liberties with the dress code here. I'm surprised HR hasn't spoken to her yet about her short skirts and blouses that dip too far down. She's flirtatious and doesn't play hard to get if you get my drift.

She stops in front of Ash, who probably knows exactly what's transpired between the two of us since she's my assistant and smarter than most. I see Nell's curves and sultry demeanor and all I can think of is Valentina. She'd never carry herself like Nell. Whether that's good or bad, I don't know, though my gut says it's a good thing.

The timer on my phone says I've been waiting a few minutes now. Any company who keeps me waiting that long can forget my business.

I hang up as Nell bypasses Ash, walking into my office uninvited. Ash stands, obviously saying something to Nell, but I raise my hand that it's okay. Nell shuts my office door behind her and stands there as if she's my favorite vice and ready to tempt me.

"How was Vegas?" she asks.

I'm not immune to Ash's displeasure as she slowly turns around and sits at her desk. She's judging us both.

I lean back in my chair. "Good."

"Miss me?" She swings her hips, placing one leg in front of the other until she reaches my desk. It's seductive, but something feels different from when I saw her last week.

"It was a bachelor party in Vegas. I was shoulder-deep in strippers." I laugh it off because truth is that I didn't think of Nell once while I was away. Shitty, I'm aware.

"And none of them made you wish I was with you?

Maybe I could have given you a lap dance with the stripper." She sits in the chair in front of me, crossing her legs and arching her back.

"I didn't get a lap dance."

Yeah, I'm dodging.

"You're making me sad." She puts on a frown to match her baby voice.

I did find this appealing at some point, right? "Sorry, I'm swamped with work, what with taking some time off. Don't have time to chat."

Her gaze scours my body for a sign that I'm interested. I'm not at the moment because I have to figure out how to get unmarried before I entertain sleeping with Nell again. If that's even something I want to do.

"My place tonight?" she asks.

"Can't. Work. But later this week maybe." I can get a quickie divorce by Friday, right?

"Don't play cat and mouse with me, Dom. I don't do the chasing." She stands and exits my office, swaying her hips so hard I'm surprised she doesn't need to make a chiropractor's appointment.

I'm dialing the next divorce attorney with a high rating on Google when my cell phone rings. *Valentina.* I hang up my office phone, walk over to my office door and shut it, then swipe my finger across the screen.

"Hey," I answer.

"Hey." Her soft voice holds a hitch as though she's upset. Unfortunately, I can probably decipher when she's upset easier than when she's happy. But that comes from trying to be her savior most of my life.

"What's wrong?" I sit back down in my chair.

"Other than the fact that we got married this weekend

and I've spent all morning trying to find out if we can claim drunken ignorance and get this annulled rather than get an actual divorce?"

"Yeah, other than that." I find my lips turning up in a smile.

"Max is..." She stops, for which I'm thankful. I don't want to hear about her ex-husband as if I'm her friend. I haven't been just her friend since we were teens. Her soft sigh rings through the phone. "Anyway. Wouldn't you prefer to get the marriage annulled?"

"What did Max do?" I ask. What can I say? Old habits are hard to break.

"Nothing. It's nothing."

"Val," I sigh. "You can always come to me to talk regardless of anything."

"Just forget it. I found an attorney who will help with the annulment. I know it sounds stupid, but I can't be a two-time divorcee."

"I thought I was handling that?"

"No you declared that you were handling it. I'm just as capable."

I inhale a calming breath. "Okay then, I'm good with an annulment. Then I'm not the divorced guy either."

I leave the Max thing off the table. He's like the kitchen sink in our fights. We fight about everything except him when he's the underlying reason for most of our issues.

She laughs. "You'd think we wouldn't care about the stigma in this day and age."

"It's not just the stigma. Our mas would implode if they got wind of this."

"True. Okay, I'll make an appointment. Is there a certain day better than another for you this week or next?"

"I'll make it work." I type my password back into my computer to bring up the charts and graphs. The market will open soon, and I need to be prepared. I realize after a moment Val didn't say anything back. "You still there?"

"Yeah, I'm here," she snipes.

"What's wrong now?"

"Nothing. It's just... you can clear your schedule for our annulment but not for a dinner date."

My head falls back on my leather chair and I stare at the ceiling. "I'm sorry I constantly disappoint you."

She blows out a breath. "I'll text you the info."

Click.

I go back over our conversation in my head, trying to figure out where it took a turn for the worse, and realize it was from the moment I answered.

I push a hand through my hair and remember the first time I saw her after the divorce five years ago. She was far from the woman she is now.

It was winter, and her cheeks were rosy. She had on a long coat and furry boots. I'd stopped in for a coffee on my way back to the office to work late, and she was two people in front of me in line. I recognized her immediately. Val has an aura to her, although she's ignorant to her draw.

She'd ordered her coffee and was lost in her phone, waiting for her name to be called. After I ordered my own, I contemplated ignoring her. I knew she'd gotten divorced and was now a single mom.

I've dissected the situation millions of times, wondering if I made the right decision when I approached her.

"Val?" I'd asked, dipping my head to her level.

Her head rose slowly—I knew she'd recognized my voice. A smile pulled at her lips. "Dom."

The way my name came off her lips made me feel like Superman. As though she needed me more than any time I'd saved her before.

My arms opened on instinct. She fell into my chest, and I held her close. She still smelled the same way—fresh laundry with a hint of berries. It's the most unique scent I've ever encountered.

The barista called her name, and I held up my finger to say we'd be right there.

I managed to get her to a table by the window, and we watched the snow cover the Manhattan streets. The hustle of the city was slower because of the weather, and I let her pour out her heart. She talked about Max and the awful things he'd done, her son who was turning defiant, and the shame of her divorce in her parents' eyes.

I sat and listened until she asked, "Dom, why are you not enjoying this? You warned me and..."

She was right. I had warned her about Max. Selfishly, because I wasn't ready to commit to anyone, but I didn't want anyone else to have her either. I should be eating the demise of her marriage up with a spoon, but she was hurt, and I'd always had a soft spot for Val.

"I'll always want the world for you, whether it involves me or not." I sipped my coffee, feeling like an idiot for saying something romantic, but it was the truth. Her swollen, red-rimmed eyes pulled at my heart.

She sat up straight and wiped her tears with the backs of her fingers. "Weren't you heading back to work?"

"Nah, it'll be there tomorrow."

For the first time in the entire conversation, she smiled. So wide. So big. So genuine. It filled me up in a way not much else can.

We closed down the coffee shop, but at the end of the night, I didn't ask for her new number. A part of me knew she could turn my life upside down and change everything for me, and I wasn't ready for it. There was money to make and ladders to climb. Valentina Cavallo had the power to make me change my life choices. And no one likes change.

CHAPTER SIX

Valentina

I sit at the curbside table of the café across the street from Mazzola Bakery. I have to pop over there to pick up bread for Sunday dinner with my parents. I'm meeting Dom here though because I'm almost positive he has Sunday dinner as well. Might as well get this annulment paperwork dealt with before we have to see our families.

The waitress sets down my coffee, and I'm enjoying it while scrolling through my phone, so I don't notice Dom approaching. Instead, I overhear the conversation between two women a few tables over, alerting me to his presence.

"That's Dom Mancini," one says.

I'm tempted to look over and make sure I don't recognize them, but I continue sipping my coffee instead.

"He's the last single one, right?" her friend asks.

I'm curious now. Someone is tracking the Mancinis? I

get that our little borough can seem small, but there're a lot of Italian men who are available, come on.

"Yeah, thank goodness. There's always been something about Dom. He seems like that quiet, commanding type. At least outside of the bedroom." The woman practically howls with laughter.

"You do like that type."

A part of me wants to rip the annulment papers out of my bag and say he's mine. But I've held on to Dom way longer than I should have.

"Good morning," he says, dropping his gym bag on the concrete. He slides into the wrought-iron chair across from me. He's freshly showered and dressed in track shorts and a T-shirt because it's Sunday and he usually plays basketball with his brothers on Sunday mornings. Except he's been picking up games with some old buddies because his brothers have limited their games to once a month now that they're involved. I shouldn't know, but I do.

"Hey," I say, peeking over at the women.

They're so busy eating up Dom, they don't even notice me.

"You have something on your face," I say, referring to his newly grown beard.

He rubs it with his palm. "You like?"

I crinkle my nose. "Not especially."

Lie. That's a total lie. Dom with a beard is a whole new level of sexy.

The waitress comes over, and Dom orders a black coffee. I glance at my chocolate croissant and feel guilty. I didn't work out this morning. I woke up late because Ryder is with Max, then I laid in bed until I had just enough time to get ready and come here. Meanwhile Dom has already sprinted across a basketball court a million times and now he's going to just have coffee.

"Feed me a bite, wifey?" His eyes zero in on the croissant. He knows exactly where my mind was. Sometimes it's scary and sometimes it's nice how well he can read me. Right now, it's nice, because I need all the humor I can get.

I pretend to look around the bottom of my chair. "Where's my ball and chain?"

He exaggerates his stare from my sandals, past my shorts, and up my T-shirt. "Damn, I knew I forgot something."

I slide over the papers before I get distracted by our usual banter. "Here's the annulment, but..." I glance at the women who were talking about him, but they're not staring. "Keep it on the down-low, because the women over there know you."

He glances over.

"Don't look," I whisper-shout.

He shrugs, turning back. "I don't know them."

"Well, they know you. Or *of* you."

"Sweet. You telling me I'm a celebrity around here?"

"Only in Carroll Gardens. Don't think too highly of yourself."

The waitress brings over his coffee, and he twirls the cup so he can pick it up with his left hand. When he brings it to his lips, his smirk is so wide, my heart hurts. It's too rare that I see it on his handsome face.

He shrugs. "Still counts."

"Ironically, they were discussing how you're the last Mancini to settle down." I lean back, sipping my coffee with milk and sugar.

"Save the best for last."

There's that grin again. My stomach flutters like

hummingbird wings. I cross my legs before I focus on the ache between my thighs.

He places his coffee down and leans over to read the papers. "So we sign and then it's done?"

"Yes, my lawyer will file them and that's it. He doesn't anticipate any issues, given the situation."

"You'll no longer be Valentina Daniella Mancini."

I shouldn't look for a sign that he wants me to remain his wife, but I am. I'm dissecting everything about this entire conversation. Still, I give him the sass he expects. "You know I wouldn't take your name."

He laughs, his eyes on the paper. Then he meets my gaze, and the papers drop from his hand. "If you were mine, you wouldn't be a Sommerland, I can tell you that much."

I kept my ex-husband's name because by the time we divorced, I'd already made my name in my business as Valentina Sommerland—my dance studios, my reputation as a dancer—plus Ryder was a Sommerland and I wasn't interested in explaining my marital status at every PTA meeting or sporting event. It's obviously still a sore spot with Dom.

"I guess that's one fight we get to avoid then." I eye the paper.

He picks it back up. "Did you tell Ryder?"

I sit back in the chair, crossing my legs. My knee aches from an old dance injury, and I rub it. "There's no reason for him to know."

He nods, his smile dying. "Gonna rain today?" He nods toward my hand rubbing my knee.

"I think it's going to be a wicked storm." My lips spread into a smile as he slides his chair toward me. He taps his lap with his hands. "Dom…"

"My last husband duty," he says, patting his legs again.

I'd usually say no way, but if it's the last time Dom's hands will be on me, I don't have it in me to refuse. So I set my leg on his lap, and his large hands wrap around my knee. My head falls back until I hear a gasp. I circle around to find the two women staring at us with their mouths open. I turn my attention back to Dom, who's staring right at me.

"If you're looking for a quickie before Sunday dinner, I think a threesome might be an option." I nod in the women's direction.

He smiles but says nothing, his fingers digging in where I need them the most. I've missed this over the months of separation and I'm going to miss this again.

"How's Ryder doing?" He distracts me from thinking about how maybe we should give ourselves a fifteenth chance.

"He's good. With Max."

"I figured."

"He turns sixteen in the fall. Can you believe it? I feel so old." I pick up my coffee and take a sip.

"Is he playing in the fall?"

I'm slightly miffed that he doesn't refute me about my age, but that's Dom. He doesn't like it when I say anything negative about myself, so he ignores it instead of saying, "You're not old," or "You're beautiful, stop saying you're not."

"Running back."

"That's great. If he ever wants any help running drills, let me know. I'm sure Enzo and Carm would help too."

"Thanks." His words are a reminder that under his hard exterior is a really good man.

He winks and pats my knee. "Better?"

"Yeah. Thank you."

"You're welcome."

I drop my leg, and he allows it to slide through his palms as though he doesn't want to pull away first. When my foot lands on the concrete again, he studies the paper and picks up the pen.

"It's been great being your husband, though I would've liked more benefits." One corner of his lips tip up as he poises the pen over the paper.

"Wait!" I say, panic flaring up and out my throat before I can stop myself. He looks up, forehead wrinkled, and I tear off a piece of my croissant and hold it up in front of his mouth. "My last wifely duty."

His lips open, and I place the flaky pastry into his mouth. He chews and swallows while his eyes devour me. I place my hands in my lap and wait until he's finished. I'd like to seal this annulment with a kiss, but that's not a good route to go. It'll end up being a quickie before Sunday dinner.

"I always do love the sweets," he says. "Thanks."

I shrug as though it's the least I could do. Then the pen meets the paper and all the fluttering in my stomach stops.

He signs and slides the papers over to me. "There you go. You're a free woman."

I take the pen and sign my name before I can do anything stupid, then I shove the papers into my purse.

"I better go." Dom stands, grabs a twenty from his pocket as though he knew he'd want a fast getaway, and throws it on the table. "Bye, Valentina."

Before I can say anything, he crosses the street. I watch as he disappears around the corner toward his parents' house. And just like that, Dominic Mancini is out of my life again.

"MA!" I announce myself as I step into my parents' house.

She peeks out of the kitchen. "Don't take off your shoes."

"I brought the bread." I slide out of my sandals and place the bread on the dining room table.

My parents' apartment never changes—the plethora of Italian flags, the cross above the front door, the pictures of my grandparents and ancestors filling the wall. And of course, a shrine to their only daughter.

"Why you take your shoes off?" Ma walks out and kisses me on either cheek. Her apron is off and she's putting on her shoes. I'm not sure what's going on.

"Where's Dad?"

She waves me off. "We have to pick some food up that I ordered."

She "ordered?" I stand in place, not understanding. Ma doesn't order food.

"Why would you order?" I ask.

She shrugs on a jacket because the woman is five-two, thin as a rail, and feels cold in ninety-degree weather.

"You don't need a coat," I say.

"Air-conditioning." She practically jogs over to the table to grab her purse.

"Ma?"

She stops and looks over her shoulder at me. "What? Come. You were late."

I glance at our, you guessed it, Italian clock. I took the long way here because I needed a minute to digest the fact that I had annulment papers in my purse. I always thought if Dom and I did marry, he'd be my forever. Even so, the clock tells me I'm still not late. What has Ma so rattled?

"Where's everyone? Dad? I don't smell food."

"I told you, I order." She opens the front door and waves for me to go through.

"I'm not leaving until you explain what's happening."

Her shoulders slump and she puts on that look. The one she's going to use to guilt me into going wherever it is she's headed. I should just agree now, but I wait.

"I woke up not feeling good. So I order food for dinner and now we're late. We need to go now."

"What's wrong?" I approach her to feel her forehead like I do for Ryder, but she shoos me away. "Where did you order from?"

"Anna Mancini. Come."

You've got to be shitting me.

Before I can argue, she's out the door and down the steps. Since she's not feeling well, I decide to be a good Italian daughter.

All we have to do is pick up the food and leave. What's the harm in that? Maybe I won't even see Dom.

CHAPTER SEVEN

Dominic

I grab a fork, poke a meatball, and put the entire thing in my mouth. I barely made it here without stopping at a bar. The dissolution of my marriage with Val was never something I imagined.

"Stop eating and wait for everyone." Ma smacks my hand and the fork falls from my grip.

She's lucky I'm still upright and not passed out. I'm starved after my basketball game.

"Where is everyone?" I ask.

My other family members should be here by now. After leaving the café, I stopped by my old high school and stared at it, letting memories of Val run through my head like some sick movie reel of the good ol' times. Why I chose to torment myself, I don't know.

"How am I supposed to know?" Ma stirs the sauce then pulls a tray of chicken from the oven.

Something seems amiss, but she's still making enough food to feed an army, so everyone must just be later than me.

"Where's Dad?" I ask.

"Out."

"No shit."

She stops, places her spoon on the holder beside the stove, and smacks me on the back of the head. "Disrespectful. I am your mama."

She's really in a mood. Usually she's brimming with happiness every Sunday, what with two of her boys bringing their significant others over.

I pull out my phone and go sit on the couch.

She pokes her head out of the kitchen. "You should change. Something nice. You're dressed like you're a teenager."

Not going to happen. I pull up the group text between my siblings and me and type out a message.

Me: *Where the hell are you guys?*
Enzo: *In bed.*
Carm: *On the kitchen counter.*
Blanca: *In A bed... not mine.*

I shake my head at Blanca.

Me: *Why the hell am I the only one here for dinner? Ma's acting strange.*
Enzo: *She told Annie yesterday that there was no dinner today.*
Blanca: *I got the same text.*
Carm: *Me three.*

Me: *She's preparing food, so there's a dinner.*
Carm: *What the hell? I'm on my way.*
Blanca: *I'll bring my new guy over. NOT.*
Enzo: *Spare us the info about your boy toy, Blanc.*
Blanca: *That's funny. It wasn't too long ago you three were all up in my business.*
Carm: *Not anymore. I can't stand to hear about your sexual adventures. They nauseate me.*
Blanca: *I had to listen to yours for years. Get used to it. I'm out.*
Enzo: *Have fun with Ma to yourself. Annie needs some help in the shower.*

Something's going on. I tap the phone on my thigh. It vibrates, and I see that Carm's messaged me in a thread with just him and Bella.

Carm: *Dude I told Bella. I'm sorry. But we don't keep secrets.*
Me: *Seriously!?*
Bella: *Don't be mad. My lips are sealed, I swear. I don't think it's a coincidence though.*
Me: *What do you mean?*
Carm: *Listen to her. She's a chick.*
Bella: *Carm, use woman, not chick please. From what Carm says you two have been circling each other your whole lives. Sometimes when everything aligns you have to listen to the universe.*
Carm: *Isn't she brilliant? Come back to the kitchen baby, I'm hungry... for you.*
Dom: *I'm done. Thanks for your advice, Bella. Carm, I don't wanna hear about your sexual shit either.*

A knock on the front door interrupts me typing the rest of my message.

Ma runs out of the kitchen, wiping her hands on her apron, then she unties it and tosses it on a table behind the plant.

"What's going on? Is Father McAllister coming to dinner?" I stand to see who on Earth is making Ma act so flustered and why I'm the only one here. Please tell me I'm not giving financial advice to one of her friends again.

Ma opens the door and there stands the reason. She's been here a thousand times before, except this time, she's my wife... at least temporarily.

Val's wide eyes zero in on me.

"Giada!" Ma opens her arms, and Val's ma hugs my mine fiercely.

The two act as though they're long-lost cousins when in reality, I bet they don't go a week without seeing one another at least three times. Val's parents own the corner grocery store.

"Anna, we brought bread. Valentina went to Mazzola's."

Ma takes the bag of bread and shoves it into my stomach before setting her eyes on Val. "Oh, look how grown up you are." She holds her by her upper arms and kisses both cheeks. "Beautiful. Simple and beautiful, Valentina."

Val shoots me a look that says, "do something," but I'm not even sure why they're here, let alone have a game plan.

"Dominic." Giada lowers her head toward me.

I place the bag of bread on the entryway table and approach her like a good Italian Catholic boy. "Nice to see you, Mrs. Cavallo."

When I draw back from our hug, she places her hand on my cheek and pats it once, smiling at me. "Such a good boy."

"Thank you."

"Come in. Come in." Ma waves the both of them in. "Dom, I haven't had a chance to put the cutlery on the table. Finish setting the table."

Val's eyes shift to her ma. "I thought we were just picking up food?"

Giada looks at Ma as though she's the ringmaster of this circus.

"Why are there only six plates?" I ask, walking over to the oversized dining room table.

"What's going on?" Val asks.

"Sit down." Ma points at me then at the chair like she did the time I trampled all over Mrs. Ricci's flowerbed when we were playing hide-and-seek as kids.

"You too, Valentina," Giada says, eyeing the chair next to me.

I slide out the chair for her, and she stares at me with "what the hell is going on?" written all over her face. But the hell if I know, so I shrug.

"We'll be back." Ma and Giada disappear into the kitchen.

Val turns to me. "What the hell? Do they know? Is this some kind of Italian setup?"

"I don't know. My brothers and Blanca said Ma canceled dinner."

Just as she's about to speak, Pa opens the front door, laughing with someone—Val's dad.

"Dad?" Val asks. She might be the only Italian girl who refers to her dad by the American name.

"Hey, kiddos," Pa says. "Oh, Valentina, you look beautiful as always."

She stands, and they kiss each cheek.

"Dominic." My name comes out of my father's mouth

like razorblades traveled up his throat, and he barely can look at me.

It's guaranteed. Our parents know something.

Mr. Cavallo puts his hand out in front of me. "Dom."

"Mr. Cavallo, nice to see you."

He nods, but I don't miss the slight flare of his nostrils. My stomach rumbles and my chest constricts as he stares at me for a second before he lets our hands drop.

Our mas come out of the kitchen.

"Perfect timing," Ma says to Dad and Mr. Cavallo. "Sit."

Between Ma and Giada, the table is filled with all the traditional Sunday dishes.

"Prayer," Giada says, holding out her hands.

Val's hand is cold as it slides into mine, and I squeeze it with the hope of relaxing her. There's no way our parents found out. This is just some "fix them up" tactic they're trying.

My dad says the prayer since it's our house, and we all say amen and our hands drop.

"How was Vegas?" my dad asks, filling his plate as the dishes get passed. "Your cousins? Good?"

"Yeah. Everything went well."

"Just well?" Giada asks, eyeing me.

I shrug. "I think the bride and groom-to-be had a good time."

She presses her lips together. "Did you know that Valentina was there at the same time as you?"

It's not really a question. She's baiting me.

"Did you talk to Carm?" I ask ma. He's such a fucking mama's boy. He can't keep a secret to save his life.

Ma cuts up her chicken. "Yes. Yesterday."

I grip my silverware tighter. "And he told you?"

"Dom?" Val whispers from next to me.

"Told me what?"

I've seen every side of Ma over the years and she's doing her 'I know, but you're going to have to tell me' act. She's not even trying to hide it.

"About Val and me?"

Val's silverware drops onto her plate.

"What about you and Valentina?" Mr. Cavallo asks a little louder than necessary.

I sigh. "Just tell me. What do you know?"

Ma places her silverware down calmly and leans her forearms on the table. "A reporter called Giada to see if she had any comment about her daughter's recent marriage."

"Why would a reporter call?" I ask.

"That's not really the point, is it?" Ma snipes.

"I'm so stupid," Val says. I look at her, and she turns to meet my gaze. "Max. Because Max is my ex, they probably have those stupid gossip sites searching marriage records in Vegas."

She's right. How did we not think of that?

"So it's true then?" Ma asks.

Before I can say anything, Val asks Giada, "What did you say?"

"I told them I couldn't be happier. That you and Dom have always been meant to be together."

"Ma! Why would you tell them that?"

"Because that's the truth."

"You're lucky your ma is so smart and can think on her feet." Mr. Cavallo grabs his wife's hand. "It's not as if we knew ahead of time. No one asked for my daughter's hand." His narrowed gaze lands on me.

"Dom and I..." Val glances at me. "We're getting an annulment."

Our mas gasp, and their faces drain of color.

Ma leans over the table as though she doesn't have perfect hearing. "You're what?"

"Getting an annulment. The marriage was a drunken mistake." I fill in the gaps for her.

"A drunken mistake?" My dad sips his homemade wine. "You're saying you didn't run off and get married?"

I sink into the chair, feeling sick to my stomach. *Shit.* My parents thought this was for real.

Valentina's staring at me to answer them.

"We ran into each other in Vegas and had too much to drink. For some reason, we got married, even though neither of us remember much."

"Excuse me." Ma slides her chair back, covering her mouth, and disappears behind the kitchen door.

"Anna." Pa sighs, then his angry eyes settle on me. "After your mama got over the shock of you not having a Catholic wedding, she was so happy when Giada called her. We thought you didn't know how to tell us, but now you say it's all a mistake and you're going to get an annulment? You break your mama's heart." My dad's chair slides back, his hands pressing on the wooden table as he stands.

"Pa." I place my napkin on the table, preparing to follow him, but he puts his hand out and continues on to the kitchen.

"Valentina, this is true?" Giada asks her daughter.

"Yes, Mama, it's true. We've already signed the papers." She looks into her lap where she's fiddling with her fingers. "It's not real."

"But..." Giada looks between the two of us. "You two were always—"

"No, Mama." Val shakes her head. "We were never meant to be."

Giada swallows, and her gaze veers to her husband. "I'm going to check on Anna." She leaves.

Now it's just the two of us with Mr. Cavallo. Great. I feel like a teenager who got caught feeling up someone's daughter.

We sit in strained silence because no one really knows what to say.

"When we got the news, I was upset because what good Catholic Italian boy doesn't ask the father to marry his only daughter." His gaze is on me. "But Giada said it must've been impromptu. That you didn't have time to call me. I thought she was crazy, but after talking with your parents about this secret wedding, I made amends with the anger because you've always looked out for our Valentina, Dominic. Looked out for us." He gives me a knowing look, and I shift in my seat. "You'd make a great husband."

Husband? I'm no damn husband.

"Now you tell us it was a mistake and that you're going to get an annulment. Valentina, that's two marriages for you. When I was young, marriage meant something. It wasn't something you do when you're drunk in Vegas and then if you change your mind, you just sign some paper-work and act like it never happened. Now, I'm going in there to comfort your mother, and I suggest the two of you think about your carelessness and how it's affected your families."

I feel like the lowest of the low right now.

Mr. Cavallo stands, leaving me with Val.

Her head drops into her hands and her back vibrates with her sobs. "I'm a disgrace."

I place my arm over her shoulder, and she turns into me, burying her face in my chest as I smooth my hand over her long chestnut hair. A few minutes later, all four parents come out of the kitchen and stop in their tracks when they take in the scene.

"New plan," Ma says.

Giada smiles, and all four of them take a seat.

Call me psychic, but I'm pretty sure I won't like this.

CHAPTER EIGHT

Valentina

From the way my dad can still give me a helluva "I'm disappointed in you" speech, you wouldn't think I'm thirty-six, divorced—soon to be twice—and raising my own child.

I turn my head in Dom's arms and see our mas taking their seats, but they aren't upset like they were before.

"What new plan?" Dom asks.

"You're going to remain married," Anna says.

"No, we're not." Dom's insistence pulls at my insecurity that I'm not enough for him. "We're in our thirties. You can't tell us what to do."

"I am your mama, and this was not a drunken mistake. The two of you got married for a reason, and you're both going to act like mature adults and deal with the situation you created. You're going to stay married and give this an honest try."

Dom scoffs and shakes his head. "You're insane."

"Don't you talk to your mama like that," Mr. Mancini says to Dom.

I'm not sure what to say, so I remain quiet, letting him handle the absurdity of our parents' plan.

"She can't make me stay married," Dom says to his father. "We made a mistake. It's over and done."

A tear slips from Anna's eyes. "What did I do to you?"

"Ma." Dom sighs, letting out a long, exasperated breath. "Nothing."

"Your brothers are all settled down. Why not you? I should be a grandmother by now. But you just work, work, work. No one remembers a man for how much money he has when he dies, Dominic." Anna points at Dom, but he's rolling his eyes like an adolescent child.

Anna shakes her head and looks at Mr. Mancini as though Dom's a lost cause.

"Valentina, this is marriage number two for you," Ma says. "We understood Max. The problems with him, that maybe the pregnancy was the cause for the marriage. But this time... why are you giving up?"

Now they're going to Catholic guilt trip me. Great.

"I'm not giving up on anything." I glance at Dom. "It was a mistake. We weren't in our right minds when we did it. I know that disappoints you and that I'm a failure of a daughter, but you can't make me stay married to someone I don't..." I stop talking because I could never say I don't want to be married to Dom. There were times I thought maybe we were meant to be together. But that was a younger version of us both.

"Listen to us. We're older and wiser than the two of you. Give this a chance," Mr. Mancini says, staring us in the eye. "You might not see it now, but there was a reason you married. Something a lot greater than the two of you did that."

"Pa." Dom throws his hands in the air. "We've already signed the papers. It's over. It's done." His curt tone startles both of our mas.

"No!" Anna stands, and although she's not big, she's still scary. "You listen to me, Dominic Anthony Mancini. You married that girl and you're going to honor your commitment. Three months. You are going to give it an honest try for three months."

"No." He almost laughs in her face. "I'm thirty-six years old. You don't get to dictate my life."

"Dominic, if I have to warn you again about your behavior toward your mama, you're going to be sorry," Mr. Mancini says, his hands clenched on top of the table.

"What are you going to do—spank me? I don't understand why you're being so ridiculous. You want to know the truth? I was drunk and saw Valentina was in Vegas, so I texted her. We got together with one intention—to have sex. Neither of us are sure how we got the marriage license, let alone got to the chapel, but we did. It was all about the sex, so drop this whole 'bigger power' and 'fate' shit."

Anna crumbles into her chair, and Ma tries to console her.

"Dom," I sigh.

His scathing eyes zero in on me as though I'm next in line to be told off. We lock gazes for a few seconds, and he cools off a bit.

He sighs. "Ma." He rounds the table and bends down in front of her. "I know you want the best for all of us. Enzo and Carm have settled down. They found their person. Val and I..." His gaze travels to me and tears well in my eyes.

I'm not his person. Is that what he's saying?

"We share a twisted past and..." He blows out a breath, his gaze staying on mine. "We're complicated. If you force us..."

Her hand touches her son's face, and his fierce bravado cracks. "Three months. That's all I'm asking."

I choke out a laugh because her boys are as stubborn as her. She's not going to accept no for an answer.

"Do you know what you're asking?" he says in a pained voice.

Anna nods. "I'm asking you to follow through on the promise you made that night."

"Give me a minute." He raises to his feet. "Val, can we talk?"

I slide my chair out from the table and follow him out the front door.

Once the door is shut behind us, he sits on the railing of the stairway. "She's not going to let it go."

"I know."

"I say we just agree to it. We'll act like we're on board, but really we're buying time until they stop with all this fate talk."

My arms wrap around my stomach. What choice do I have? My parents already think I'm a failure. At least if I pretend to give this marriage a chance, it'll soften the blow of having a daughter who's been twice married.

"Are you sure?" I ask.

He nods. "My cousin's wedding is in five weeks. We keep it up until it's over so my ma can save face. Then we file the annulment. Tell them we can't do the three months. It's not working and we need to go our separate ways."

Dom's business side is alive and kicking right now. There's no emotion in his decision. It's strictly about reaching the goal of making his ma happy and getting our annulment.

"Sure."

"They'll make us attend Sunday dinners together. We'll have to pretend we're actually trying."

"Okay."

His arms fall into his lap. "I'm sorry, Val."

What is he sorry for? The fact that he doesn't want to be married to me or that we have to keep up a charade for a few weeks?

"Let's go agree and make them happy." I open the door, but he pulls on my elbow and I fall into his chest.

He tucks a strand of my hair behind my ear. "If you don't want to do this, just say the word."

The smell of Dom overwhelms me in the best way possible. I'd never deny him when we're this close. "It's fine. Five weeks is nothing."

Our eyes lock, and a whole slew of emotions float back and forth between the two of us. I'll never figure out what he thinks in that beautiful mind of his.

"Thanks."

My hands slide down his chest until they're resting on his hips. "You're welcome."

I circle on my heel and open the door. Our parents are eating, and I spot the annulment papers on the table, which means someone went through my purse. I swear there's no privacy in this family.

"Okay, we're going to give it a try." Thankfully Dom is doing the lying. I'm not sure I could do it.

"Oh, Dominic!" Anna stands and rounds the table. "My good boy. I love you." She hugs him, and Dom's smile says he'd do about anything for his mama.

Ma leaves the table and comes over to embrace me. "Valentina."

I catch my dad picking up the papers from the middle of the table. Mr. Mancini grabs a sterling silver tray and a match, then he lights the papers on fire.

"Welcome to our family," Anna says to me, the two mothers changing spots.

"Thank you." I ignore the stabbing feeling in my chest over this not being real.

"Now, next line of business. You'll probably want to move in with Valentina because of Ryder," Ma says.

Dom's head swivels toward me. Looks like Mr. All-Business-All-the-Time didn't think about that.

I secretly want to high-five Anna for playing a good hand.

CHAPTER NINE

Valentina

"You can't just tell him you're taking him to Europe and not talk to me first," I lower my voice. The last thing I need is for someone to take our damn picture again and splash it on a magazine so I can read about how Max Sommerland and his ex-wife were fighting in a restaurant. Then again, maybe that's better than when we actually got along for a brief moment and they said we were getting back together and poor eleven-year-old Ryder thought his wish had come true.

"He's my son. I pay support. I hold his insurance. He's turning sixteen and I want to experience a trip to Europe with him." He cuts up his steak with a smile. This is the fake Max Sommerland who, even when he's seething, can plaster on a brilliant white smile.

"All court-ordered. As is the fact that I'm the primary caregiver. I know we've been lax with Ryder's schedule as he's gotten older, but a six-week trip right before school starts? I won't see him for the rest of his summer break."

"You had him for the first half. It's not my problem if you'd rather go all over God's creation teaching girls in tutus to twirl." He brings the fork to his mouth upside down and slides the piece of steak off it.

God, how I loathe him.

"Undermining my profession again? Get a new script. I guess making old women laugh with your stupidity every morning is saving the world?"

He winks. "Let's remember who funded your first studio."

"Let's remember who raised your son."

"Let's remember whose money allowed you to do it."

I grip my napkin under the table, surprised it's not in shreds by now. Leaning back in the chair, I catch an older woman pointing at Max, her eyes sparkling like diamonds. "One of your admirers is about to approach."

I sip my wine and watch the woman cautiously smile as if she needs my permission to approach him. She rises from her seat and walks over.

"Max Sommerland?" she asks with a pen and a receipt in her hand.

"In the flesh." He puts down his fork and knife, wipes his mouth with his napkin, and holds out his hand for the pen. Meanwhile, I'm gagging from the endorphins he gets whenever this happens.

"Can my husband take a picture?" She waves him over, this time without permission.

The poor man sighs, looks at his meal, and stands.

"Of course, but my friend can take it." He signals to me.

He's got to be kidding.

"Friend?" I clarify, but his permanent smile is on display, though his eyes are cold as they stare me down.

I smile and accept the phone before snapping the picture. I pass it back to the woman. The poor husband came over for nothing, but he does put his hand out for Max.

"Thank you," the woman says. "I hope the rumors aren't true, because you guys make a beautiful couple."

"Thank you," Max says.

"Rumors?" I ask.

She stops a foot away.

"Oh, stop with your gossip. Let's go finish our meal," her husband says, grabbing her hand.

"That you got married this weekend," the woman says. "Congratulations."

Max chokes on his piece of steak because he couldn't wait until she actually walked away to continue eating.

"I'm sorry?" I ask with wide eyes.

"Vegas. This site I follow said you got married and sadly not to Max. My gals and I were hoping for a reconciliation." Her lips dip as if we're the favorite boy band who just announced their breakup.

Max gulps his water and reaches for his phone on the table. After dinner with my parents, I scoured the internet and could only find a few mentions about me getting married in Vegas on some stupid little nothing blogs.

"Nice meeting you," I say as she walks away.

"You got married? And you're pitch-forking me over a trip to Europe?" Max's fingers are flying over the screen.

I didn't figure people actually read those tiny blogs.

Max's thumbs stop moving and his eyes scan down the screen. "I thought you were smarter than this."

I pluck the phone out of his hand.

"Guess I shouldn't be surprised it's to Mancini. That man put a wedge in our marriage the size of the Grand Canyon." He goes back to eating his steak because he doesn't give one shit that I married Dom as long as the blog doesn't make him out to be a monster.

"I don't see why it's news in the first place."

"You're my ex-wife. Did you really think they wouldn't figure it out? The media combs through every marriage license in Vegas. Either that or they pay off someone who works there. Hell, there's probably a picture."

I recall the picture stuffed into my nightstand behind my favorite unicorn vibrator. "The keyword is ex. I should be off the radar."

"I think once you make it onto the list of names they scan for, you probably never make it off." He winks again and my stomach hollows out. "Who would've guessed you'd be associated with my name your entire life whether we're legally bound or not."

The satisfaction he's gaining from this information is wearing thin.

"It could've been you." If he'd been able to keep it in his pants.

"Nah. You ruined the forever after shit. I'm going Dom's style. Or at least his old style. Different flavors all the time, wasn't it?"

Now he's hitting below the belt. I gulp down the rest of my wine. "Are you insinuating I'm one of his flavors?"

He finally finishes his steak and moves on to his green beans. The man only eats one food group at a time. He's basically a toddler.

"Don't get upset. You're his favorite flavor." Max shrugs. The waitress comes over, and Max doesn't even bother asking if I want anything else before he says, "Check." She walks away and he sets his eyes on me as if he didn't metaphorically jab me with a knife and I'm not bleeding out all over the floor. "I have to be on set early."

"We need to discuss this trip." I don't budge.

He pulls out his wallet and places his card on the edge of the table. The hell if we're going dutch when we wouldn't be here if he'd act like a mature adult and consult me when it comes to Ryder. I'll let him pay for my meal.

"Go play house with Mancini for a while, and I'll take Ryder to Europe. See how civil I'm being?" He wipes his mouth again before putting the napkin on the table.

His words remind me that if my son is around all summer, I'll have to tell him about my impromptu marriage. Dom and I have yet to decide where we'll live. If Ryder goes away with Max... "You can have Ryder on one condition."

One of his perfect eyebrows rises. "This should be good." He leans back with a smirk and folds his arms.

"You take Ryder to Europe, but don't tell him about Dom and me. Let me have the six weeks to decide how and when to tell Ryder when he gets back."

He pretends to think it over, his head tilting from side to side and his eyes toward the ceiling.

"Otherwise I say no to taking Ryder, and you know very well what the papers say about taking him out of the country without my permission. I believe it's called kidnapping."

"Always a hard bargain with you, Val. Fine. Deal. But don't blame me if he finds out on his own."

The waitress returns with a credit card machine, and he puts on his reading glasses to read the screen.

"Please, you're not that big of a celebrity. It's not like it's going to be on *Entertainment Tonight* or something."

He looks over the rim of his glasses, testing me, but he

knows it's the truth. "Fine. I've already booked the tickets. We're leaving this weekend."

The snake thought he had me from the get-go. Was he really willing to lose the money for those tickets?

"I'll get him packed."

He slides his card back in his wallet, along with the receipt the waitress gives him. "I'm not sure what Mancini has that I don't, but good luck figuring out whatever it is that you have to figure out."

I could list a whole spreadsheet of reasons why Dom is a better man than Max, but he's doing me a favor, so I'll play nice. "Thanks, Max."

"Sure. Never say I'm not a nice guy."

We leave the restaurant, and he puts me in a taxi. I was terrified to tell Ryder, so this buys me time. By the time he returns Dom and I will have moved forward with the annulment and there won't be anything to tell Ryder—except maybe a lesson as to the perils of drinking too much.

"SWEETIE!" I walk into my condo to the sound of music blaring from Ryder's room.

He doesn't answer, so I drop my purse onto a kitchen chair and walk down the hall, where I knock on Ryder's door. The music quiets and he opens the door. He's dressed in sweats and a T-shirt, freshly showered after being out with his friends.

"What's for dinner?" he asks.

"I've eaten, but I have something in the fridge for you. How was your day?" I try to peek into his room, but he steps out into the hall and shuts the door, blocking my view.

I'll just go in later when he's not home.

He shrugs as an answer to my question.

"I'm assuming your dad called you?"

"Yeah. Thanks for letting me go, Mom." He puts his arms around my neck as we walk down the hall. He's been taller than me since the eighth grade.

I nod. "Well, make the most of it."

I dig Anna Mancini's meatballs and pasta with chicken marsala out of the fridge. Thanks to that horrible dinner yesterday, my son can eat tonight.

"Will you be okay here?" Ryder asks with real concern in his voice.

The poor boy always feels responsible for me. The first weekend he left me to go to his dad's after the divorce, he kept thinking of reasons he couldn't go. He'll be going off to college soon, and the last thing I want is for him to stay close on account of me.

I glance over my shoulder after placing a plate in the microwave. "I'll be fine."

"Dad said we could go to..." Ryder continues to tell me about all the promises Max made.

For my son's sake, I hope his dad does spend the six weeks getting to know Ryder better and not finding exotic women to sleep with. I nod and smile and encourage him while my insides ball up into a big messy knot. While he's gallivanting around Europe, I'll be moving in with Dom.

Once Ryder's busy eating his dinner, I shoot a text to Dom.

Me: *Ryder is going to Europe with Max for six weeks. I'll move into your place since you have an extra bedroom. After Luca's wedding, we say it doesn't work and I'm back home before Ryder returns. And he never finds out what I did.*

The three dots appear.

Dom: *You sure you don't want to share my bed, WIFE?*

I roll my eyes but school myself before Ryder senses anything is amiss.

Me: *Positive.*

Not really. My body is like a magnet to Dom's. Just because we live together doesn't mean I have to be there all the time. I'll sleep there and that's it.

Easy peasy.

CHAPTER TEN

Dominic

Every Thursday, I meet my brothers at the Trading Post for lunch. Today they decided to bring along their girlfriends. Now I'm stuck at a table with all of them. There's no fun in this, so I send Ash a message to call me with an emergency in twenty minutes. By then I should've already finished my lobster mac and cheese.

"I can't believe you're married." Annie sits next to me, Enzo across from her. "I think it's romantic." She pats my shoulder.

"I love the spontaneity of it." Bella looks just as dreamy-eyed as Annie.

Carm beams a smile toward Bella, and his hand disappears under the table.

"Don't get too excited. We're giving it five weeks. We'll pretend until after Luca's wedding, then we'll break it to our parents that it's not working." I sip my drink.

"What?" The horrified expression on Annie's face is like she just saw the ending of a romantic movie being stripped away. "Why?"

"Because we were drunk. We didn't plan for it to happen. We're both in agreement."

"Are you sure about that?" Bella asks, straightening her napkin in her lap. "Because the woman I saw in Vegas was very interested in you."

"Really? I wish I would've had more time with her that night." Annie pouts at Enzo, who shrugs.

"I don't," he says, picking up a piece of his goat cheese pizza.

Now that I think about it, those two disappeared halfway through dinner.

"There was something between you. I can't describe it. I don't know... it reminded me of turbulence."

"Turbulence?" Annie asks.

I check my phone. Five minutes until Ash calls me.

"That doesn't make sense," Enzo says over a muffled mouthful of pizza.

"Let her explain," Carm says, protective over his girlfriend.

Bella smiles at him, but still holds an expression that says *I've got it, but thanks.* "It felt like there was a lot of unease between the two of you. Worry about when the next big dip will come that has you gripping the arms of the seat, but even though you're scared, you enjoy the thrill at the same time."

Annie snaps her fingers and points at Bella. "Makes total sense."

Annie turns to Enzo, and he's nodding. Seconds later, she pulls out her notebook and the two of them end up in a conversation about an idea for an ad pitch brought on by Bella's little speech.

"We've lost those two." Carm kisses Bella's cheek. "Have I told you how much your brain turns me on?"

Bella giggles and slaps his chest. "What doesn't turn you on?"

"True story."

"Anyway, I think you should hold out until you're through the turbulence, you know?" Bella says to me. "Putting a time limit on it seems like a horrible idea."

"Believe me, there's a lot between me and Val you don't know."

She holds up her hands. "I know it's none of my business, I'm just telling you what I, as an outsider, saw. I mean, I never would have thought Carm would be the one."

"There's history." I continue to make excuses when I should just shut up. It's none of their business, but I kinda want to know more about what Bella saw in Vegas. Because when I look at Val, all I see is a woman who hates me but wants me in the same breath. I have no idea what goes on in her head, but one thing is certain—she started the annulment process. That means no matter how much she might want to fuck me, she doesn't want to be married to me.

"History is the basis for the best relationships sometimes. I think that Mama is right. You can't argue that there's a reason why the two of you married. Drunk or not," Carm says.

The waitress walks by our table, and I signal for my bill. Poor Katie, who was our waitress for years, decided not to take our table when Carm walked in with Bella. She liked him, we all knew it, but Carm never felt the same way. Which means that if the girls keep attending, we might need to find a new restaurant for our Thursday lunch dates.

I look at my phone again. Ash should've called by now. It's not like her to not follow orders.

"Okay, we're out. We've got to get back. Congrats on the wedding, big bro." Enzo stands and sets some money on the table. "Let us know when you guys register."

I flip him off, and he laughs.

"Bye, guys." Annie hugs and kisses everyone before following Enzo out of the restaurant.

As my gaze follows them, I blink because I can't be seeing what I'm seeing.

She knows this is where I lunch on Thursdays. How many times last year did I stop by her studio for a quickie after lunch?

Val's in ballet tights, small skirt, and a leotard. She has a small wrap to cover her curves, but it's not enough to keep the other patrons from appreciating her body. Our eyes catch, and her shoulders fall. Without a smile, she weaves through the tables, followed by a trail of gazes checking out her ass. I'm not happy with the way other men look at her as she makes her way to me, and by the time she reaches the table, I'm annoyed.

"It's my new sister!" Carm stands and embraces Val in a huge hug, swaying both of them. "I knew it was just a matter of time."

"Carm, are you sure you're not the leak?" She allows him to kiss her on each cheek before she gives the opportunity to Bella.

"So good to see you." They embrace, then Bella looks at Carm. "We should get back."

Carm, the asshole he is, acts as if he doesn't understand. "I want to spend time with my new sister," he pretends to whine, all while opening his billfold and laying money on the table. "But I do have things I'd like to do rather than play mediator between the two of you."

I roll my eyes and say my goodbyes to Bella.

"See you at Sunday dinner." Carm's laughter echoes through the crowded restaurant, and I catch poor Katie watching him and Bella walk out.

"May I?" Val signals toward an empty chair.

"You are my wife. Would you like me to pull out the chair first?"

She rolls her eyes and sits down, keeping her purse attached to her arm and sliding closer to the table. She's not here to eat, I guess. "I ran by your office, forgetting that you're here. I thought maybe with your brothers' new girlfriends..."

"That we didn't meet anymore?" I ask.

She shrugs. "That maybe you didn't have hook-up war stories to swap anymore."

"Nah, now we just talk about how I married someone in Vegas and how Ma is making me stay married to her and how she's moving into my condo this weekend."

"About that..."

"Do you have a plan where we don't have to move in together?"

Her eyes stay trained on me, and she shakes her head, worry furrowing her brow. "No, unfortunately, I'm still arriving first thing Saturday morning, after Max picks up Ryder. But I figure we need to set some ground rules first."

"Ground rules?" I inhale a deep breath, sure that this conversation will annoy me to no end. I pick my fork up to get back to my lunch.

Our waitress approaches again. "Did you want anything?"

"No, I'm leaving shortly," Val says with a smile.

"Okay, let me know if you change your mind." The waitress leaves.

"Listen, I get that we're doing this whole fake marriage thing for our parents' sakes. I don't want to disappoint mine as much as you don't want to disappoint yours. But I can't live with you while you're sleeping around."

My fork drops from my hand into my bowl of mac and cheese. "I thought you were talking about cleaning up the kitchen at night or making sure to put the toilet seat down. Not where my dick goes."

"All of those are up for discussion too, but I won't allow you to embarrass me." She lets her statement hang there for a minute as we lock eyes.

I know what she's not saying. She's already been through that once before when Max was her husband.

"I started thinking about it at work... how it would look and how'd I'd feel if that happened and I started to panic a bit. So if you can't commit to that, then I'll be straight with my parents about what this is and to hell with them being mad at me. I'll tell Ryder about my mistake in marrying you. But one sighting from someone in the neighborhood of you with another woman and suddenly I'm a bigger embarrassment to my parents and once again I'm the naïve and unsuspecting wife."

I sip my drink before I answer to give myself a moment to cool down. "I won't."

"Even at the office." She gives me a pointed glare.

"The office?"

"There was a very attractive trader, Nell, hanging around Ash when I dropped by. She was asking when you'd be back, and I didn't get the sense that it was for stock tips."

"She's a co-worker." I stab a piece of pasta with my fork and shove it into my mouth.

She tilts her head and stares at me until I break.

"I don't have to apologize."

"No, you don't. But please refrain from screwing her for at least five weeks."

I push away my bowl of lobster mac and cheese.

Val surprises me by picking up the fork and stabbing a few noodles and a clump of lobster. "I assume you're done?"

"What's yours is mine, right?"

"Cute." She stuffs the forkful of pasta into her mouth.

One thing I've always loved about Val and me is how comfortable it is between us. Maybe too comfortable at times, and that made us too honest.

"I won't sleep with anyone else during our honeymoon phase." I pretend to cross my heart with my finger.

"Thanks. I'll do the same."

"That's nice of you. Don't bust into my room if you hear me groaning though. My guess is I'll be beating off nightly."

Hell, sharing a condo with Val and not screwing her is going to give me a permanent case of blue balls. Not being able to fuck anyone else will make this excruciating. But I won't hurt her like Max did.

"Same here. I might just buy myself a new toy." She smiles over another mouthful of pasta.

"Thanks for that visual."

She reaches for my glass, and I allow her to take it. After she swallows, the smile and friendly banter between us dies. "We can do this, right? I mean, with no lines being blurred or crossed?"

I want to say let's just sleep together and enjoy the five weeks while we have it, but I know where I'll be after that. Not in a good place. And I swore after the end of us in the Hamptons last year that I'd never do that to myself again.

"Of course. We went nine months without sleeping together before Vegas."

She stares at the table then looks back at me. "And then we got married."

I laugh. "We went thirteen years before we started hooking up."

She nods. "Okay then. Do you have any rules you want me to follow? Especially since it's your place."

"Is asking you to walk around naked taking it too far?"

She laughs then stands. "God help us. If you keep thinking that way, we won't make it past day one. Bye, hubby."

She blows me a kiss and saunters out of the restaurant. Half the men are gawking at her ass and I can't even say it belongs to me.

Yeah, my hand and my dick are going to be best friends for the next five weeks.

CHAPTER ELEVEN

Valentina

New York City is dark and dreary as I join Ryder on the elevator to meet Max.

"You have your passport? Don't lose it. Stay near your dad and always be aware of your surroundings."

He puts his arm around me. "I'm gonna be fine."

Isn't that what every fifteen-year-old would say? They all seem to think they're invincible.

"Keep your phone charged so I can call, and no matter the time difference, call me if you need me or if you just want to talk. I put a battery pack in your backpack just in case."

He laughs and turns me toward him, placing his hands on my shoulders. I stare up at him and try to remember exactly when the little boy who called me Mama left. "Stop watching the news."

This time I laugh. "You should try watching the news and not ESPN all the time."

"ESPN is the sports news."

I can't argue with that.

"I'll be back in six weeks, Mom."

The elevator dings and the doors open.

Max is waiting for us. "Stop with the tears, Val. This trip is going to be shorter than your kitchen remodel."

I roll my eyes as we step out the door of my building. A black sedan waits outside for them. I hand Ryder's big duffle bag to Max.

"What did you pack? Jesus. I'll let the two of you say goodbye. Don't drag it out, Val, we have a flight to catch."

"Come here." I hug Ryder and flip off Max behind Ryder's back. No need for him to see our animosity. "I love you and I'll miss you, but I want you to have fun. Just not too much."

He chuckles. "I love you too. If you need company or anything—"

I draw back from our hug because I am going to break down if we don't make this snappy. "Stop."

He smiles. His gorgeous wide smile full of perfectly white teeth that cost me a fortune.

"I'm good. I have a lot of reading to do."

He nods, rocking back on his heels.

"Go." I move in for one more quick hug then step back, sucking back the tears that want to fall.

He walks toward the car, looking back at me every second step. Max packs the last bag, and right before Ryder ducks into the sedan, he waves. How did we produce such a great kid? I wave back as the car pulls away from the curb into the New York streets.

"Always sad to say goodbye," Ben says from behind his desk when I go back inside the building.

"He's gone for six weeks," I say, remembering that I need to discuss me leaving with him.

"Sounds like a great adventure for a father and son."

I shrug. I'm sure it will be an adventure. I just want the adventure to end with my son safe at home. "Hey, Ben, I'm going to be staying with a friend for a little while. I'll pop by for my mail once a week, but in case anything should seem suspicious, could you give me a call?"

"Of course, Ms. Sommerland."

"Thanks." I step over to the elevator and press the up button.

"I hope you enjoy your time with Ryder away. Sometimes moms need a vacation too."

I smile and turn around, stepping into the elevator. He has a point. The break will be good—if only I didn't have to spend it with Dominic Mancini.

I KNOCK on the door to Dom's condo, my bags dropping to the creases of my elbows.

The door swings open and he spreads out his arms. "Welcome home, honey."

I blow the strand of loose hair off my forehead and step into his space. A space I'm familiar with. A space where memories of us naked and screwing are present in every room and on every piece of his expensive furniture. I drop my bags by the door. He's nice enough to wheel in my big suitcase.

"Is there a moving van with the rest of your stuff?" He laughs and steps away from the door and into the kitchen.

His stainless steel gourmet kitchen.

One thing most people don't know about Dom is that he's an excellent cook.

Do you know how intimidating that is for an Italian woman who can barely follow directions on the back of ramen noodles? I was raised thinking the key to a man's heart is through his stomach. Maybe that's why I've never fully won Dom's heart.

"I made you something." The timbre of his low voice pulls me from my thoughts.

He's busy chopping an onion, and when I look at the breakfast bar, I spot piles of chopped up veggies and garnishes.

"Mongolian beef?" I ask. "With lo mein?"

The man can cook anything from Chinese to Indian to Italian. His curry is out of this world.

"Still your favorite?" he asks.

I join him by the cutting board and sneak a piece of the meat sizzling in the pan. "Only yours."

"Are you saying you only like my meat?" He looks up from what he's doing and grins at me.

If we were still that couple who pretended they were just fuck buddies, I'd lay my hand over his crotch and whisper in his ear exactly how much I love his meat. But we're not. We're... married now. Somehow that changes everything.

"How are you doing with Ryder gone?" He doesn't allow me to answer his sexual innuendo because it was meant to make me feel uncomfortable, not as an invitation.

"I'll miss him."

"You can always use me as a good distraction." He drops all the vegetables into the pan with the Mongolian beef and flips the pan over the open flame. His forearm flexes from the weight and it's so damn sexy I might have to call a truce on that deal we made about not sleeping with others.

"Are you going to keep making sexual advances?"

"I'm not making sexual advances."

I slide up on his counter, my feet dangling. His gaze skips over my body for a second. "You keep throwing sexual comments out there."

"That's because I've always loved your blush."

"I thought you hated me."

He sighs. "I'll never hate you, Val."

I watch him stir the veggies and meat then take the noodles from the water and place them in another frying pan with soy sauce and garlic that's already simmering. It's so unbelievably hot, admiring him in the kitchen. The amount of ease and trust he has in his capabilities. I once asked him why he learned and he said that it was because his work was so stressful, he wanted to excel in something he could set the pace around. Being the perfectionist he is, he kept finding new cuisine to master.

He picks up the frying pan and shakes the contents, the muscles in his forearm and bicep flexing as he does.

"Ugh!" I jump from the counter. "You're playing dirty."

"Dirty?" His smirk says he knows exactly what he's doing.

"You know what your cooking does to me." I scramble over to the front door and grab my bags, then I weave back behind the big sectional couch he's had me on in multiple positions.

"I'm just being nice and making you a welcome meal."

I drop my bags in the guest room and storm back down the hallway. "Tell me you don't want to sleep with me."

He shoves the pan to the back of the stove, turns off the burners, then walks toward me. "I always wanna fuck you,

Val. Feel me right now and you'll find out. But me making you this meal isn't a way to get you in my bed... again."

I throw my hands in the air. I know Dominic Mancini and I am not seeing things that aren't there. His sexual comments. All the 'wife this' and 'welcome home baby' shit. He's an agenda kind of guy. There's always an end goal in mind.

"Then stop. I'm not going to survive five weeks if you keep doing nice things and saying stuff like that to me. Just keep your distance. We need to keep this platonic."

He laughs and shakes his head. "There's nothing platonic about us."

His light eyes search mine, but I have no clue what he's looking for. I swallow the lump in my throat and will my feet to stay in place. *Don't run to him. Don't jump into his arms and kiss him until his hands run along your body and he walks you to his bedroom.*

I use every ounce of my willpower to stay grounded. If we cross that line, I'll only end up devastated again.

"You've got your wish." He raises his hands. "I'm officially your roommate only." He goes back to the kitchen, scoops the food onto a plate, and slides it in front of a breakfast stool.

"Dom." I step forward now that he's not looking at me, because it's safer now. "I just want us... you know as well as I do that if something happens—"

"I know, Val." He walks to the entry table and grabs his computer bag, sliding his wallet into the back pocket of his jeans. "You don't have to remind me. It was honestly just dinner. I knew you'd be upset about Ryder. It was a way for us to find our way back to the friendship we had, not a way to sleep with you."

Before I can respond, he opens the condo door and

shuts it behind him softly. Somehow, the absence of a slam or bang makes me flinch harder.

I eat the meal he prepared, package up the leftovers, then clean the dishes because it's the one thing I can do well in the kitchen. It isn't until two in the morning that I hear him come home. With my door closed, I hear him drop his keys onto the table and open the fridge. He always has a water next to his bed at night.

The shadow from the hallway light I left on is interrupted by his shadow on the other side when he stops at my door. I want to tell him I'm awake. To come in so we can talk this out. But I don't say anything, and the shadow disappears.

I roll over and curl into a ball. How will I ever survive five weeks of this?

CHAPTER TWELVE

Dominic

Nell is hovering again. She's walked by my office five times this morning. I told Ash to tell anyone who inquires that I'm busy. Even so, there's probably no time like the present to nail this coffin shut. Nell needs to know that what was going on between us is over.

I straighten my tie and smooth it down my chest as I leave my office to head to Nell's down the hall, but when I round the corner, she's right there. I jerk back in surprise.

She giggles. "Did I scare you?"

Nell's upped her game today with a short black skirt and a red blouse with a lacy cami underneath that she has no problem showing off. My guess is that's probably because I didn't message her all weekend. Since Vegas, I haven't approached her, even after she left her panties in my desk drawer.

"Yeah, a little." I get the sense that this could move into

boiling bunny territory if I'm not careful with my wording. "Can we talk?"

She looks around and, not seeing anyone, steps closer, her red polished nails sliding down my tie. "Supply closet?" She pulls me toward her by my tie. I put my hand over hers, but she grips the fabric harder. "Come on. I miss my guy."

Her baby voice never turned me on, but it didn't grate on me the way it is now.

"Nell..." I'm tempted to screw her. I can't lie. Val has me so twisted that I want to fuck someone else imagining that it's her. Even if I know it'll do me no good. I haven't slept the past two nights now that she's right next door to my room.

"Come on." Her hand slides down the front of my slacks and I step back.

"Sorry for interrupting."

Instead of stepping back, I jump this time. Nell's hands slip from my tie and my junk.

I spin around. "Val!"

Though she's smiling, I can tell she's not amused. She's in a pair of yoga pants and an oversized sweatshirt that falls to the side, revealing one bare shoulder. I want to yank it down to expose one of her mouthwatering tits, but there's a time and place for everything.

"Honey, you forgot your wallet this morning." She taps it against her lips. "I thought I'd bring it by. You know, being a good wife and all."

"Wife?" Nell asks, her face now ghostly white.

Val smiles and weaves her arm through mine. "Is Dominic keeping that all to himself? We got married two weeks ago. It was a Vegas thing, but we have a long history together." She looks at me with a Stepford wife smile.

"I didn't know." Nell looks her up and down, but Val

isn't one to be intimidated. One thing Val has is self-confidence.

"You know our Dominic. He likes to keep his secrets." Val pats my cheek. "I'm still getting used to this facial hair thing." She shakes her head at Nell. "We've known each since pre-puberty and I always loved him with smooth skin. Reminds me of the Dominic who once scaled a tree to save me. Remember that, honey?"

Her use of a pet name says she's selling this hard. Nell is clearly taken back by the new revelation.

"I should go," Nell says. "I have work to do."

Val puts out her hand. "It was nice meeting you."

Nell shakes her hand, then looks at me as though she needs more clarification. I try to convey to her with my eyes that this is what I was going to talk to her about.

"Nice meeting you... Val, right?" Nell says.

"Yes. Valentina Som—well." She giggles and lovingly looks at me. "Valentina Mancini now. Still getting used to my new name."

"Let's not pretend you haven't been scribbling that name since we were thirteen." I purposely up the ante.

Val's eyes narrow slightly. Her hand stays on my cheek, and she gives it a tap that's closer to a slap. "What can I say? Guess I've always loved you." Then she pinches my cheek and I know it's going to leave a red mark.

"You just had to find a way to catch me." I turn to Nell. "She had to get me drunk in Vegas."

Val's shoulders tense next to me. One thing about her is that she can't hold her temper for long. "I think you're mistaken. Remember, you tracked me down and messaged me." She smiles at Nell. "As I'm sure you know, our Dom isn't that romantic." She lays her head on my shoulder. "But I still love him."

"I'm happy for the two of you. Sorry, I have a meeting to get to." Nell slides by us.

Val straightens, removes her arm from mine, and says to a departing Nell, "We'll have you over for dinner sometime."

"Nice act." I signal for her to go.

Val laughs, walking in front of me. We round the corner and I open my office door.

"Ash! How are you?" Val opens her arms and Ash stands, eyeing me from over Val's shoulder.

It's been nine months since Val's been to my office. We used to do lunch. She'd come to my office to pick me up or bring me a surprise. Sometimes the surprise was that she was the lunch.

"Valentina," Ash coos as if they're long-lost friends. "How are you?"

"Good." Val sits on the edge of her desk, and Ash sits back down. "Ryder went to Europe with Max and it's driving me crazy. I already miss him, and it's only been a couple of days." She leans forward and touches Ash's arm. "What about you? How's little Molly?"

Ash grabs her cell phone and holds up a picture of her daughter, Molly.

Val takes the phone. "Not so little anymore. Where are her chubby cheeks?"

Ash leans back, and I stand in the doorway of my office. Ash and Val became quick friends. Mostly because my meetings ran late or I had to cancel last minute on Val. Basically whenever I put work ahead of Val.

"I know. They grow so fast. I think I might be ready for another." Ash bites her lip and looks at me as if she needs my permission.

"Just give me a heads-up, okay?" I push off the door frame and stand up straight.

"We both know Dom can't function without you." Val and Ash laugh, their eyes shifting to me.

I signal for Val to join me in my office. "Let's go."

"What's the rush?"

"I have to work."

Val rolls her eyes, pushing up off Ash's desk. "You shouldn't work all the time. It isn't healthy."

Ash watches us for a second. "Are you two...?"

Figures. She might be the only assistant in New York who isn't afraid of her boss. Not that I want her to be afraid of me, but I wouldn't mind if she refrained from asking personal questions.

"We're married," Val says.

Ash's mouth drops open, and she glances at Val's left hand.

Val catches the shift. "Oh, no, it was a quickie wedding in Vegas."

"Vegas?" Ash sits up straighter.

Val is next to me now, and all I smell is her. The scent turns me into a lion smelling its prey.

"Yep. We're getting it annulled, but our mas—"

"She doesn't need to know everything," I grumble.

"She's your assistant." Val turns to me briefly before circling back to Ash. "Our mothers want us to give it an honest effort, so I've moved in with him."

Ash's forehead crinkles. "You both agreed to that?"

"It's called Catholic-Italian mama guilt. It's a real thing." Val looks at me with an expression that says, "pipe in here."

"It is," I confirm. "Can we go into my office now?"

I scour the area to make sure there's no one else around.

Ash, I can trust. She's kept more than her fair share of secrets. But anyone else in this office? No way.

"Huh." Ash diverts eye contact.

"What? I know it seems ridiculous. That's why Ryder leaving for Europe was a blessing in disguise. We can pretend to do this for our mothers, but we're not really anything." Val waggles her finger between us. "Five weeks is nothing."

Ash nods but stays quiet.

"Let's go." I signal with my arm, swinging it toward my office once more.

"Bye, Ash," Val says, finally stepping into my office.

"Bye, Mrs. Mancini." She's laughing, but Val doesn't hear her because she's already sitting on a chair inside.

"Nice," I say to my assistant.

Ash shrugs. "You know as well as I do that this isn't some fake marriage, but I'll play along if you want." She slides her chair so her back is to me and her hand is on her computer mouse.

Instead of arguing, I walk in and shut my office door. Then I make my way over to my desk and sit across from my wife.

"I'm still surprised you were screwing another broker." Val crosses her legs and I chance a glance at her long limbs. She's trying to catch me off guard, but I meet her gaze straight-on.

"Why?"

"You always said you didn't sleep with people you worked with. That it complicated things."

I vaguely remember that conversation, but that was before Val broke me. Nell presented herself as a way to get over our break-up.

I shrug. "Things change."

"Good to know your values can shift as dramatically as a pendulum."

"Technically a pendulum swings with precision."

She rolls her eyes and juts out her jaw. "Whatever, Mr. Smarty Pants."

"Okay, Miss Jealous."

She scoffs. "I'm not jealous."

"Don't worry. I take it as a compliment."

She points at me. "Stop it."

I bring my hands up in front of me. "I'm not doing anything."

She stands and tosses my wallet onto my desk. "Here."

"Thanks." I slide it into the inside pocket of my jacket. "I can take you to lunch as a thank you."

"You'd leave work to take me to lunch?" Her condescending tone makes me want to say forget it.

"What can I say? Marriage has made me a changed man."

She rolls her eyes again.

"Keep doing that and they're going to get stuck."

She sticks out her tongue. "I have to get back to work. Young bodies to build into dancers."

I nod. "Thanks for the wallet."

"No problem. Isn't that what all good wives would do?"

Val pauses by the door, and for some reason, I can't let her go without explaining who Nell is. "She was just a casual hook-up. Nothing serious."

For a moment, I don't think she's going to turn around, but she does, seriousness transforming her face. "You don't owe me an explanation."

"And for some reason, I want to give you one. She was a way to get over you. That's all."

She turns back toward the door. I want to beg her to ask

the question—did it work?—because in this moment, I'd tell her the truth. *No.*

"I'll be late tonight." She opens the door and leaves.

She gives Ash a hug and they exchange some words, then hug again before she heads toward the elevators. I lean back in my chair, unable to concentrate on work. I fear I'm getting sucked in all over again, and I promised myself after the last time that I'd never let that happen.

CHAPTER THIRTEEN

Valentina

Dom and I stay out of each other's hair during the week. He's figured out my schedule, and when I'm at the studio for night classes, he's already in his room when I come home, and vice versa on the days he works late.

Weekends pose a different problem. This one, we're due to have a big Sunday family dinner at the Mancinis'. Our parents insisted on our presence this week because they fear the truth—that we're going through the motions but not actually trying to make this marriage work.

Dom returns home on Sunday around noon, a sweaty mess from playing basketball with his brothers. I feel like a slacker since I'm binge-watching *Good Girls* on Netflix with my coffee and the donuts I had delivered out of pure laziness.

He eyes me and drops his duffle bag next to the entryway table, his keys hitting the ceramic dish a second later. I pretend not to notice so I don't have to engage. I've had long sex droughts in my life, but being around Dom all the time makes it feel as though I've been celibate for twenty years.

"Good morning," he says, walking into the kitchen.

"Afternoon."

He glances at the microwave clock. "So it is."

I look away again and try to get back into my show. I hear him open the fridge, but I don't know what he's doing until he plops down beside me on the couch.

"What are you watching?" He opens one of those green drinks that scream good health and probiotics, then downs half of it.

"Just a show on Netflix."

"Is that what it's called? *Just a Show on Netflix*?" He eyeballs me then my bag of donut holes, smirking.

"No, it's not. What?" I crumple up the bag and set it aside, sipping my coffee.

"You and your sweets." He smiles as though it amuses him.

"Yeah, yeah. Whatever, Mr. Health Nut."

He's really not. I've seen him consume bags of taco-flavored Doritos.

"I prefer when you call me hubby more than these stupid mister names you keep making up." He pulls the ottoman closer and puts up his feet. He's barefoot, but I can see the outline from his socks and shoes from when he was playing basketball.

"Sorry I don't please you."

"I'll let you please me if you really want to." He opens his arms and looks at his lap. When I toss a pillow at him, he laughs. "Are you gonna share?"

I pass him the bag of donut holes.

"So what's the show? What am I missing?"

Clearly, he's not going to let this go, so I pause the show. I don't want to miss anything—especially if Rio has a scene.

"I'm still on the first season. It's about these three women who all need money and decide to rob a grocery store..." I tell him about the series.

He pulls two donut holes out of the bag—a glazed and a red velvet one—and pops them into his mouth as he listens. He actually looks as if he's interested in what I'm saying.

"All right, cool. Press Play." He leans back and wiggles his ass into the couch as though he's going to spend the rest of the afternoon there.

I press Play, and we watch television together for a while. It isn't until the break between episodes that he asks me to pause it for a second.

"I'm going to make a sandwich. You want one?" He disappears into the kitchen.

"Sure, but I can make it."

"Val, let me make you a sandwich. There's no hidden agenda in it. I promise."

"Okay."

He doesn't ask what I want because he knows. One of my favorite times with Dom were the nights when we'd have sex then eat. That's when I learned what a talented cook he is and when he found out how sexy I find him cooking. We usually ended up having sex again before he was finished preparing the meal.

"I booked the tickets to Luca's wedding. We're leaving on the Thursday night because of the rehearsal and coming home late Sunday. And I have bad news about the hotel."

I swivel in the corner of the couch and look back at him. "Let me guess, we're sharing a bed?"

"I could lie and say they only had king-size beds, but I

scored two double beds. That's the bad news." He winks, and I hate that I wish there was only a king room left. "If you want to take our chances, I could try to get us two rooms, but if Ma finds out..."

"We'll manage. Just let me know what I owe you."

He moves from the fridge to the counter, then he's heading back over with two plates and a bag of taco-flavored Doritos. "It's *my* cousin's wedding. You don't owe me anything." He hands me my plate.

"Thanks. But I'd like to pay my way."

"Stop it." He rests his plate on the coffee table and sits next to me. Opening the bag of Doritos with ease, he smiles at me. "It's not a big deal."

"And we'll be done pretending after the wedding?" I take a bite of my roast beef and turkey sandwich, complete with mayo, lettuce, and a hint of Dijon.

"I guess we will be." He leans forward and bites his sandwich. "Let's watch more. We don't have to be at my parents' until four."

I press Play and pretend that the idea of our fake marriage being over doesn't bother me. We spend the afternoon watching television, and though I yearn to snuggle up to him in the hopes that something more might happen between us, I stay on my side, tucked into the corner, while he sprawls out as though he has no issue trying to keep us platonic.

I guess I'm the only one who still feels something between us.

———

AT THREE-THIRTY, I walk down the hall to find Dom waiting in the living area, dressed in shorts and a T-shirt.

This time they aren't gym shorts but a nice greenish-blue, and a gray V-neck. His hair is gelled after being freshly showered.

His gaze falls down my yellow summer dress with skimpy straps. It shows off my dancer body and I knew when I took it off the hanger that Dom would like it on me. A heavy breath leaves his lungs, and hunger spills from his eyes. How many times this week have I begged him in my mind to take me? Too many to count.

"Ready?" he asks, his voice cracking as he opens the door.

"Yeah." I arrange my purse crossways over my body and walk out of his condo.

We make it down the elevator and past the doorman.

"Subway or taxi?" he asks once we're on the street.

I'm busying staring at the blue sky as the sun warms my exposed skin. "Um... subway?"

"Okay." He heads in the direction of the station.

I'm surprised he's willing to take the longer way to his parents'. "If you'd rather—"

"No, it's fine."

We walk side by side without saying much other than commenting about a store or some other mundane topic. When we reach the subway, the train is just pulling into the station and we hop on. Forty-five minutes later, we're in Brooklyn.

Once we get off at Carroll Street and we arrive in our old stomping grounds, Dom's hand slides into mine. I look between us and he says, "For appearance's sake."

My insides do cartwheels as he guides me down the street.

"I feel bad for not coming over earlier and helping," I

say as we round the corner. "That's what a good Italian daughter-in-law does."

"She's got Annie. She acts like an Italian daughter-in-law even though I think she's part German or something."

"She and Enzo seem happy."

"They are."

"And Bella and Carm too."

"Yep."

"How's Blanca?" I saw her in Vegas, but my mind was a million different places, so I didn't get to have a long conversation with her.

"The usual. Single."

"Maybe the two of you can move in together when you get older." I laugh, trying to picture it.

He glances at me from the corner of his eye. "Why?"

"You know how brothers and sisters do that after their parents are gone if they don't have their own families?"

He stops at the light, and we wait for the pedestrian sign to appear on the pole across from us. "I'm not going to live with Blanca. Plus, I'm sure she'll get married one day."

"But not you?" I'm poking the bear, I know, but I can't help myself.

"I am married." He smirks at me.

"Not for long. I always wondered what the turnoff was for you. Whether you were against the institution of marriage as a whole or—"

He shoots me an expression to say, "You want to talk about this now?"

I nod.

"I enjoy my work. I like money. I'm not good at multitasking. I tend to be laser-focused on one goal at a time to the detriment of everything else."

"I think you're wrong about the multitasking part, but I

agree that work and money are what you're most obsessed with. But you can have that and a wife."

"Technically, I already do."

I tilt my head in a "come on" manner.

"We both know that when it came to you, my work was our Achilles' heel. It was our weakness in spite of our overall strength, and it destroyed anything we could've built."

I swallow past the lump in my throat at the reminder that once upon a time, he chose work over me. "Maybe one day you'll meet a woman who will make you feel differently."

He stops us before we hit his parents' street. Backing me up into an alley, he positions me against the brick wall. "Let me be clear. If there was a woman in this world who could change me, it'd be you."

His eyes lock with mine, and though I can't read what's in them, I lean forward, wanting to kiss him. All those feelings for him haven't died inside me—I just try to ignore them. But with his admission, I want to believe that I could be enough for him. Enough for him to put work aside and make me his priority. But since he stays upright, not showing any signs of admitting anything to himself, I choose to quiet my heart.

Without any other words, he takes my hand and pulls me back onto the street. We walk in silence up the steps of his childhood home and he opens the door to a packed house. We both smile and play our part as spouses. For the first time ever, I realize with certainty that there's never going to be a happy ever after for Dom and me.

CHAPTER FOURTEEN

Dominic

By the time dinner is over, I want to go home and pass out. The emotional drain of pretending Val and I are a happy couple is wearing on me. The only bonus of the situation is being able to touch Val whenever and wherever I want.

After saying our goodbyes, we head back to the subway station. We walk past the alley where I pressed her against the brick wall on the way over. I wanted to smash my lips to hers after divulging that she's my one. The one I was meant for but am still not good enough for. Because until I know with certainty that I can give her exactly what will make her happy, there's no future for us. I'll never break her like Max did.

Heading down the steps of the Carroll Street station, I take her hand. Not for appearance's sake but because I've grown used to touching her and I'll use the excuse while I can.

After we sit down on the subway train, she rubs her knee absentmindedly.

"Come here." I pat my leg.

"No. It's fine."

I slide her legs over my lap. She doesn't protest but shifts so that she can lean back. The silky fabric of her dress restricts me from using my thumbs and digging into where she needs relief, so I slide one hand under the hem of her dress, judging if she's okay with it. She says nothing, so I continue with my second hand, keeping one on her knee for stability and one for massaging.

"It's funny when you think about it," she says with her eyes closed.

"What is?"

"How many people hate their in-laws and vice versa? Here we are with both parents pushing us together." Her giggle turns into a moan when I press on a sensitive spot.

"True."

"Circumstances aside, it's nice the way your family kind of pulls mine in. Mama is so happy to be part of a bigger family again. With everyone back in Florence, it's been hard on her over the years. I haven't seen her as happy as she was today cooking with your mama and aunts, in a long time." A small smile forms on her lips. "I wish she could really have that."

"You know my family. Bigger is better."

"Thank you. Even if Ma only gets to experience it for a short time. I just... it was nice is all."

I've never thought much about the fact that a lot of my family from Italy is over here. Val's family is small, and with her parents running the corner grocery store, they aren't able to get back to Italy very often. I take it for granted that I have so many loved ones surrounding me.

"You know they're always welcome. My parents have an open door."

"We both know that once we announce the end of our matrimonial bliss, that'll be done. It would be weird if either of us ever marry again."

The thought of her with someone else is like swallowing glass, but I respond how I should. "Then I guess you have to find yourself a man with a big Italian family."

She opens her eyes and stares at me for a second, then slides her legs off my lap. "Thank you."

I'm pretty sure I saw a flash of hurt in her expression, but we've been over this. We've tried how many times to be together? And every time we've failed. She can't possibly agree with everyone else that it's some sign that we ended up married.

Our stop is announced, and I exhale a breath of relief. Conversation over.

Pretty soon we have to address the elephant in the room, but I'm going to toss a blanket over it for tonight because I need to get myself under control. Being this close to her all the time makes it hard to think. I've always been a practical guy who weighs risk against reward—that's basically my job as a trader. But at this point, my dick is going to overrule common sense soon.

I WAKE up on Monday morning to overhear Val talking to someone on the phone.

"I have a meeting with a guy on Broadway about some dance instruction for his new musical this morning. I can come over right after... Mama, calm down. I'll call someone."

I walk out of my bedroom, rubbing my eyes. I'm an early riser, but I swear it's still dark outside. I lean my shoulder on her bedroom door. "What's going on?"

"Sorry." Her eyes widen when she sees me. "Mama, I gotta go. I'll call someone."

She clicks her phone off. She's wearing a cute silk shorts-and-cami pajama set and her nipples are poking through the thin fabric. Her eyes dive down my bare chest and shit... yeah... I'm fucking hard.

"It's morning." I shrug.

"I know."

"I mean..."

"I know, Dom. Don't worry, I don't think it's because of me."

But it is because of her.

"What's going on with your parents?"

"Sorry if I woke you. A pipe burst or something at my parents' store. They're frantic. My dad's trying to figure out what the issue is, but we all know he isn't a fix-it man and I have this—"

"I'll go." I push up off the doorframe.

"No!" She stands and shakes her head violently. "I can handle it. I woke you. Go back to bed."

"I'm not going back to bed, and I have no pressing meetings today. I can do it."

Her shoulders slump. "Are you sure? I mean, it's Monday. You're usually all chipper on Monday mornings to start your week."

God, she does know me well.

"It's fine. Call your ma and tell her I'll be there in an

hour. My dad has a friend who's a plumber, so I'll call in a favor."

"You're a lifesaver." She rushes toward me and throws her arms around my neck.

My arms beg me to pull her close, wrap around her and don't let her go. But I stand there until she feels awkward that I'm not hugging her back and that my hard dick is pressing into her stomach.

"Sorry. Thank you."

"No problem." I head into my room to change and call my dad about his friend so I can get the fuck out of here before I storm into her room and show her the only thing that will quench my dick—her.

An hour later, I'm back in Brooklyn. I walk into the corner store, and sure enough, my dad's friend is already there. It's good to have a big family with connections.

"Dominic!" Giada runs toward me.

The water damage is somewhat extensive. Two aisles full of food have wet drywall caked all over them, and the ceiling is open where the weight of the soaked drywall fell through.

"Hi, Mrs. Cavallo. Wow, this is bad." My phone vibrates in my pocket, but I ignore it.

"I know, I know. Valentina had that meeting and I know it's important, but this..." She puts her hands out, signaling the mess. "It's a lot. We'll have to throw away and restock."

The sadness is clear in her tone and her face. If I stay here, this will be an all-day venture. I can already hear Mr. Cavallo micromanaging my dad's friend. I'll have to help them clean up then figure this out. I look down at my suit.

Fuck.

My phone vibrates again. I put my finger up and step away, pulling my phone from my pocket and seeing my office number. "I'll be right back." I answer the call. "Ash, did you get my message?"

"Yes, I got your message. You forgot about your meeting, I'm assuming?"

"Meeting?"

"The meeting that was rescheduled on Friday? The one where you're supposed to present the portfolio?"

"Shit," I murmur.

Mrs. Cavallo is thankfully trying to take care of a customer now, filling them in on what happened and what won't be available today.

"I'm in Brooklyn."

"You're where? It's Monday. You usually beat me here." There's an impatience I've never heard in her tone.

I look at the mess and at Mrs. Cavallo telling the story to the customer. The tears leaking from her eyes. She looks so much like her daughter, it's scary. If I want to know what Val will look like in twenty-five years, I do.

"I'm going to have to reschedule. See if you can set it up for tomorrow. My hands are tied."

She huffs. "You want me to go in there and tell them what?"

"Tell them I'm sick or that I have a family emergency. Yeah, just say family emergency."

"So lie."

I push a hand through my hair. "Not really. It's Val's parents' store with the problem and Val's my wife, so it's family. Not a lie."

"You mean I'm not lying so you can screw some random chick all day? You're not coming in because you're helping someone?"

The surprise in her tone pisses me off. Just because I'm a workaholic doesn't mean I'm a complete asshole. "Yes.

There was a plumbing issue and I have to help them figure this out. Val had an important meeting and—"

"Say no more. I'll handle it. I'm sure everyone will understand."

"Thanks?" A second ago, it sounded like she wanted to rake me over the coals.

"You're welcome. Now go help your in-laws. I'll call if anything else arises."

"Thanks a lot, Ash."

"It's what assistants are for."

She hangs up, and I tuck the phone into my slacks before taking off my jacket and laying it over a bag of chips. My phone vibrates again as I roll up the sleeves of my expensive shirt. I pull it out and see that it's Val.

Val: *How bad is it? I can come.*
Val: *I'll reschedule. This isn't your problem.*
Val: *I should've just canceled the meeting.*

I shake my head because this is Val. She hates inconveniencing people, yet she's the first one to inconvenience herself if someone else needs her help.

Me: *Not bad. I'm good to handle it. Just worry about your meeting.*
Val: *Are you sure? Ma said something about the drywall falling and food being destroyed?*
Me: *Just an over-exaggeration. You know our mas. I'll probably only be an hour late to work. Good luck with your meeting.*
Val: *Oh good. Thanks again. I owe you one.*
Me: *Can I put in a request? ;)*

She doesn't respond and I didn't expect her to, but I can't stop making sexual innuendos because sex with Val is the only thing on my damn mind. I want her any way I can have her, and the longer I live with her, the more I crave her. Lately, I see no way of getting out of this without destroying either my dick or us.

CHAPTER FIFTEEN

Valentina

I walk into my parents' store still in my heels and pantsuit, and I blink to make sure I'm seeing things correctly.

"Valentina!" Ma coos, rushing toward me with a huge smile.

My dad is refilling the shelves, and my eyes catch on Dom in the corner of the store, his dress shirt rolled up to his forearms and his tie gone. His hair isn't gelled back like it usually is, but instead, it's messy like after we've had sex all day. He glances at me then back at the man he's speaking with.

"It looks good," I say, watching a man on a ladder mudding and taping the new ceiling.

"Dominic, he took charge."

"I thought it wasn't anything big?" I don't look at Ma because I'm too busy scouring what has happened in such a short amount of time. My meeting went well and since I was last up, I accepted when they asked me to lunch because I thought Dom would be long gone and everything would already be resolved.

"I told you. The whole ceiling fell through." She gestures to the man on the ladder as if that explains everything.

"But Dom said it would only be..." I huff, a smile pulling at my lips.

Who would've guessed? Dominic Mancini lied to me for my own gain.

"That's the insurance guy," she says. "Dominic's negotiating what we're going to get because he paid out of his pocket to get this all fixed, so we didn't have to wait."

A customer comes in and ma rushes to them to see if they need help, then she rounds the counter to check them out. I walk around the aisles toward the refrigerator cases. I see a garbage can full of dented cans with ripped and drenched labels at the end of the aisle. There are a few more bins of ruined food by the back door of the storage room.

"You married a good one," my dad says when I approach. The shelves he's stocking aren't chipped or aged like the ones that have been present since I was a child. They're brand new.

"It was bad, huh?"

My dad stands up, holding his back, which tells me he's been working hard all day. "They say it was a plumbing issue from upstairs, but Dom's guy said we're good now. He replaced some of the plumbing and said it won't happen again." My dad swings an arm around my shoulder. "Dominic took care of everything. The clean-up crew, the plumber, the construction crew. He bought new shelves and helped us get new food in. We have no choice but to wait on some items but..."

As my dad brags on about all Dominic has done in such a short amount of time, my vision veers to him. He's pointing at a contract and handing receipts to the insurance representative. They're disagreeing about something and Dom doesn't look like he's about to back down.

But why would Dom do this? A man who can't leave work early for dinner took an entire day off to help my parents?

I desperately want to believe he did it because he's lying to himself and his feelings for me haven't diminished but are alive and kicking under his hard exterior. But it could all be because we're acting like we're married, and in any Italian family, the son-in-law would help his wife's parents no matter the cost. Or maybe it's just because in our culture, you help someone when they're in need.

I chew on my cheek, and he glances up as though he can sense my gaze on him. A small grin pulls on his lips and ignites that fluttery feeling in my stomach.

Bending, I help my dad stock the rest of the shelf, wishing Dom didn't do nice things like this. It makes me believe I might be enough to change him. That one day he'd pick me over his work. But I have to remember that times like this are the exception, not the rule.

DAYS LATER, right after I get home—or not home, but Dom's—there's a knock on the door.

I head over to the door, nervous about who it could be. I still fear that one day, I'll open the door to Nell wearing a trench coat and nothing else, asking for Dom. Rising on my tiptoes, I look out the peephole and fall back down to my heels before opening the door.

"Ma?"

She walks in, her arms filled with bags of food.

"What's going on?" I ask.

I move to shut the door, but Anna Mancini comes in right after. Which explains how they got past the doorman.

"We're going to teach you how to cook Dom's favorite meal." Ma unpacks her groceries on the large island.

Anna drops her own bags before hugging me. "He loves my gnocchi. He tries to act like a meat-and-potatoes guy, but he loves the pasta." She beams at me and helps Ma locate all the cookware they'll need.

"You need to learn to cook if you're going to be married," Ma says, pointing at me with a wooden spoon she's pulled out of a drawer.

"Dom's a great cook. He can be the chef in our marriage." I slide onto the breakfast stool. I'm not resorting to the typical nineteen-fifties housewife role.

"But he took off work to help us. Your parents. You need to thank him." Ma's eyes beg me not to embarrass her in front of my new mother-in-law.

And with an Italian mama comes guilt, so I slide off the stool and round the island.

Anna pulls three aprons from her bag. "Step one, you do not get dirty." She puts an apron over my head and spins me by placing her hands on my hips before tying it in the back.

I look down to see what my apron says, and I shake my head with a chuckle. "Kiss me, I'm Italian" with the Italian flag underneath.

"You can both wear it." Anna beams. "Here, Giada."

I tie Ma's apron that reads, "I'm the sauce boss."

Lastly, Anna puts on hers, and Ma ties the back. "Your opinion wasn't in the recipe" is faded on the front and there are a few stains, which means she bought aprons for Ma and me, but hers is one of her own. It's a sweet gesture, and the hug Ma gives her conveys how much she loves this. She's had friendships, but she wants family. Always has.

"Now." Anna spins me toward the sink. "We wash hands. Hot water and soap."

I'm slightly offended she didn't think I knew that much, but I keep my reaction in check. We wash our hands and dry them with paper towels after she scolds me for using the dishtowel because it's "not sanitary." I nod and throw away my paper towel, feeling all kinds of uncomfortable and incompetent.

"When will Dom be home?" Anna asks.

I look at Ma as if I'm ten and someone asked me a question I have no answer for. She waits—because this is the kind of information a wife should know.

"He usually comes home later," I say, which appeases Anna. She's familiar with her son's obsessive work hours.

"He'll be so happy when you present him this meal." She shares a smile with Ma as though if the two of them could rule the world, they'd match up all good Italian singles. "I got these ready beforehand. They're just cool enough. But next time, you just bake the potato." Anna holds out a few baked potatoes. "You know how to use the oven, right?"

Ma eyes me like "don't embarrass me because I never taught you to cook." Blanca can probably make the seven fish meal for Christmas Eve and I can't boil water. Italian mamas teach their daughters, but my mother was too busy when I was growing up.

"Of course she does," Ma says.

I've heated pizzas. Hello, I have a son to feed. Although there were a lot of Lunchables and takeout through the years.

"Okay, 'cause Blanca acts like I handed her a map and told her to get me to California when I to cook with her. She's lost from the time I say go. The boys know more than her, which isn't much. Except for my Dominic."

I laugh, and my anxiety lessens now that I know she might not have as high expectations as I thought. Ma smiles too, now that she doesn't feel bad for having a daughter who can't cook.

As Anna is instructing me how to scoop the potatoes out of the skin, the key in the door alerts us to Dom's imminent arrival. They both look at me for an answer as to why Dom is home when I said he'd be home later. All of our heads shift toward the microwave clock at the same time. It's four-thirty. He shouldn't be home.

But the door slowly opens, and Dom stands there, staring at us in bewilderment. His tie is loose but still knotted around his neck. Other than that, he's just Dom. Put-together and gorgeous with the weight of the world on his shoulders. He places his keys into the dish and his bag on the chair.

"Hello, everyone," he says, toeing out of his shoes. "Ma." He walks into the kitchen and kisses her cheek. "Mrs. Cavallo." He hugs her and kisses both cheeks.

The two of us stand there because to show our mas we're trying, he should kiss me hello, but he just stands there.

"Hey, babe," he finally says and hugs me, kissing the side of my neck.

I slide into his large frame with the same ease I always have, and I find it as warm, welcoming, and safe as it's always been. But he steps back quickly, inspecting the counter.

"Gnocchi. I love you." He smiles at Anna.

"Valentina is going to prepare the meal," Ma says with a huge smile.

Dom places his arm around my waist, pulling me into his side. "Really? I'd like to see this. The other day she changed the clock time on the oven because she couldn't figure out how to turn it on." He chuckles, as do our mothers.

I swat his stomach. "You have these fancy appliances, that's why."

"Sure, babe. Sure." He kisses my cheek and leaves me standing there in a mush of goo. "I'm going to change."

"Then you can come and help," Anna calls. Her body language says we need to hurry as though there's a surprise party and the guest is about to arrive.

"I made the sauce." Ma raises her hand. "But I left the recipe for you, Valentina, and we'll show you that later. Let's get it heated though." She pours the sauce into a waiting pot on the stove.

"Oh, Giada, it smells wonderful," Anna says.

Our mas talk about my ma's sauce and her grandmother's recipe that keeps getting tweaked. They discuss how, back in the day, you couldn't change a recipe at all but how all their ancestors probably changed them through the years anyway.

I'm busy scooping out potatoes and my mind is on so many things that I don't notice Dom's rejoined us until his chest hits my back. His hands extend around me, taking the potato and the spoon, showing me how to get the most potato out. Shivers run up my spine and I close my eyes from the scent of his cologne.

"That way you get it all," he whispers.

"Dominic? You know how to make gnocchi?" Ma asks, leaning her hip on the counter, watching him teach me.

"He's quite the cook," I say. "All different cuisines."

"Really? When do you find the time?" Ma asks.

"I'm a night owl." He's lying. The truth is he practices on weekends when he's counting the minutes until Monday morning. His voice is low in my ear and I can't help but let myself fall back into his strong chest as he says, "Then you take the potatoes and add some flour, egg yolks, and salt."

He manipulates my hands to crack an egg, and the egg white drips from our hands.

"Now you need to wash," Anna the pseudo health department inspector lectures.

We wash our hands while Anna takes over kneading the dough.

"Ma, that's the fun part. Let Val," Dom says.

Anna smiles at him as though he's the Pope, and she steps aside. Dom resumes his position behind me, his hands on mine. Is he doing this for our mas' sakes? Because if so, I'd like to ask them to move in with us so I can do this every night.

We roll the dough out, and he cuts it into small pieces.

"I have the water going," Ma says.

"Perfect." He runs the small nuggets of dough along a fork. "This is for the sauce to soak into the gnocchi more." Again, he uses my hands as though they're his, directing me to do what's needed. He puts a handful on a plate, and we turn toward the stove where the water boils. "Now we go over to the water. Heavily salted?"

I'm surprised our mas aren't offended. But they nod, watching us as though we're the latest romance movie.

"You drop them in, and when they float, we're going to take them out." He hands the plate to me.

When I drop in the noodles, hot water splashes on me, and I draw back my hand.

"Be careful." He takes my hand and inspects to make sure I'm not hurt.

Our eyes catch for a moment. I want to kiss him. Tell him thank you for taking over. That cooking with him is ten times better than with our mas.

"They're ready," he whispers, interrupting my little bubble of thoughts that are a jumbled mess.

He uses a shallow strainer to remove the pasta from the water. Then he pours the sauce and forks a gnocchi before putting it in front of my mouth. As I slide the pasta off the fork, our mas sigh. It's not the pasta I have an appetite for right now though—it's my husband.

Who knew that could be such a problem?

CHAPTER SIXTEEN

Dominic

Where one Mancini goes, they all go.

All three women are across from our gate at the airport, scouring the shelves for magazines to take on a two-hour flight to Chicago for my cousin's wedding. If I was actually with Val, I might suggest we use the first class bathroom ourselves, which my two dickhead brothers are playing rock, paper, scissors for right now.

"I win, and Bella and I get the bathroom." Carm's hand is on his palm, ready to play.

"Why do we have to resort to this childish game? I say whoever gets there first wins," Enzo says.

"You're in the first row. How's that fair?"

"I have an idea," I say. "Try going two hours without fucking your girlfriends."

They both crinkle their brows as if they don't understand how my last name is Mancini.

I sip my coffee, watching the stock market results scroll across my phone screen. Two days off work for a wedding seems absurd. Originally, I was going to fly in late on Friday, but with Val and I having to put on a good show, it felt unfair to rush her.

"One." Carm interrupts my thoughts, smacking his fist against his open palm.

I'm surprised Enzo agreed to this.

"Two."

"Three."

Carm shoots paper.

Enzo shoots rock.

The bastard can't win to save his life.

"Woo hoo!" Carm places his hand in front of me for a fist bump.

I ignore his outstretched hand because the mile-high thing is stupid. You can't get a woman off in a restroom outside the cockpit. Carm will give it his best shot though.

"Nice. Ma and Pa will be two rows back. Look forward to answering those questions." I roll my eyes.

Carm tosses me one of the napkins he picked up at Starbucks. "You're just jealous. Just have sex already. You're an even bigger dick when you're abstinent."

I grab the napkin before it flutters to the floor. "I'm not jealous. I'm saying it's a bit juvenile to join the mile high club."

"Seriously though, why are you not having sex right now?" Enzo asks.

"Because it's disrespectful. If people think we're together, how will it look if either of us is seen with someone else?"

Enzo nods in understanding.

"Well then, why not have sex with each other? I mean, you've had sex with her before, right?" Carm asks.

I've never been completely honest with my brothers. They know about high school of course, but they have no idea that the girl I was seeing last year was Val. Maybe it's about time it comes out. "Yeah. Remember the woman I was sleeping with who didn't want anything serious?"

Carm's eyes widen to the point that I fear they'll pop right out of his head if he opens them any wider. "Shut up! You and Valentina? She was your hook-up?"

Enzo leans back in his chair with a smirk. Maybe he's smarter than I give him credit for.

"You knew?" I ask Enzo.

His facial expression says he did. "Annie and I ran into Valentina in the Hamptons last summer, and I wondered at the time if she was the woman you were hooking up with."

"Why? There's a zillion women crawling around there in the summer."

"Yeah, but the way you were so hot and cold, I knew whoever she was, she was more than just a hook-up. Val seemed to fit. I thought it was a far-off idea, but then the rumors about her and Max reconciling—"

"Wait!" Carm leans over the table. "You said that you and your hook-up broke up before we started going to the Hamptons last summer."

This is why I didn't mention it to my brothers. I knew it would turn into a *thing*.

"She called it off last spring. Said she was confused and needed more than I could give her. But when we ran into each other in the Hamptons that summer..." I shrug. "You know how it is."

Enzo glances behind me, presumably to make sure the

girls aren't in earshot, then he leans in. "Did you know she and Max were getting back together?"

"She told me." I clench my fist in my lap. Just the sound of her ex-husband's name grinds on me.

"Dom?"

Enzo's eyes are asking me to give him more information, but I'm the oldest. I don't show vulnerability or weakness. "It wasn't a big deal. I pushed her toward him. They share a son."

"But?" Carm asks.

I put up my hand. "It's over. Or at least it *was* over until I ran into her in Vegas and ended up in this mess."

My brothers look at one another.

Carm clears his throat before speaking. "Are you sure there's not more between you guys? She's not with Max anymore and you guys ended up married, drunk or not."

"Exactly." I point at him. "We were drunk." I look back over my shoulder and seek her out in the store. She's laughing while they all flip through the magazines.

"When I'm drunk, I'm honest," Carm chimes in beside me.

Enzo is surprisingly quiet as he sits across from me.

"You also do stupid shit when you're drunk," I say.

Carm shrugs. "True. But if I married someone, I think I'd wonder if it meant something more or not."

"Did you think it meant something more when you pissed on April Wilson's front door because she refused your advances? Or how about the time you let April Wilson spend the night after she forgave you for pissing on her door? You broke your spend-the-night rule for her. Was that a sign?"

He looks at the ceiling as though he doesn't remember

any of it, including April Wilson. "I was passed out. That's the only reason she spent the night."

"You took her to breakfast the next day," I deadpan.

"For the pissing on the door thing." He grows more agitated the longer this line of conversation continues.

"But that wasn't a sign?"

"No. Whatever, man. We're talking about you." He points at me.

"What about Dom?" Val asks as the girls join us, each of them saddling up next to their Mancini brother.

Poor Blanca heads toward my parents where they wait closer to the gate.

"Nothing. What magazines did you get?" Enzo puts his arm around Annie's waist and guides her to sit on his lap.

Bella sits on Carm's lap, and I look at Val. No way can she sit on my lap unless she wants to feel the half chub that hasn't gone away since I walked into her room this morning without knocking and found her wearing only a lacy bra and panties. The image has been flashing in my mind all day.

"Let's go join my parents." I stand, grab her hand, and lead her away from the lovebirds.

I don't want her getting any ideas.

CHAPTER SEVENTEEN

Valentina

"Would you mind zipping me up?" I turn my back to Dom and I hold my hair up off my neck.

His fingers, which were busy fixing his cufflinks, grab my zipper and pull it up so fast that I don't feel any goose bumps or shivers like in the movies where it's an intimate moment between two people. I let go of my hair, and it cascades over the open back of my fitted black dress. I put my foot into my high heel, then the other one.

"So..." Dom clears his throat behind me.

I'm afraid to look at him because I know he's going to look hot as hell and my body doesn't need another reason to want to be closer to him. The act so far with his parents here is painfully pleasant. I get to be close to him, smell his cologne, and feel his body next to mine. But there's still a wall between us. We hold hands, but he doesn't rub his thumb along my pointer finger like he used to. He wraps his arm around my waist, but he doesn't squeeze my hip. He looks at me when I speak, but the hunger that used to be present isn't there any longer. It makes me yearn for him all the more.

I have no choice though, so I circle around to face him. My jaw drops when I see him holding a jewelry box with a ring inside. "Dom?"

"I figure my family will wonder, so I got you a ring." He takes it out of the box and holds it out.

I'm so busy gawking at the huge oval diamond on a silver band encrusted with diamonds that I don't feel him grab my left hand and hold the ring over my first knuckle. He waits a second and nods toward my hand, silently asking if it's okay.

"Yeah, probably." I choke on my words because this is too much.

He slides on the ring. "You're officially Valentina Mancini, ring and all."

"What about you?"

"I'll say I don't like wearing jewelry. Lots of men don't wear wedding bands." He drops the ring box on the desk and turns his back to me.

I thought for sure he'd make a joke about this, some kind of witty comment about owning me or something. Stepping toward him, I put my hand on his back. "Thank you."

He nods. "Don't get attached. It's a loaner."

My heart plummets into my stomach. Of course it's a loaner. How could I be so stupid to think he'd lay down this kind of cash for a fake marriage? His words serve as the reminder I need to remember that all of this is a charade. "Yeah. I didn't think..."

He turns around, never even glancing at my hand. "Ready?"

I nod so fast I fear I look like a bobblehead, but I'm about five seconds from tears. The truth is, I've imagined Dom giving me a ring many times. When I turned and saw him holding one, I was swept away by the moment—fake or not.

Get ahold of yourself.

"I'll just grab my clutch." I scramble to my suitcase and shove the contents of my purse into the clutch.

Dom waits by the door, holding it open as though I'm making him late.

I rush over. "Thanks."

"You can stop thanking me. I'm benefiting from all this too," he murmurs.

The slam of the hotel room door behind us startles me. Where did the Dom who cracks jokes and enjoys sexual innuendos go?

WE MAKE our way to the hotel down the street for the rehearsal dinner, and we're not there more than a few minutes before we're put on the spot about our marriage.

"Congratulations!" Mauro's wife, Maddie, approaches after spotting us from across the room. "Anna told me about the impromptu wedding." She looks at Dom, but he grunts.

"Thanks." I glance at Dom to see if he wants to add anything.

"I'm going to get a drink," Dom says. He leaves me with Maddie, and his cousin Mauro quickly kisses my cheek before following Dom.

"Let me see." Maddie reaches for my hand, excited because she thinks it's real. She inspects the ring, the overhead lights in the restaurant where the rehearsal dinner is being held making it glimmer and shine. "It's gorgeous! Of course Dom would spend a small fortune on your ring."

I glance at her ring and see that it's classic and simple. Though I don't know her well, it seems to fit her and Mauro perfectly. "Thanks."

"Did someone say ring?" Bella comes over with a glass of champagne. "Hey, Maddie."

The two hug.

"You haven't seen Valentina's ring yet?" Maddie asks Bella, her forehead scrunched.

Bella eyes me for a second, then her gaze falls to my left hand. "Oh, yeah... of course. That ring."

Maddie picks up my hand to look at it again.

"Wow, I keep forgetting how big it is." Bella covers her eyes. "I think I should razz Dom and ask if the diamond is the same size as his heart."

We all laugh. They don't know Dom like I do, but I kind of like that. I get the homebody side of him. The one who walks around barefoot and loves thunderstorms. Who spends a whole night perfecting a dish. The man who will binge-watch a television show with me while pigging out on junk food.

"Congratulations, I just heard." Cristian's girlfriend, Vanessa, saunters over in an elegant, form-fitting dress with an off-color heel. She hugs me, her perfume crisp and light. I swear she could be a supermodel.

"Thank you."

"How is married life, Maddie?" Bella moves the conversation away from Dom and me. Thank God. But she purses her lips, sneaking looks at me. I haven't really talked to her or Annie about the marriage being fake, but from the way she's acting, the boys know, which means they do.

"It's good," Maddie says. "Not much different than pre-married life, but—"

"She's already knocked up," Vanessa spills the gossip.

"Wow, congratulations!" I say.

Maddie runs her over her stomach. "It's early, so..." She shoots Vanessa the evil eye.

"What? Maria knows, so everyone will know by the end of the weekend, and you're four months along."

Maddie smiles and shakes her head. "If anyone has any questions, I'll be sure to send them your way. Thanks for telling everyone my news."

Vanessa grabs a champagne glass off a passing server's tray. "Welcome," she says without an ounce of regret.

"How are the happy couple?" Bella asks, staring ahead at where Luca and Lauren are talking with a priest.

"Let's see, the wedding has been pure drama so far. Those two fight like two heavyweights, but one minute they're disagreeing on who sits where and the next we find them in the closet, half undressed." Maddie rolls her eyes then shrugs. "That's just them."

"Zia looks very happy," Vanessa says.

All of our eyes shoot to Anna escorting Annie around the room, introducing her to everyone.

"Annie's her favorite," Bella says.

I glance at Bella, hoping she doesn't really think that. "She's been in the family longer." I knock my elbow against hers. "I'm the newbie."

"You have a ring. You're the Mancini daughter-in-law," Maddie says.

Bella chokes on her champagne.

"Are you okay?" Maddie asks.

Bella nods, trying to swallow. "I'm just so excited for

Val and Dom." Bella places her hand on my arm. "Vanessa, did you see the ring?" She pulls up my arm.

"Sweet Jesus!" Vanessa's mouth hangs open. "That's huge."

"That's Dom." Cristian steps into our circle. "Ladies." He goes around and hugs us and kisses our cheeks. "Always such a show-off." Once he's at Vanessa's side, he stares at her.

She blushes as if they're having their own conversation. With a small shake of her head, they both concentrate back on us.

"Dom!" Vanessa hollers, seeing him approach. "You outdid yourself."

He looks confused for a moment before Vanessa signals to the ring. Then his eyes, cold and hard, turn to mine as though he's reminding me that it's nothing. He didn't buy it. It's a loaner he probably borrowed from one of his hot-shot clients.

"Thanks." He sips his scotch neat, looking anywhere but at me.

The lights dim and go back on.

"Dinner's ready. Thank goodness, I'm starved," Maddie says. "Afterward, the guys are taking Luca out and the girls are heading to a suite. You should all come. Grab Annie too."

Dom never said anything about that to me.

"We'll see. Thanks." I smile so Maddie knows I appreciate the invitation.

Maddie spots Mauro coming to find her, and she makes her way over to him. He leads her by the small of her back into the banquet area where dinner will be served. What that must be like? I find myself jealous of all the relationships in this room.

"Come on, we're over here." Bella signals us to our table, though Carm's voice could be our navigation. She must notice too because she says, "He's so damn loud."

Dom stays two paces back. His hand doesn't guide me, and when we get to the table, I'm surprised he picks the chair next to mine.

Luca and Lauren stand and grab the microphone that's been set up at the front of the room. "We just wanted to thank everyone for coming..."

They continue thanking everyone, and my mind wanders, the metal on my finger cold and unwelcoming because it's not real. All of this is fake. Why did I ever sign up for this? What am I, thirteen years old? Mama guilt shouldn't still force me to do something I don't want to do. We're both thirty-six.

My gaze slides over everyone in the room and stops on Anna. She smiles wide and bright. Because she believes that I love Dom. She's always watching us, always dissecting what we're doing. With Dom's arm over the back of my chair and me slightly swayed toward him, we look like a couple. He's really good at pretending when he needs to, which frightens me.

"We also want to offer our congratulations to our cousin Dominic, who just got married."

Everyone claps, and Anna signals for us to stand. Dom slides his chair back and lightly grasps my elbow, helping me up. I feel my cheeks heating as everyone looks expectantly at us.

"Thanks, Luc," Dom says.

Then Carm taps his glass with a utensil and Bella joins in. Soon the entire room is clinking their glasses with their silverware.

Someone should tell them to stop. Please stop. I'm hanging on the last inch of a very thin thread.

But no one stops. The clinking and calls for us to kiss only become louder.

Dom's large hand slides against my skin to cup my cheek, and his head dips down to mine. He doesn't ask before his lips press to mine. At first there's a hesitancy and I think he's going to leave it at that. A light kiss to appease the crowd. But the longer his lips remain on mine, the closer his body presses to mine. His free hand slides around me, pulling me into his hard chest as his tongue slides along the seam of my lips. I happily open them, and our tongues reunite with a taste so sweet and divine, I moan. His hand grows firmer, his fingers threading through my hair, and he pushes harder against me as his tongue slides faster.

My hands seek anything to grab hold of, and I find it as my fingers dig into the waist of his slacks.

"Okay, this isn't your wedding," Enzo says.

Dom stops the kiss like a motorbike—fast and skidding to a stop. Our eyes catch, and the heat overflowing his sparks every cell in my body to life.

"Well, congratulations you two. Now go to your room next time," Luca says over the microphone.

I look down, embarrassed for making such a spectacle.

"As delicious as always," Dom murmurs but untangles from me, holding out my chair.

I sit down, unsure of what to do. I reach for my water goblet and catch Bella and Annie staring at me with dumbfounded expressions.

Shit. That was so believable, I almost thought it was real.

CHAPTER EIGHTEEN

Dominic

Fuck. What did I do? I could've left it as a short peck on the lips. No one would've said anything. But I lost control. Me. The disciplined guy who makes sure every box is checked, and everything is in order just mauled his fake wife in front of an entire room full of family.

Val's quiet beside me, and the waiter has refilled her water glass four times now. When she excuses herself between dinner and dessert to go to the restroom, I'm relieved because all I can think about is pulling up her dress under the table and seeing how wet she is from that kiss.

I can't even stand to look at the ring on her finger. So I dodged her all night—until everyone clanked their glasses. We didn't have a choice. The more you deny them, the more they clink.

Ma and Pa get up from the table to go say hello to someone, and Enzo and Carm slide over next to me.

"What the hell was that?" Carm asks. "You were about two seconds from clearing the table and laying her down."

Enzo laughs.

"It's an act." I take a sip of my scotch, staring straight ahead so I don't have to look at them.

Enzo raises his eyebrows. "That wasn't an act. You need to face the facts, bro."

I take another sip of my scotch. "Val and I are not an option, but I can't deny that I want her."

"Then do it. Have sex," Carm, the least responsible of us, chimes in.

"I can't."

"Why? You guys are fighting some crazy chemistry." Carm shakes his head. "Maybe you're both just horny. You put that stipulation in place that you can't have sex with anyone else. And then the two of you are living together? I can't imagine how you're holding up. Pornhub?"

I nod.

"That's not gonna work for long. If you guys had casual sex before, why not now?" Carm asks.

"That's stupid," Enzo says. "It's because he clearly loves her."

"Whoa." I hold up my hands. "I don't love her."

Enzo blows out a breath. "You're delusional."

"I get that I fell for her once upon a time maybe, but we're friends now. Childhood friends. I might have love *for* her, but I'm not *in* love with her."

Enzo sits back in his seat. "Bullshit."

What is it about people who've found love wanting everyone else to have the same? It's irritating as hell.

"Then that's perfect." Carm shrugs. "Screw her and get it out of your system. You guys will get the annulment after all this and that's it. I have no idea why you're second-guessing yourself. It's pretty simple."

Huh. He could have a point. After last summer, I should be good at leaving my heart out of the equation. No point in being sexually frustrated when I don't have to be.

"You might be the smartest brother." I wink at Carm.

He winks back, beaming at Enzo like "take that."

Enzo rolls his eyes. "You're both idiots. And when you lose her and you're devastated, don't come crying to me. Carm can handle that all on his own." He stands, pats Carm's shoulder, and walks away.

"Thanks," I say to my youngest brother, perfectly happy to go ahead with this plan.

"Any time." Carm shakes his glass and the ice inside clinks. "I gotta go get a refill. Go find your woman and make it happen."

He leaves, and I think his advice over again. Every big decision deserves a second thought. But when it comes to Val, I think I've done enough thinking.

So as the waiters take away our dinner plates, I stand, planning on having my dessert upstairs.

CHAPTER NINETEEN

Valentina

I'm reapplying my lipstick when Annie and Bella enter the bathroom. There's a small lounge area, and they sit in the velvet chairs facing the large gilded mirror.

I stop applying and meet their quizzical eyes. "What's up?"

"You know we know, right?" Bella says. I think she's the more outspoken of the two.

"I figured." I drop the lipstick into my clutch and turn to face them, leaning against the small counter.

Annie's eyes hold a note of sadness.

"What I'm wondering is... is all of it fake?" Bella crosses her legs.

"Bella, it's none of our business," Annie says, which I'm thankful for, but to be honest, I'd like their opinion.

My mind is a jumbled mess and Lulu is so occupied with motherhood and pregnancy that I've gotten away with telling her we're moving forward with the annulment without having to go into any detail. Dominic Mancini's name alone tends to make her blood pressure skyrocket and she doesn't need that right now.

"Dom and I... we're complicated. I'm sure the boys have told you that we share a past we have a hard time walking away from." I sit on the third chair tucked into their corner.

Bella stands and moves her chair to face me.

Annie still looks as if she just watched the ending of *Titanic*. "Isn't that the best part though? That you guys have so much history? Maybe you're meant to be."

I laugh until I realize they aren't. "I don't know if you noticed, but Dom isn't a father-of-two-and-a-white-picket-fence kind of guy."

Annie nods, but I'd really like to hear her thoughts on this matter.

"Not yet," Bella says. "But Carm didn't want to settle down either. Or Enzo, right, Annie?"

Annie shakes her head. "The Mancini brothers are hard nuts to crack."

Bella laughs so loudly, she startles two older ladies walking through the door.

"That kiss, though? There was nothing fake about that kiss," Bella presses, keeping her voice down now that we have company. Strands of her red hair fall from her updo because she's so animated when she talks. She and Carm are so alike.

"No, there wasn't." I can't refute it. My toes are still tingling, and my knees are still regaining their strength. It's like a movie playing back in my mind, over and over again.

Bella points at me. "See."

"Bella," Annie sighs.

Bella's head swivels in her direction. "What? You

coerced me and Carm to get together. From that duckpin bowling to the house in the Hamptons. Why aren't you on my side here?"

I wonder how close Bella and Annie are. They have no idea I was part of Dom's life while they were getting together with the Mancini brothers. At least I don't think they do.

"Because it was different. Dom is..." Annie's gaze shoots to mine. "Different."

"See." I hold out my hand toward Annie. "She gets it."

"Different isn't bad. He's like any other guy," Bella insists.

"She has a son," Annie says. "She can't take a chance on a guy who works every hour of every day."

"Yeah, but he's, like, almost sixteen, right? It's not like he's going to grow super attached to Dom and ask him to be his Little League Coach." She shoots me a look as though she's asking me to side with her.

I nod. "No, but I do have to worry about who I introduce him to."

"Okay, forget the kid."

"Forget the kid?" I question.

"No, not like that. I mean, the kiss was hot. I bet you guys had hot sex too."

My mind travels over our history of sexual exploration. From when we lost our virginity together to last year when he made lo—screwed me in the backseat of our rented car outside a winery. Still, I raise an eyebrow. "Your point is?"

"You probably don't get it a lot, what with being a mom, right?"

I laugh.

"Bella," Annie sighs.

I smile at her to say it's okay. "True. My unicorn cock vibrator goes through its share of batteries."

"Then take advantage of it while you can. If you both have your reasons why it won't work out between the two of you, then just be fuck buddies in the interim."

"You can't be serious?" Annie leans forward as though she has to look into Bella's eyes to see if she means it.

"I am. Look at them. They could barely control themselves out there."

Annie presses her lips together.

I shake my head. "We tried that last year and it ended horribly."

"Wait, what?" Bella holds up her hand and looks at Annie.

But Annie isn't surprised. She knew. I let that sink in. She knew. Maybe that's why she's so against us now.

"You're the reason he kept disappearing on the weekends in the Hamptons?" Bella asks.

I nod.

"And what happened?"

"It just didn't work out." I'm not willing to go into specifics.

Annie looks as though she's still screaming, "JACK!" in her mind. "How did Rose not save you? There was room for two of you on there."

"Why not?" Bella asks, pinning me with her gaze.

"I told you. We're complicated." My shoulders sag as I think back over our long and sordid history of on-again and off-again.

Bella nods. "Okay, then I definitely say screw one another and have fun. Your son is gone for how much longer? How often do you have this kind of time to yourself?

You don't need a vibrator; you need the real thing. Might as well enjoy it while you have it in the next room."

"I feel like I don't even know you," Annie says, standing and heading to the mirror I was just using.

I watch Annie reapply her makeup, her eyes skittering to mine every once in a while. She doesn't think a fling is a good idea and I can't say I blame her.

"Work him out of your system," Bella says before she joins Annie at the mirror.

I contemplate their advice, or really Bella's. Could I sleep with Dom again without getting all up in my feelings? Our kiss runs through my mind again, and yeah, I think it's at least worth a try. Being around him all the time and not being able to have him has been torture.

Besides, I already know what it feels like to have Dom walk out of my life. I survived before, and if I do grow attached, I can survive again.

I follow Annie and Bella out of the women's restroom, and there stands Dom, leaning against the wall with his hands in his pockets. When he sees me, he smiles.

If there were any doubts in my mind, they float away like a helium balloon on a windy day.

CHAPTER TWENTY

Dominic

"Go get her," Bella whispers as she walks by.

"Bella, seriously!" Annie scolds, the two walking back toward the banquet room.

Val approaches me, her eyes fixed on mine. That has to be a good sign. With any luck, our kiss is still affecting her as much as it is me.

"Hey," she says as though she didn't see me moments ago.

"Hi." I take her hand. "We need to talk."

"Talk?" She doesn't fight as I drag her toward the doors.

The doorman opens the doors when we approach, and we step out into the Chicago humidity. At this moment, I wish my cousin had had his rehearsal dinner at the hotel we're staying in, but the wedding is there tomorrow, so I can't complain.

"Taxi?" she asks.

But as fast as I want to get her back to the hotel room, we can't just dive into this again. We need to set some boundaries like we had before. "No, we're going to walk."

"Have you seen my heels?"

I glance down, and yeah, I noticed her heels earlier when I was envisioning myself drilling into her with the pointy ends poking into my ass.

"It's not far." I take her hand, and we cross the street.

"Isn't your family going to wonder where we went?" She steps up onto the curb with me.

"They're going to think we're doing exactly what we will be doing." I let go of her left hand and go to walk on the opposite side of her, grabbing her right.

"What are we doing? Exercising?"

"Right now sure, but soon I'll be fucking you." She gasps, and I stop us. "Is that a problem?"

Her eyes widen, and she shakes her head. "No."

"Good. I figured we were on the same page." I start us walking again.

"And that page is...?"

"I have a proposition for you."

"Did the ring come with stipulations?" she asks, slowing her steps again.

"No." I tug her forward. I'm hoping we can settle the rules before we make it back to the hotel. Once I'm behind closed doors, I'm going to be done playing the polite fake husband. "This no sex thing isn't working for me. I have no release, and everything you do is turning me on." But I stop walking because I have to see her eyes. If there's any chance things will become weird or awkward if we do this, as bad as blue balls are, I'll stop myself. "I want the same agreement we had last year. Fun and fucking. No strings. No sleep-overs, except now you'll be in my guest room. No dates. And most of all, no feelings."

She looks into my eyes, probably judging whether I'm the one who can handle this. I look away briefly and see our hotel one block over.

"Are you sure? I mean, after the Hamptons last summer..."

"I had to if you were going to give it a try with your ex. You can't have a fuck buddy making conjugal visits if you're trying to reconcile with your husband."

She flinches. I know we were more than fuck buddies. It just about killed me to walk away from her, but she doesn't need to know that. That's for me to take to the grave. All she needs to know is that I want to do it again. I want the incredible sex she offers but no relationship. No relation-ship means no feelings means I don't have to suffer through all that again.

"And what happens after Ryder returns? We still get the annulment?"

I glance at her ring and wince. I hate that fucking thing and what it represents. "Yeah."

She nods and looks at the sprinkling of stars we can see past the skyscrapers. "I'm worried."

"You're worried you're going to get hurt?" The last thing I've ever wanted to do is cause Val pain, but unfortu-nately, I've done my fair share of that over the years.

"Well." She studies me, searching for a hint I might want more from her than sex. So I splash on a sexy smile to mask my true feelings. "No. I just—"

I end the conversation with a kiss. She's worried about me because of last summer. Our last night together is vivid in my mind. I made love to her and promises fell from my lips, then bam, her ex-husband showed up the next morning saying he'd learned the errors of his ways and wanted to try again.

I need us to forget all that and move forward. I'll never let myself get there with her again, so there's no point worrying about it.

She pulls at my shirt, yanking me to her.

I didn't think this through. I should have her at the hotel already.

Stripping my mouth from hers, I grab her hand. "We need to get to the hotel, pronto."

Somehow, we make it through the hotel doors and up the elevator to our room.

I hold the room key above the sensor, examining her one more time. "You're sure about this?"

"I'm a thirty-six-year-old woman, Dom. Let me make this decision." She takes the key from my hand and slides it over the sensor. It beeps, the light changing to green. She pushes open the door and pulls me in by my tie. The door slams shut.

"Do me one favor?" I ask, pulling her toward me. "Take the ring off."

The hurt in her eyes almost cuts me, but I have to. After sliding it off her finger, she puts the ring on the desk next to the box it came in, then she slips out of her heels and moves her hand to the zipper in the back.

"Let me," I say, turning her around.

She swipes her hair off her back, resting it all over one shoulder. I find the zipper and slowly lower it until I see the top of her thong. My dick twitches at the first sight of the lacy fabric separating me from her pussy. My hands splay on the bare skin I've missed since last summer. Yeah, there was Vegas, but that was a drunken mess I only half remember. This time, I'm going to savor the moment with her.

When I slide my palms up her back, she arches, her head falling forward as my fingers dive under the fabric of her dress at her shoulders. It slides off and down her arms, and I lean forward, allowing my lips to taste her. The smell of her body wash pulls at my memories of us together. She leans back into my chest, and I push the dress off her torso, freeing her arms. A moan escapes her throat. With her head on my shoulder and her mouth so close to my ear, a shiver runs up the back of my neck.

"Always so beautiful," I mumble, happy to see she went sans bra today. Her nipples are already peaked, but I squeeze them between my thumbs and forefingers and her back bolts up off my chest for a moment. "How do you want it?"

She turns her head and kisses the hollow of my neck. "I'm not picky. As long as it's you I get."

All those questions about whether we should or shouldn't do this finally dissolve. Having Val in my arms again is like picking that one crazy stock that everyone thinks will crash but soars.

My hands glide down her thin dancer's frame, pulling the dress until it falls off her hips and cascades to the floor.

"I have to see how wet you are." I tease where her panties meet her skin. I almost want to save this part to make it last, but I'm way too greedy. Her body softens when my finger dips into her folds. "Tell me if this happened after our kiss."

She raises one arm up and around my neck. "I've been wet for weeks around you. The kiss might have been the final straw, but..."

"Come here."

I bend closer to kiss her and she turns in my arms, both her arms around my neck. Our kiss is slow and gentle. I can't explain why I want to go ape-shit crazy on her, but at the same time I need to take my time. The thought that I'll never have her again is scary. She's only ever in my life for short excerpts.

"You're way overdressed for this occasion." She smiles, pulling at my tie. With my help, I'm quickly stripped down from the waist up. When her hands land on my belt, her fingers dip under the fabric to graze my skin. "I've missed him."

I chuckle and shake my head. Her incessant need to refer to my manhood as though it's a third party between us always gives me a laugh.

"He's missed me too, I bet." She lowers to her knees, her eyes on me.

I watch her undo my belt and pants, unzipping them carefully.

"Yes, he did." She palms my hard length over my boxer shorts, and her other hand pushes my pants to the floor. After she runs her cheek over my bulge, her teeth tease me.

A groan echoes in the room, and I'm not sure if it was her or me.

"Come here." I try to bring her back up to me, but she shakes her head, looking at me.

"You're not the boss here, Mr. Mancini."

My hands find the edge of the desk and I grip so hard my palms ache, watching her take me out of my boxer briefs. Just like we both knew would happen, my dick springs out like a panting dog when his owner returns home. Pre-cum rests on the tip, indicating my excitement. She twirls her hand over my cock, opens her mouth, and slowly accepts all of me until the tip of my dick slides into the back of her throat.

"Val!" I'll have little restraint if she keeps doing that. No one can get me off with a blowjob like Val can, and if she continues, this night is going to end early.

She draws back with a satisfied smile, and I pull her up under her arms so we're face to face.

"Another time." I don't want her to fight me on the topic, so I take her lips with mine and slide my tongue in. She doesn't complain as I backstep her toward the bed.

When the backs of her knees hit the bed, she falls down then slides up the mattress, dipping her fingers over her pussy. I toe out of my shoes, take off my socks, and push my boxer briefs down the rest of the way.

"Still have an IUD?" I climb up the bed.

She nods. "Are you clean?"

I tilt my head because of course I'm clean, but she found out about Nell and who knows if she slept with anyone else... Damn, I can't even think about her and someone else without wanting to kill someone.

"Yeah," I bite out.

Her legs open farther. "Come."

"I plan on doing just that, but I think I need to get you to like the beard first." I nestle between her legs, my arms wrapping her legs over my shoulders as I kiss the insides of her thighs.

Her hands grab the pillow behind her head. The smell of her pulls memories of other times I've been in this position with her to the surface. Moments I took for granted. I'll never do that again.

When I run my beard over her inner thigh, she yelps and grinds against me.

I chuckle. "Not so bad, huh?"

"Not at all."

I swipe my tongue up her center and watch for her reaction.

Maybe this wasn't a good idea. I'm already thinking of all the ways I'm going to take her, and it's going to take a hell of a lot longer than we have left together.

CHAPTER TWENTY-ONE

Valentina

His beard feels amazing on my thighs, and when he runs it over my clit? I'll have to tell him I was lying when I said I didn't like the way it looks so he doesn't get rid of it.

Dom's tongue slides along my folds until he hits my clit, then he twirls his tongue over my bud before sucking it into his mouth. I buck up and he chuckles into my depths, placing his hand on my pelvis to keep me on the bed. He quickly brings me to the brink because he's mapped me before. He knows what gets me there. As my hand grabs the pillow, fisting it, he draws back and stares at me.

I hate this game.

"Don't," I warn.

He smirks. "Don't what?"

"You know what."

"Enlighten me." He blows on my clitoris while staring at me. "I'm doing what you love."

"I do *not* love the 'come, oh wait no, don't come' game."

"That's not the game." His finger runs through my wetness and he teases my opening without inserting his finger.

"Then what is it?"

"It's called delayed gratification. It's fun."

"For you." I prop up on my elbows, and he bites his lip, getting a laugh out of this. "There will be payback."

"That's where we're different. You love satisfying me, and I love watching you." He buries his head between my thighs again, his beard creating the best friction along my skin.

As he masterfully climbs me up that ladder again, I anticipate that he won't let me come, but he inserts his fingers while his tongue moves at the perfect speed and applies pressure along my clit.

"Dom," I sigh and bite my lip because I don't want to give him any sign that I'm about to come.

My toes curl along his muscular back, and blackness creeps in at the edge of my vision. I clench and he pulls out his fingers, his mouth leaving my clit.

"I'm going to kill you!" I scream.

He laughs, blowing on my wet bud again, his finger slowly gliding down my center. "Don't worry, I always deliver." His cocky smile is annoying.

But he's right. He always does deliver. In spades.

When he dives back down this time, my hands entwine in his hair so I can keep him where I want him. But he ups his game, adding another finger and sliding his thumb between my clit and my opening. With his tongue, it's like a trifecta. My hands fall off of his head to the sheets, grabbing and gripping until my knuckles ache.

"Don't stop. Please, Dom, don't stop," I beg just like he probably hoped I would.

I soar into another dimension, as though I'm floating in a galaxy without gravity, and he doesn't relent. I clench around his fingers and he moans, his tongue circling and shifting, then with one long suck on my clit, my orgasm explodes. I cry out and buck against his face, and he eases the pressure on me until I float back down.

When I come back to Earth, Dom places a kiss right below my navel, then he climbs up my body. "That was worth it, right?"

I have no words because he knows me way too well. I take his head and pull it down to mine in a ravishing kiss. My taste on his tongue is too much to bear, and another climax starts like a bass drum between my legs.

"I need you." I pant when we tear apart.

His lips make their way over my jaw, my neck, my ear until he comes back and captures my mouth again. He pushes inside me, my wetness coating him. "Shit, Valentina, you feel so damn good."

He thrusts immediately and I'm not complaining because I want him to use me for his sexual pleasure. I don't want lingering kisses or touches right now. I want him to grip me, grind me, flip me, fuck me.

He never disappoints, as though he knows what I need before I do.

Pulling my legs up to lay flat on his chest as his hands grip my hips, he drills into me over and over, sweat forming on his face and glistening on his muscular chest.

"Harder," I say, and he obliges. With my legs up, he's so deep and my climax crashes over me without any warning.

When I open my eyes, he's smiling, staring at me and probably mentally tallying that that's number two.

Dom allows my legs to fall, then his hips find their way back between my thighs. He kisses me once before his face lands in the crook of my neck, his breathing increasing, panting and swearing and telling me how I'm made for him. He pumps hard, then with a groan, he stills inside me.

We're two sweaty messes on the hotel bed, but he kisses me slow and unhurried until I wrap my arms around him, wishing this wasn't just sex. When I decided on this, I forgot how much he owns my body.

Times like this, it feels as if I was made for him and he was made for me. But if that's the case, how come we're so wrong for each other?

DOM'S LIPS trail kisses down my spine when he wakes me the next morning.

"Mmm." I smile into my pillow, my eyes remaining closed.

"Are you sore?" he mumbles, his naked limbs sprawled over me like an octopus.

Dom always flirted his way into getting more from me unless I kicked him out. Which I did well for the first few months we were hooking up. I couldn't take the chance that I would want more from him. But gradually, as it always does, he'd stay for a few hours. We'd share a meal that he'd make. And then on the weekends that Ryder was with Max, our hook-ups turned into a full weekend of sex and lounging around.

"Not bad." Truth is, I relish the delicious ache between my legs from last night.

He rolls on top of me, his hand brushing my hair so it lays on the pillow while he kisses across my shoulders and up my neck. I feel his hardness pressing into my ass cheeks. "That's good news. I ordered breakfast. Should be here in about an hour."

"An hour, huh? How will we ever fill the time?" I grin.

He chuckles, using his strong palm to roll me over. He situates himself between my legs, his hard length already poised and ready at my opening. "I have a few ideas."

"What about the wedding?" I ask, tilting my head as his lips travel down my throat.

"Right now I'm thanking God that I'm not a groomsman."

"Do you think we need to talk?" I ask, unable to ignore the obvious—me being here this morning because we're sharing a hotel room doesn't make this feel like a hook-up.

"No, I don't. This might not be part of the plan, that I actually get to feed you breakfast, but when we get back to New York, we'll get you moved out of my place and figure out the annulment."

Of course Dom has it all already figured out. He always does. Always one step ahead.

"Okay." I'm not going to argue. When I agreed to sleep with him again, I knew the score. That's the problem when you go back to someone a second time. Who they really are isn't a surprise.

Just as Dom's sliding down my torso and I'm losing any fight as to why this might be a bad idea, a knock sounds on the door.

"An hour, huh?" I ask when his head pulls up from between my thighs.

Dom puts up one finger and calls, "Who is it?"

"Carm, jackass. Open the door."

"Sorry, busy."

"Yeah, yeah, but cousin duty calls."

I look at the alarm clock. "It's eight o'clock."

Dom gets up and puts on his slacks from where they rest in a ball on the floor. His back flexes when he runs a hand through his hair. "Don't move." He points at me.

I slide up the bed so my back hits the headboard. Dom leaves the bedroom and heads into the living area. The locks clink, and I hear the brothers talking.

"This is like déjà vu, am I right?" Carm laughs.

"I'm busy."

"I can see that. First I want to thank you for putting pants on this time."

"Get to the point." Dom's impatience has me holding back a smile.

"Luca can't dance."

Now I do smile. He probably can but thinks he can't. Men are so weird about dancing, whereas most women I know go out there and do their own thing.

"And why does that concern me? All he has to do is hold her and spin in a circle."

I shake my head.

"I'm guessing Val is in there naked in bed?" Carm asks.

"You assume wrong."

"Okay, sure. You're standing here smelling like sex, but she's not in there?"

I hear a scuffle, then Carm is standing in front of the bed with his eyes covered. I pull the sheet up over me.

"Carm!" Dom scolds. "What the fuck? What if I did this to you?"

"I'm sorry," Carm says, turning around with his eyes covered. "It's an emergency."

"We're busy." Dom digs through my suitcase and tosses me the pajamas I should've been wearing.

"He's your cousin. It's his wedding. We can't leave him hanging."

"Luca doesn't seem like a guy who can't dance," I say.

"Can I look now?"

I get up off the bed and shimmy on my shorts. "Go ahead and turn around."

Carm does, but his gaze scatters over the room. "I was expecting clothes hanging off the lights and condom wrappers everywhere."

"Talk, Carm," Dom snaps, and I laugh.

"Sorry, jeez." Carm's eyes set on me. "Val, how long would it take to teach Luca?"

I shrug. "What's he looking for? Just a basic box step? It depends how fast he can keep it up. Plus, I'm not a ballroom dancer."

"You're the best we got." He inspects a chair before sitting down.

"Don't sit down," Dom says.

I smile at him. Carm narrows his eyes. I always did love their relationship. It's amusing to watch.

"Relax, big guy, it's like a second. You'll get your orgasm this morning. Won't he, Val?"

I ignore his question. "Let me eat breakfast. Is he here at the hotel before the wedding?"

"He's at his parents' house. The church is over that way."

I nod. I didn't mind the idea of spending the day in bed with Dom, but the distraction is probably good. "Okay. Tell him we'll be there mid-morning."

"Thanks." He stands from the chair and pats Dom's back. "See? That was, like, five minutes." Then he stops before walking down the small hallway back to the suite door. "Don't tell Annie, but you're my favorite sister-in-law."

I raise my eyebrows. "Technically I'm your *only* sister-in-law and—"

"Nope." He puts up his hand. "Let's not speak of the foreseeable demise of Vominic."

"Vominic?"

"Your couple name. Like Brangelina?" Carm shrugs.

"I get it," I say.

"And it's stupid." Dom takes Carm by the shoulders and pushes him down the hall.

"I think it has a nice ring personally. Bella and I are going with Barmelo. Awesome, right?"

"You're just taking one name and replacing the first letter with the first letter of the other person's name. That's not really how it works." The door opens and Carm's voice fades.

"Not true! I came up with Lorenzie for Annie and Enzo." His voice is as prideful as a kid coming home with an A on their spelling test.

"Perfect. Go interrupt them. I'm sure they'll be happy to hear what you've come up with," Dom says.

The door shuts as Carm screams a thank you to me.

Dom appears at the doorway of the bedroom. "Take those back off."

He undoes his slacks, stepping out of them on his way to the bed. The flutter in my stomach as he stalks toward me is a bad sign, but I can't stop myself. I'm an addict when it comes to Dominic Mancini.

CHAPTER TWENTY-TWO

Dominic

Val and I step out of the Uber in front of my zia's house. Flowers still line the sidewalk up to the front door, but the gate isn't white anymore. It's black wrought-iron now. The hanging baskets boast colorful flowers that clash with the large Italian flag hanging from the porch railing.

"I remember running along these streets when we'd come for vacation." I link my hand with Val's mostly because I want to, but it's nice to have the excuse that we're supposed to be happily married.

"It must've been so great to come from a big family," she says.

I hear the sadness in her tone. Val was alone a lot when her parents had to work at the store. It's how we were thrown together—ma met Val's ma at a church function and volunteered to watch her. Ma had no clue that from that

moment forward, Val's and my lives would be like tree roots
—entwined forever.

"You always have us."

She frowns. "Not for long. It's almost time for us to
part."

"When does Ryder get back?"

"Next weekend."

I let go of her hand, and she walks up the concrete steps.
She's wearing a sundress. The fabric is light and clingy and
gives me a perfect view of that ass I love to bite.

I knock on the screen door. I can already hear loud
conversation coming from inside.

"Val!" Zia comes to the door with her robe on. "Come.
Come." She opens the door and hugs Val. "This is so my
boys. Waiting until the last minute. Lauren asked Luca to
take ballroom lessons when Maddie and Mauro did, but
Luca thought he had it handled." She shakes her head.
"Dominic." She pats my cheek, smiling at me. "Look at you
two. You could be on a magazine, you're such a gorgeous
couple." She waves us inside. "Downstairs. You know the
way, Dominic."

"I do, Zia. Thanks." I kiss her cheek and again entwine
my hand in Val's.

The basement stairs creak on our way down to the
finished basement that Mauro moved into when he was a
teen. All three of my cousins are on the couch in front of the
Xbox, playing *Madden*.

Mauro has on his tux pants but no shirt. Luca's in track
shorts and a T-shirt while Cristian's wearing jeans and a V-
neck T-shirt. If I didn't have a better body than Mauro, I'd
demand he get dressed in front of Val. But let's be real, he's
put on a few happy pounds.

"Boys," I say.

Mauro and Luca glance up from the television, their fingers moving across the controllers as they shout at one another.

"What's up, Dom? Thanks for bailing Luca out, Val. You'll come to find out he's the baby of the Bianco family and acts just like one." Cristian ruffles his younger brother's hair and Luca slides out from under his touch.

"He's jealous because I'm the better-looking one." Luca's eyes are still on the TV screen.

"I thought we were here to teach you how to dance?" I motion for Val to sit on the plaid chair, and I stand by Cristian.

She crosses her legs and watches the game. Silent but observant.

"The girls at the hotel?" I ask.

"Nah, they're at Luca and Lauren's, getting ready before they head to the church," Cristian says, since the boys are too busy playing their video game.

"Nice. So when will you be visiting the altar?" I slap Cristian on the shoulder.

He smiles. "Van's not ready yet. I let her dictate how fast we go. She just got another new store to take on her designs, so I'm waiting until next year maybe. But I won't be making a big deal of it like these two. We'll be eloping."

I chuckle. "Zia gonna like that?"

"After these two, Ma won't mind. Maybe we'll have a small reception, but I don't want all the fuss. I want the wife with no wedding. Plus, her ma died when she was young, and I think it'd be painful for her to have a big to-do."

I half smile at Cristian because out of all the Biancos and Mancinis, he's the one who always puts others' needs before his own. Not that we're assholes, but Cristian's like hero territory. Which probably explains why he's a police officer.

"I gotta say, I was surprised to hear about your nuptials." Cristian keeps his voice low, but Val turns ever so slightly, so I know she heard.

"Yeah. Val and I have known each other a long time, so..."

"But marriage?" He shakes his head. "I always envisioned you as the forever bachelor, Uncle Dom who brought home girls half his age."

I chuckle and Val stifles a giggle, still trying to act as though she's not eavesdropping. "Gee, thanks."

"No offense." Cristian shrugs. "But I'm happy for you. You guys sneaking off last night must mean things are good."

Val turns toward the television. "How much longer?"

The boys are arguing about a touchdown.

"Give me two minutes to kick his ass," Mauro says, standing from the couch. His body moves side to side as his fingers press on the remote.

"We're good," I say in answer to Cristian's question.

Luca stands up next to Mauro, his fingers just as fast. A second later, he drops the remote on the table with an 'I'm the best' attitude. "Winner!" He raises his hand toward Val and she high-fives him.

"It's his wedding. Can't let him walk down the aisle thinking he sucks." Mauro laughs and Luca tries to put him in a headlock.

Mauro wraps his arms around Luca's torso, and the two wrestle on the couch.

Val laughs and looks at me.

"Yeah, we wrestle sometimes too," I answer the question she didn't ask.

"I figured," she says.

"Come on. We don't have all day. Luca, get your ass up," I say.

His red face peers up through Mauro's arm, then he slips out of Mauro's grasp and straightens his T-shirt. "Sorry." He shoots a warning glare at Mauro, who's too busy laughing to care. "I just need to know enough to not make a fool of myself."

She stands and comes over to where I am, since there's more space. "Play some music, Dom."

"What kind of music?" I ask, pulling out my phone.

"I'm assuming you have a mother-and-son dance along with the first dance for you and Lauren?"

Luca nods.

"Are they fast or slow?"

Luca glances at Cristian.

"How would I know?"

Luca's vision shifts to Mauro.

"It's your wedding."

Luca throws up his hands. "It was weeks ago that we met with the DJ and Lauren already had a song picked out for me and Ma, so I went with it."

"Do you know the song you're dancing to with Lauren?" Val asks in a patient tone that still suggests *step it up, you're the groom.*

This is Luca. His attitude toward the wedding has no bearing on how much he loves Lauren. He's probably arranged for something to be delivered to her already this morning. Their honeymoon will be awesome. But he doesn't care what they dance to. All he cares about is her.

"I'm not a complete dipshit." But he pauses to think, and when his eyes light up, we all sigh. "'Thinking Out Loud' by Ed Sheeran."

"Okay." Val nods to me, and I search for it on my phone. "Now, you're going to hold your ma much differently than Lauren. Let's do Lauren first since we have the song." Val holds out her hands, waiting for Luca to step into her space. "Come."

"Oh." Luca steps forward.

"One hand on the small of my back, the other hand clasped with mine."

Luca does as directed.

"Now she might move her arms like this." Val links her hands behind Luca's neck. "This is great, but I feel like you can be just as intimate with your hands linked." She moves closer, tucking her hand back in his. "Great, now that we've got the position, let's work on the footwork."

For twenty minutes, we play the song over and over while she shows my cousin how to do the box step. I'm surprised how long it takes Luca to learn such a basic step. Val stops him once he has the step down. Mauro and Cristian are still in the basement with us, looking bored.

"Great job getting the step down, but you need to be the one to lead her. Take control. Here, watch me and Dom," Val says.

Mauro looks up from his phone. "Dom knows how to dance?"

"Well, I taught him." Val sheepishly looks at me.

I place the phone on the table and take Luca's place.

"Can't wait to see this." Luca joins his brothers on the couch.

Oh, now everyone can put their phones away.

Val easily steps into my space like that night she taught me almost two decades ago. My hand slides around her hip to her lower back, and she raises her arm to wrap around my neck with our entwined hands tucked between us.

"Ready?" she asks.

"Yeah."

Thank God I had her last night, because if we did this before we slept together, I'd probably have a raging hard-on and make a fool of myself in front of my cousins. I never realized what a turn-on dancing is. And I'm not talking about grinding my dick against her ass at a club.

"You have to maintain control, Luca," Val continues teaching as I circle us around the small basement. "Dom is leading me..."

I whirl her and the song ends. "Perfect" by Ed Sheeran starts next. The lyrics sink in as I hold her, and her directions to Luca fade into the background as I soak in the feeling of having her in my arms again. The lyrics hit home —not knowing she was the one because we were kids when we first fell for each other.

When I first met Val, she was all metal braces and long legs. I was boney and hairy. But over the years, we've emerged from our adolescent cocoons as beautiful creatures. Valentina especially. Her teeth are straight and white, her long legs slender and graceful. I'm not sure if the lyrics are speaking to her too, but she leans her head on my shoulder, her fingers running up the back of my head.

Is this all for show? I don't even care. I can't afford to care. It's hard to admit it, but that summer in the Hamptons when we split, I was a fucking mess, destroyed by mourning the death of something that was never fully realized. I'll never tell her that though. Because it doesn't matter. I'll never allow myself to be in that position again.

CHAPTER TWENTY-THREE

Valentina

I'm not surprised that Dom remembers how to twirl me around a dance floor without making it look as though he's concentrating on what he's doing. The universe seems set on tormenting me, what with the Ed Sheeran's "Perfect" starting up after Luca and Lauren's song. It's a song that only makes me think of Dom. It could've been written as our very own love song.

Nostalgia sets in. This basement feels familiar—like the one in the Mancini house. They lived in a rare three level semi-detached and were one of the only people I knew who had a basement growing up. A basement we played Monopoly in on rainy days, or hide-and-seek when we were much younger, spin-the-bottle once we got older. My first kiss with Dominic happened in his basement, and three years later, I lost my virginity to him there. There was nothing especially romantic about the scene, but it felt romantic just the same.

My parents had inventory, so Mrs. Mancini had said that I could spend the night with them. They had a bed in the basement for family members or friends who spent the night.

Mrs. Mancini set me up downstairs and made sure I was comfortable. I lay in bed with a movie on the television to help me fall asleep. I hadn't slept over at the Mancinis' since I hit puberty, and I was positive there was a reason for that.

Around midnight, I heard the third stair creak, and I didn't have to look to know who it was. Dom appeared in a pair of track shorts and a T-shirt. His hair was everywhere. I wondered if he'd fallen asleep before he came down to join me.

"Hey," he said, walking across the basement toward my bed. "You doing okay?"

Back then, and still I suppose, I loved the way he acted like my own personal bodyguard, always making me feel as though I wasn't alone. "Yeah, I just can't sleep."

He glanced at the TV, where My Best Friend's Wedding *was playing, then shrugged and sat on the edge of my bed. "Seriously? You haven't watched this enough?"*

I poked him with my toe. "It's a cute movie."

"It's stupid. Who makes a pact to marry someone by a certain age?" He leaned his back against my headboard, his long legs stretched out in front of him.

It felt intimate, sitting that close to him on a bed.

Being teenagers, it wasn't a luxury we could often enjoy.

"Why do you think they didn't marry earlier?" I ask.

"They're friends. They both want careers. I don't plan on marrying anyone until at least thirty."

I drew back as though he'd offended me. That was the first I'd ever heard him say anything like that. "Why?"

"What's the point of getting married if I can't take care of my wife and kids? I want them to have everything, and for that to happen, I need to have a stable career."

At that point, I had no idea what I wanted to do with my life. I loved to dance, but I knew there was a slim chance I'd be able to make a career out of it. But Dom was nothing like me. Maybe it because he was the oldest, but he already knew he wanted to work with money and make money early on. He knew what he wanted to do and what school he wanted to get into.

"What if you lose the love of your life in the process?" I held my breath for his response.

"If she's the love of my life, she'll still be there at thirty." He was cool and casual and certain. It scared me to think I'd miss out on the love of my life.

"Maybe there's more than one love," I offered.

He stared at me, the glow of the television making him look somehow older. "I think there's only one true love for everyone."

"Dom." I elbowed him, but his eyes never left mine. "What if you never meet them?"

"What if you meet them too young?" he asked.

"Answer my question."

His eyes dipped to my lips, then his tongue slid out of his mouth and he licked his lips. A tingle shot through my body. We'd kissed before—a few times— but we'd never gone further than some heavy petting. Still, I was cognizant of something stirring deep inside me, a desire and a want I wasn't accustomed to.

"I don't know what happens if you never meet them. My problem is that I worry I met mine too young." Talking in code had always been Dominic Mancini's MO. The man never laid his cards out, because he could never show vulnerability.

"And who is that?" I was afraid to hear the answer, but I needed to know.

He tilted his head, his eyes never leaving mine. "You know who."

"Are you talking about Lulu?"

Lulu was another neighborhood girl. We'd been friends for years, but she was the complete opposite of me. She wore bows, and her hair was always perfectly curled. When we were younger, she played in dresses and was always trying to pull me away from the boys to play house or Barbies. At sixteen, I wasn't climbing trees anymore, but Lulu was still the kind of girl that most boys in our grade gravitated to.

"Stop it, Val, you know we're meant to be together."

What had started as a tingle now felt like a full-on blaze about to ignite my entire body. Dom was finally being straight with me and I couldn't stop hope from sprouting.

"We're sixteen."

He tucked one strand of my hair behind my ear. "And you'll be my wife someday. You just have to let me conquer the world first. Promise."

Our eyes locked, and all I wanted was for him to seal his promise with a kiss. Just as I hoped, our faces drew closer and our breathing was the only sound I heard.

"How could you ever think I like Lulu?" He smirked right before his lips brushed mine.

His tongue slid along my seam and I opened, allowing him to enter. The kiss became more intense, and soon my back was flat on the bed and Dom was half on top of me, his hand about to slide up my shirt.

"Is this okay?" he asked before touching my breast.

I arched my back and nodded to grant him permission.

My Best Friend's Wedding played in the background as we explored each other's bodies. Dom raced upstairs to retrieve a condom from his bedroom and then we took off our bottoms. I didn't look when he put it on, and I still had my shirt on as he slowly pushed inside me. He kissed me to drown out my pain, and for a moment, the painful sensation was masked by my love for him.

It was awkward and sloppy, but it felt magical all the same. Because anything that involved the two of us was always good.

He stayed with me until sunrise, when we heard his dad getting up for work. His lips landed on mine, *and he acted as though it tore him to shreds to leave the bed.*

Later, I told his ma that I'd gotten my period in order to explain the sheets and she gushed over me to make sure I was okay. I'm not sure what Dom did with the condom. I never asked.

At breakfast that day, Carm played Duck Duck Goose with Blanca even though none of us got up to chase them. My eyes caught Dom's, but then we'd look away from each other. I was certain of one thing when I left the Mancinis' that weekend—I'd wait forever if it meant having Dominic Mancini.

Dom's feet slowly stop, pulling me back to the present like a bucket of cold water. He releases me as though he didn't realize himself that I was still in his arms.

"Whoa. You guys are good," Luca says, pretending to do what we did.

Mauro yawns and stretches. "I'm hungry." He barrels up the stairs without another word.

Dom turns off the music and stuffs his phone into his pocket. "There you go, Luca."

"I'm not sure I'll do as well as you guys, but..."

I walk over to Luca, happy for the distance from Dom. "Just love her out there and your feet will do the work. If all anyone sees is the love between the two of you, they're not watching whether your footsteps are right."

"Thanks." Luca stares over my shoulder at Dom. "I never would've guessed that you'd be one to sink."

"Sink?" The heaviness in Dom's voice almost sounds like he wants to say fuck off.

"You're drowning in love. It's great to see." Luca smiles

then nods toward the stairs. "Ma made some food. Want to join us? I eat when I'm nervous."

"Give us a minute," Dom says, putting up his finger.

"Sure." Luca barrels up the stairs with Cristian in tow.

I try to keep my eyes focused forward when I hear his footsteps growing closer.

"You okay?" Dom's hands land on my shoulders.

I desperately want to lean back, assured that his strength will keep me up, but I force myself to stay upright. "I'm fine."

"You look like you saw a ghost." He's quiet and his hands run up and down my biceps.

"Just memories." I turn around, but his hands stay on my arms as he peers down at me.

"What memories?"

I can't take us down memory lane. We can't afford to get lost there. "Nothing. Let's go."

I walk toward the stairs, but he grabs my hand, pulling me back to him. "Valentina, what is it?"

I shake my head. "All this pretending brings up a lot of stuff from the past at the same time as it brings reality to the forefront. Come on."

I tug and he follows, letting us pretend that any feelings we might have for one another are all part of the façade. That's the thing about Dom—he'll never let me see his vulnerability. It's always been the one part of him I can count on.

CHAPTER TWENTY-FOUR

Dominic

We say goodbye to my parents at the airport. I watch them climb into a taxi, and when they drive away, so does any reason for me to hold her hand, kiss her cheek, or wrap my arms around her.

She's quiet on the way to my condo. The countdown until Ryder returns feels like a bomb ticking off the seconds in my head.

"Busy day tomorrow?" I ask, keeping my head buried in my phone as the cab makes its way to my condo.

She doesn't look up from hers. "Yeah, we're doing a rehearsal for the recital this coming Saturday."

"Right, I remember you mentioning that now." I was going to take her to dinner on our last night before Ryder returned, but I guess that's out now. How do we end this? With a handshake?

"I'll probably be late most nights this week." She gives

me a half smile, and I'm not sure if that's an 'it sucks, I'd rather be screwing you' smile or if it means something else.

"I'm behind on a few things. I've taken off more time this past month than the last ten years," I say.

She nods, her thumb running over the screen.

We're quiet the rest of the way to my condo. When the taxi stops at the curb, I exit first, offering her my hand. She accepts, but it still feels like we're a disgruntled couple who's been married for twenty-five years and silently loathe one another. How can the energy between us change so much from one city to the next?

I open the condo and she heads to her bedroom wordlessly, so I head to mine. After I shower and change into sweatpants and a T-shirt, I decide to pay her a visit. I'll never be able to concentrate at work if I don't know what's going on in that beautiful head of hers.

I knock on her bedroom door, and she says come in. When I open the door, I see that she's also showered and in her pajamas, which consists of another pair of silky shorts and a lacy cami that turns her nipples into a beacon for my gaze. She's putting lotion on her arms and only spares me a brief glance.

"Talk to me," I say, sitting on the edge of her bed. "What are you thinking?"

She shrugs, concentrating on working the lotion into her skin.

"Valentina?"

"The wedding was our timeline, right? It's over, so we can contact the lawyer about the annulment and get things rolling again." She moves to her legs, propping one up on the bed.

"Is that what you want?" I could kick myself for asking.

"Ryder's returning. That was the deal."

I put my hand on hers, and she looks at me. "I asked if it's what you want?"

She stops and sits next to me, blowing out a breath. "Why is everything so complicated with us?" There's a hitch in her voice.

"I have no idea, but I'm not ready for this to end. We have a week. Let's make the most of it."

It's a bad idea, and her skeptical look says she knows it.

"And after Ryder returns, then what?"

"It'll be easier. You'll be back home with him and we'll just coexist when we see each other. You know when we're in close proximity we can't control ourselves, but..."

She pumps the lotion again and rubs it on her other leg. "It's still not going to be easy to walk away."

"I know. But I'm not ready to say goodbye tonight." This is the most honest I've been with Val since I was sixteen and stupid. I still blame my dick for saying that sappy shit about her being my one and only.

"I'm not ready either."

I shift to face her better. "So we'll enjoy ourselves this last week. Fuck like teenagers. And come Sunday morning, it's D-day?"

She bites her lip and nods.

"Perfect," I say. *It's anything but perfect.*

I lean in, my lips pressing to hers, and she falls down on the mattress as I position myself on top of her. Her one leg winds around mine. I've never been happier to be free-balling it under my sweats.

"We're the stupidest people. You know that, right? What everyone must think of us."

I press my finger to her lips, my other hand sliding her silk cami up and over her breasts. "We don't care what other people think. All we need to think about is what we want." I take one of her nipples into my mouth, my teeth scraping the sensitive bud.

Her hand weaves through my damp hair, her heels digging into my ass. "Bite me."

I nibble on her skin, leaving a mark right above her nipple, and she groans, pressing my head into her breast.

"Harder."

I find a new spot to torment, always loving that she's just as into the biting and sucking as I am. I didn't figure that out until right before she married Max. I bit her and she came. After that, it's always been that way with us. Whether it was slow or fast, I've always marked her.

I grind my hard cock against her center, and she rocks into me, meeting me thrust for thrust. At some point, I raise up on my knees and she pulls me out of my sweatpants, palming my hard dick.

My lips hover above hers as I pull aside the silky fabric of her shorts, allowing the tip of my dick to pierce her opening. Kissing Val is like kissing no other woman. Feelings I've ignored for most of my life emerge, and for a moment while our hands explore and our tongues slide, I think that maybe we could win this fight.

Then I push all thoughts out of my head. Her soft skin is under my fingers and I roll onto my back, bringing her over to straddle me. She positions herself above me and my hands mold to her hips.

"Ride me?" I ask.

She takes no time to guide my dick back inside her warm entrance. She rocks over me and I latch my mouth onto a nipple, playing with the erect bud with my tongue before falling back onto the mattress.

I watch her above me. Her long hair is pulled into a bun on top of her head, she's bare-chested, and her shorts are still slid over to make room for me. She's so beautiful, I can barely stand to look at her with the thought that I might have to go months without seeing her again.

With my thoughts getting out of control again, I flip us back over and tear her shorts off her body, kicking off my own sweatpants. Kneeling on the bed, I use her ankles to pull her back to me, thrusting hard inside her again. The delicious friction does us both in and she grabs a pillow then scrapes her fingers along my torso like it's killing her not to touch me.

"Dom," she sighs.

My balls tense because my name coming off her lips is as hot as the sweaty mess she's becoming under me. Somewhere in the mix, I fall on her, unable to resist kissing her again. The sweat mixes between us and my eyes are closed, my mind, my heart, and my soul filled to the brim with all things Valentina. She shatters underneath me. Two seconds later, I thrust, pumping into her and explode inside her.

I roll us over, and we lie on her bed on our backs until our breathing returns to normal.

"Hungry?" I ask, because it's a reason to get me out of this room.

"If you're cooking, always."

I kiss her shoulder and crawl off the bed before grabbing my sweatpants from the floor. Before I leave the room, I'm about to ask if there's anything in particular she feels like eating, but Val disappears behind the door of the bathroom.

I guess I'm not the only one who wants to pretend that the idea of ending this isn't torture.

CHAPTER TWENTY-FIVE

Valentina

I'm exhausted by the time I insert my key into Dom's lock on Monday night. I was up most of the night before with Dom, eating, having sex, and watching television. I feel as though I need to soak up every second we have together before the week is over.

I push the door open, and a woman's voice stops me in my tracks until I see Blanca on the couch, typing on her phone. Dom turns toward me and smiles. I can't even explain the feeling that courses through my body when his smile is directed at me. He's usually so guarded, he downplays a lot of the enjoyment.

"You're home earlier than I thought." He rises from the couch to greet me.

"I finished up some admin stuff faster than I thought, and I don't have to teach tonight."

His lips press to my cheek and his strong palm to my

lower back. "She's staying for dinner," he whispers in my ear.

"Okay," I say. Blanca was like my little sister until I ended up as a mother and a wife.

"Wine?" he asks, already heading to the kitchen, where a bottle and one glass sits on the island.

"Val!" Blanca finally notices and stands, holding her own wine glass. "How are you?" She gives me a hug and a kiss on each cheek before sliding into a chair in front of the breakfast bar.

Dom pours me a glass of white wine and opens the oven, checking on whatever he's making. He got home early enough to cook?

I glance at the microwave clock to find it's only six o'clock. It isn't like him to leave early on a Monday. I swear it's his favorite day of the week.

"Thanks," I say, accepting the glass. An electric current rushes between us as our fingers brush.

"How's married life?" Blanca asks.

I tilt my head and study her. Surely, she knows this is a ruse?

"It's good. Ryder returns next week from Europe," Dom says.

I can't tell if he's changing the subject on purpose.

"Oh, I saw his pictures on Instagram. I really need to get my ass in gear and get over to the Motherland." She laughs before sipping more wine.

I sit in the chair next to her. "You follow Ryder on Instagram?"

"Yeah, is that a problem? He friended me a few years ago after we figured out you were the common denominator. He's good friends with my friend's little brother."

"Who?" I ask.

"Ty Ricci. I'm friends with his older sister, Jemma."

I nod, remembering Ty from Ryder's grade school before we moved to Manhattan permanently after the divorce. It's embarrassing that I didn't know they were still in contact.

"We both ended up at the Ricci house once, and I said how you used to date Dom. I hope that was okay?"

"Of course, no worries." I touch her hand in a reassuring manner.

Dom doesn't turn around from whatever he's doing at the stove.

"And look, you two ended up together." She eyes my hand. "Where's your ring?"

I stare at my left hand. My bare left hand. Wearing it felt weird since our charade is supposedly over. Dom turns around, staring at me with questions in his eyes.

"Work. I didn't want it to snag any of the dance outfits. You know all those delicate fabrics."

Dom gives us his back and Blanca stares at me like "okay whatever."

"Go put it on now. I'm sure it kills you to take it off," Blanca says.

I slide off the stool. "It does. I'll be right back."

Heading down the hall, I snag my purse on the way, pulling out my phone.

Me: *Does Blanca think our marriage is real??*

No response.

Me: *Dom!?*

Finally I hear him tell Blanca he's got to return this email and to give him a second.

Dom: *She doesn't know. She'll tell Ma.*
Me: *I hate all this lying.*
Dom: *It's just Blanca.*
Me: *She's your sister.*
Dom: *Exactly, my sister.*

I throw the phone on the bed and sit down. Why am I annoyed that he's keeping our secret from his sister? He kept it from his cousins. He kept it from the people at his work. I won't see Blanca again until this charade is over.

I dig the ring out of my underwear drawer and slide it onto my left hand. It really is gorgeous—exactly what I would've picked—but I hate that it represents our fake marriage. I fist my left hand as I walk back into the main living space.

"Your blog is great. Why haven't you told any of us about it before?" Dom's leaning over the counter with a computer in front of him. Three plates with a chicken dish and garden vegetables sit to the side.

"Because I went to school for business. I should do something with my degree. This is just for fun."

"What is it?" I sit on the stool, and Dom swivels the computer my way.

"Blanca writes a blog." He steps aside and opens the silverware drawer.

The blog is well organized with a bright logo that reads "Post College, What Do You Do Now?"

"I started it anonymously when I graduated and was searching for a job. I needed to vent to someone and who better than strangers? Once I found the job in banking and started making money, I blogged about what it's like to start your life journey after college. You know dating, finding an apartment, how to stretch a dollar."

I scroll through to find that it's very professional and screams Blanca. "Who's your photographer?"

She laughs. "Me."

"Really?"

She nods. "Do they look amateur?"

I shake my head. "Not at all."

I skim a few articles, and it's clear to me that she has a way with words. I want to eat up each and every one of them and I'm not even her target audience.

"I only have time to write in it four times a week now because of my work schedule. I find myself missing it."

I slide the computer back toward her, planning on looking it up later and reading all her posts. "A lot of people make money off blogging."

She shrugs. "I had a few people reach out to sponsor me. Makeup and health people mostly. They send me their goodies and I promote them. But trying to make this a bigger source of income would be a huge jump and my parents spent a fortune on my college degree. How do I just walk away from that?"

I nod, understanding all too well.

"I'll handle our parents. Blanca, if you don't love banking, then don't do it. You'll never succeed if you don't love it."

Dom's words surprise me, and I lean back, sipping my wine.

"Easy for you to say. You love a lucrative career." The corners of her lips tip down in a way that reminds me of her brother when I've said something he doesn't like.

He shrugs. "Yeah, but money is the driving force for me. It's different."

That doesn't surprise me. Why he always felt the need to make so much money, I never understood.

"Don't we know it." Blanca rolls her eyes at me.

"Let's remember who loaned you money before you found your job." Dom scoops up the silverware and brings it over to the dining table.

Blanca nods and looks down. "It's just such a risk."

"Let me tell you about starting a non-lucrative career," I say.

Blanca turns to me while Dom takes the three plates to the table. He says, "Come and eat while you tell us the story of Valentina Daniella Cavallo."

I stick my tongue out at him for using the running joke about my name from our childhood and he chuckles, heading over to the sofa to grab his wine. We all settle around the table and Blanca waits for me to speak.

"I wanted to be a dancer, and I was in my last year of college. I had a few leads to be in a chorus on Broadway, but I became pregnant with Ryder."

Blanca nods because everyone in Carroll Gardens knows my story. How I married the wrong man after getting knocked up. What an embarrassment it was to my parents.

"After I had him, I knew there was no way I'd be able to dance again. Dancers keep strange hours and I had no one to watch Ryder. Your body changes after a baby and I didn't have the time to dedicate to keeping in shape the way I needed to. By the time he was three, I decided I had to do something in dance, even if I wasn't dancing myself. So Max agreed to fund my first studio."

Dom's knife slides on his plate, and a huge screech reverberates around his condo.

"Sorry," he mumbles.

"I had so much to learn. I had never taught small kids before and I had to figure out how to keep the books and what to charge to make sure I was in the black. How to schedule classes and keep the parents happy. How to make sure I was hiring employees who would represent the studio in a good way. There were some hard years but look at my business now. I have three locations, and though I'm not making a name for myself as a dancer, I am as a dance director. Sometimes you have to alter your plans, but that doesn't necessarily mean it's a bad thing."

She pokes her fork into the vegetables. "Who taught you all that? The business side of things."

I eye Dom because he did help me until we realized we couldn't be around one another. It was a brief month of meetings during his lunch hour or after hours. I'd have Ryder with me, and to this day, I hate that I hid it from Max. Nothing inappropriate ever happened, but the energy between us was palpable, and I think we both knew that if we continued spending so much time with each other, the outcome wouldn't be good.

"Just books and stuff." I shrug.

"Dom would've totally helped you, I bet. He helped me do a budget after I got my job. Set me up with how to save and..."

I'm sure he did—because she's his sister. I was the woman he wanted in his bed, but back then, I wore another man's ring.

"Just do it, Blanca. I'll help you if you need it," Dom says.

"You're young. Don't waste your future on something you don't really care for. It won't end well." I feel like a fraud for giving her advice without telling her Dom and I are acting.

But she nods, and we leave it at that. We fill the rest of the meal with talk about Luca's wedding and how happy Maria was to show off the women her boys have found love with.

At the end of the evening, Blanca hugs me goodbye. Then she rises on her tiptoes and hugs Dom, whispering something I can't hear. She leaves with directions from Dom to text him when she makes it home. When the door shuts, Dom pulls me to him, his fingers threading through my hair and his lips locking on mine.

Once we come up for air, he rests his forehead against mine. "I've waited all day for that."

At times like this, I wonder how good of an actor Dom is, because he seems like he desperately means the words, but there were no hidden touches or longing gazes over dinner.

"Six days and counting. Let's make the most of them," I say.

He flips the lock and turns off the lights before carrying me to his bedroom.

I'll face reality in six days. But who's counting?

CHAPTER TWENTY-SIX

Dominic

"You're late from your meeting, and your wife left you lunch." Ash follows me into my office.

It's Thursday, and although Val and I have been enjoying one another physically all week, we've been careful not to cross that line. Whoever's bed we fuck in, the other person leaves to sleep in their own bed afterward. At this point, I look forward to seeing her in my home at the end of the day, which means there's going to be a transition period once she leaves.

"Thanks." I take the bag and walk into my office, where I set it on my desk.

"She said it's probably her last time seeing me?" Ash sits in the chair on the other side of my desk.

I loosen my tie and glance at the Trading Post bag. I couldn't meet my brothers today because of a meeting with a client I couldn't move. I pull the container from the bag.

Just as I thought, it holds the lobster mac and cheese I eat every week.

"Is that a smile?" Ash asks.

I straighten my lips. "No."

"It is so. You're smiling."

"She brought my favorite meal." I told her this morning how I wouldn't be able to make my usual lunch with my brothers. I sit down and pull the plastic cutlery from the bag. "Don't you have a lunch of your own to go to?"

"Answer my question."

"What question?" I pop the lid off the pasta. Condensation drips from the lid.

"About why I'm not going to see Val again?" She crosses her arms.

I take the fork and dig into the pasta because if it gets too cold, it will suck.

"Dom?"

I finish chewing and swallow. Ash won't like this, but so what? She works for *me*. "Ryder returns this weekend, and once that happens, we're going to get an annulment."

"What?" Her mouth drops open.

"You knew the circumstances."

"But—"

"This time is being deducted from your lunch hour right now."

She waves me off because she'll take as long as she wants. "You leave early every day now, which you *never* do. She brought you lunch. Your brother's Instagram has a picture of the two of you at the wedding and you both look so happy."

"There's a picture of us on Instagram?"

"That's what you got from what I said?" She drills me with an exasperated look. "You clearly love her."

"Whoa. Whoa. Whoa." I raise my hand, wiping my mouth. "I don't love her. I mean, I do as a person, but I'm not *in* love with her. There's a difference."

"You're either blind or you're stupid, because you do love Val. You have for the past two years, and if I knew your history, probably longer than that. Why are you so afraid to admit it?"

"Ash, this is personal." It's clear from my tone that this is not something I'm going to discuss with her.

She stands. "Fine. Don't talk to me. I shouldn't care if you're going to throw away your chance at happiness."

She storms out of my office, and I watch her grab her purse and stomp off toward the elevators. Once she's gone, I pull up the Instagram app I barely use. Sure enough, I find the picture under Enzo's account. Annie probably posted it though. There's the two of us, and I'll admit, we do look happy.

Me: *Thanks for lunch.*
Val: *You're welcome. I had hoped for a quickie in the copy room.*
Me: *I would've happily obliged.*
Val: *Maybe another time.*
Me: *I'll hold you to that.*

My chest constricts because I know there won't be any other time for us. If it doesn't happen in the next couple of days, that's it.

Val: *Have a great day. Enjoy the Mac N Cheese.*
Me: *I'm leaving the office at three today.*
Val: :(*I won't be home until late. Rehearsals.*

Me: *I'll stay up.*
Val: :)

I put my phone on the desk and stare at the meal she came all the way uptown to bring me. Yeah, come Sunday, there's going to be some adjustment needed because I've done the one thing I promised myself I wouldn't do again—I'm invested.

Any trader knows that you have to balance the risk with the reward, and Val proved last summer that she's too much of a risk. So what the hell am I doing?

———

SINCE I KNOW Val won't be home until late, I decide to stay at the office. It's not like I don't have a shit-ton of work to do. Ash was right, I've been leaving early lately—early for me being five or six o'clock.

At six-thirty, I close my computer and get my stuff together because I've pretty much succumbed to the fact that I'm a pussy now and want to be home when Val arrives.

I reach the elevator as Nell approaches from the opposite side of the office. She's given me space since she found out about Val, but I still catch her walking by my office and peering in way more than necessary.

"Hey," I say, waiting for the elevator to open.

"Good evening, Mr. Mancini." She nods, but it's so dramatic she might as well have bowed.

"Cut the shit."

"You are technically higher up than me."

"You don't work for me, and I might have more years here, but we're the same."

"You could've told me you were getting married." She pouts.

The elevator dings and the doors glide open. We both step in. "I was about to. It happened in Vegas."

I could tell her the truth, but I'll use my impromptu marriage as an excuse to get her off my dick.

"I'm not opposed to a more secretive arrangement." She steps closer, and I freeze. I've never been put in this position, a woman coming on to me after knowing I'm already in a relationship.

"Nell."

"What? I think there's a reason you didn't tell me."

I step back and hit the elevator wall. "I assure you I just hadn't had the opportunity."

She's so close, her tits are a millimeter from pressing against my chest. The elevator doors ding and open on the ground floor, and I turn my head, ready to make my escape.

There stands Val in her dance gear. Her bag slips off her shoulder and falls to the floor with a thud.

"Val!" My voice is high and shocked and makes me sound guilty as fuck.

She picks up her bag and stares me down.

"We were both working late." Nell saunters out, touching Val's arm lightly as she steps past her. "Bye, Dominic. See you tomorrow." She waves, and her smirk makes it appear like she's the winning bidder and I'm the prize.

I step off the elevator. Val and I stare at one another wordlessly until Nell is out the doors of the building.

"Nice," she spits out like venom.

"It was nothing," I say like every other man probably does when it actually *is* something.

"I asked you for one promise! And here I thought you'd

actually keep your word and not see anyone else." She spins on her heel and rushes to the door, pushing it open with force.

"You said you had to work until seven."

She stops and studies me. "So that's a pass for you to fuck around behind my back?"

"I wasn't fucking around," I grind out between clenched teeth. "Do you really think I'd do that to you after what happened with Max? Jesus, just when I think maybe we're getting somewhere." I throw up my arms, pissed off that I constantly get such low expectations from her.

"I don't know what you'd do because the fact is you *were* screwing her."

"I made you a promise."

She steps out onto the sidewalk, stopping before she hits the street. Her shoulders deflate and she circles around to look at me. "I just..."

I approach her cautiously, just in case I ever do want to father a child someday. "Why do you find it so hard to believe that I wouldn't do that to you?"

She swipes at a tear and looks away. "I never know where I stand with you."

"You stand on the first pedestal. It's always you, Val. Always." My hand cradles her cheek. "I stopped things with Nell as soon as you came back into my life."

She nods, and her hand holds mine to her cheek. "Take me home?"

I step closer to her while raising my hand for a taxi. "Always."

The taxi stops at the curb, and I open the door for her to slide in first. She tries to stay on the far side, but I pull her along the vinyl seat toward me.

"Tell me what you want me to do to you when we get

home," I whisper in her ear. My lips travel along the soft skin under her ear.

"Show me how I'm number one."

Her lips find mine. I'm not opposed to public affection, so I kiss her back, sliding my tongue between her lips. Our kiss starts slow and easy. My finger runs up her thigh and she parts her legs, allowing me access. Her leggings are thin enough that I should be able to get her off in here, then I'll really take care of her back at the house.

I glance at the cab driver, who has AirPods in and is speaking animatedly in a language I don't recognize to someone on the phone. He's not paying us any attention.

"Dom, we can't," she whispers so softly I barely hear her.

Usually I can keep my shit together until we reach the elevator of my condo at least, but I'm desperate to show her that Nell means nothing to me. I push my finger into her center, and she bucks into my hand.

"Just relax." I kiss her jawline then capture her lips.

I try to position us so that the cab driver will think we're just making out, but she's squirming as I apply more pressure to her clit. Her breath hitches, the thin fabric acts as a barrier so that she doesn't get the ultimate relief she's seeking, and she circles her hips and presses her body closer to mine. I bite her earlobe and her body sinks into mine.

"I'm going to mark you tonight. When you look in the mirror tomorrow, you'll know I was there and know whose bed you belong in."

Her hand slides down my arm, gripping my wrist.

"Go ahead." I grant her the permission she's looking for.

Using her hips and the pressure of my fingers, she gets off, controlling her movements and the pace. Her ass rises off the bench seat, and I watch her eyes flutter shut, the pink of her cheeks turning bright red, and her body falls back down as the orgasm takes over. She's so damn breathtaking when she comes—even if it is silent by necessity. No wonder I never get enough.

Her head falls to my shoulder, and she slides her hand in mine as though she didn't just see stars or fireworks behind those eyelids. As I'm composing myself, she tilts her head and presses her lips to the hollow of my neck.

"I'm sorry for questioning you," she murmurs.

Her apology should make me happy, but that time bomb is still ticking toward Sunday, and when it blows, it's going to shatter me to pieces.

CHAPTER TWENTY-SEVEN

Valentina

"Gia, it's okay. It's just a fun recital for the parents." I kneel down to eight-year-old Gia's level.

"Why have you been dodging me?" Lulu says from her seat, sipping her iced coffee as it rests on her big belly.

"I'm not dodging you." I stand, moving Gia back toward the rest of the girls in her class. My employee Libby is demonstrating the dance one more time. "You shouldn't be worrying about me. You should be worried about why my goddaughter is so stressed."

The answer to that question is in the classic cliché that the apple doesn't fall far from the tree.

"She's a perfectionist. Blame Vinny. Anyway, I figured you got the annulment and needed some time to yourself because that's usually how it goes down with you. Imagine my surprise when I stop by your parents' store and they brag about their new son-in-law." She slurps her iced coffee, judgment resting deep in her dark eyes.

"I was going to tell you," I lie. I would never tell Lulu. She hates Dom.

"No, you weren't." She pins me with a stare. "I get that I've given you hell over the years about the guy, but you can't go through this alone. You cannot manage the Dominic Mancini waters solo. You get blinded by his beauty and that dick of his and forget that he's a shark until he swallows you whole."

I glance behind me to make sure none of the kids heard her. The last thing I need is for one of them to go home, say the word "dick" and tell their parents they heard it here. The music is on as they run through their ballet positions on the other side of the studio though, so we're safe.

I blow out a breath, watching the girls practice for the recital that'll start in a few hours and wishing my best friend would've felt too sick or too pregnant to come torment me. "I'm thirty-six. I get that I was once blind, but I'm all eyes-wide-open this time around. Trust me. Plus, it's a mutual agreement between the two of us."

Just the thought of waking up in Dom's bed this morning shoots tingles along my flesh. I can't think much of it. We were both spent last night, and when I slid to the edge to return to my room and he put his arm around my waist telling me to stay, I knew it was a bad decision. Lately, I can't seem to make any good ones.

Lulu looks bored. "It's the same story on repeat with you two. Always is."

"Just relax, we're friends."

"You and Dom are many things. Friends is never one of them."

I glance at her. "That's not true."

She pretends to yawn before grabbing my hand to help her out of the chair. "He's already sunk his claws into you. I'm too late. Damn, before all these kids, I would've sensed something was wrong, but any time I thought about it and was going to call you—bam, it's three days later." She touches her stomach. "Now I'll have another one to keep track of."

I laugh and lead her down the hall to my office. Libby has the girls under control, so I decide to take this conversation somewhere more private. "I'm good with it this time. I mean, we're in a different stage of our lives, *we're* different. There was an understanding from the get-go—"

"Do you hear yourself?" she asks as she settles into a chair.

I do hear myself and I know I'm making excuses, but the truth is, I'll suffer the heartbreak just to have him while I can. That's always been the way I feel when it comes to Dom. Pathetic maybe, but I've never been able to give up the hope that maybe this is the time it will work out.

"Lulu, enough." I'm curter than I mean to be.

She rears back, her legs wide open with her belly between them. She's the biggest she's been of all her pregnancies and I kind of wish she'd go into labor right now before I have to piss her off even more. "What?"

"You know the reason why I'm with Dom, so don't pretend you don't. I know I'm probably making a huge mistake, but it's *my* mistake." I point at myself. "And don't worry, I won't call you to pick me back up if things go south."

She mocks offense. Lulu is hard to offend. "Of course you're gonna call me and of course I'm gonna be there for you. But it's also my responsibility to warn you in advance because otherwise I'm a shitty friend." She inhales a deep breath, clutching her stomach. "You think I don't know. I do." She points at herself, wiggling to the edge of the chair. "Truth is you and Dom are blind as bats. That's what makes it so damn frustrating. You two are the ones who don't know, but everyone around you does."

She stands, and I move from behind my desk to help her up because she's sweating now. "Lu, are you okay?"

"I'm fine. Just Braxton Hicks. Had them two nights ago." She shucks my hands off her. "Listen, you're wasting your life if you two won't be real with each other, and if Dom was here, I'd tell him the same. But he likes to play hide-and-seek from me because every time I see him, I call him out on his bullshit."

"Calm down, you're scaring me." She's sweating even more now.

"Oh shit." She grabs her stomach with both hands and bends at the waist. "I'm not so sure this is false labor."

Right as she looks at me with resignation in her eyes, water drips down her legs, puddling below.

"Yeah, not false. I have to get you to the hospital."

Lulu is oddly calm. "Damn, I thought I had time." She stops at the doorway and digs through her purse. "Let's call Vinny, because it'll take him a while to get here. I'll drop Gia off at Nonna's, and then if you don't mind, you can drive me over to the hospital."

"Mind? Of course not. Where's the boys?"

"At my in-laws for a few weeks. They offered since the baby was due soon and I'm too smart to turn them down."

Lulu waddles out of my office, and Libby must notice something is amiss when we reach the studio because she tells the girls to keep out of our way.

Gia, being her mother's little replica, ignores the instructions and runs over to us. "Mama, is it time?"

Lulu pats her head. "Yep, so grab your bag and I'll take you to Nonna's."

"But what about the recital?" Gia whines.

Lulu looks at me. "I don't know, baby. Maybe if your brother comes fast."

"Lu," I warn. Even if she delivers in record time, she's not going to be attending the recital this evening.

She rolls her eyes as though I'm shooting down a viable plan. "I'm sure I'll see pictures and video."

Gia crosses her arms and pouts. She's so her mother, it's uncanny.

"Don't do that, Gia," Lulu says. "I have to call your dad."

I snag the phone from her hand and run through her contacts, clicking on Vinny. It goes to voicemail. As Gia is standing statue-still with a pout that would give a professional British nanny a hard time, Lulu is encouraging her to grab her bag. Vinny's obnoxious voicemail where he pretends he's actually answered the phone but hasn't, plays in my ear and I wait for the beep. Libby is trying to get the girls back in order and to stop running over and asking questions about what's happening. My dance studio has turned into a disaster—and who decides to step into the mix at this moment? You guessed it. The one and only Dominic Mancini.

He stops in his tracks, soaking in everything that's happening. He probably wishes he could turn around and leave. This is a clusterfuck and Dom is not a patient clusterfuck kind of person.

As I leave a message, Gia stomps, and when I say stomp, I mean she could probably be a cast member in *Stomp*. Lulu is still dripping amniotic fluid. Dom is holding an iced coffee I'm pretty sure is for me and a small bag from the bakery I love.

I have no chance to reach him and talk to him before Lulu's voice booms through the studio. "DOMINIC MANCINI."

He smirks. He and Lulu have an unusual relationship, one born of hate and respect. Like two African lions fighting over a lioness.

"LUCIA MILANO."

They stare one another down for a moment.

"The baby is ruining everything," Gia whines.

"He's your brother. Nonna will bring you to the recital. She can't wait to see you." Lulu attempts to put a positive spin on the situation, but I know Gia well enough to know that there's going to be a giant guilt trip that will probably cost Lulu a pretty penny at the American Girl store.

"Whatever." Gia stomps out past Dom.

His gaze follows her. "Talk about a mini-me."

"Jealous?" Lulu walks up to him. "You could've had your own by now, but oh that's right, you don't want marriage and kids." She's sneering at him, and I roll my eyes.

He scoffs. "Who would want a mini-me?"

I want to raise my hand, but I smartly keep it at my side.

Lulu snaps her fingers. "That would be no one. Could you imagine a kid walking around making deals and counting his money in a suit?" Her eyes trail down his body. "Are you breaking out in hives without the high silk content of your professionally tailored suit jacket?"

Oh, Lulu. You just can't help yourself. It's Saturday, so he's in shorts and a V-neck T-shirt, but he still looks handsome as always. I suppress a grin.

He stares at her stomach. "You're having twins? I didn't know."

Shit, below the belt, Mancini.

Lulu jabs him in the arm. "Fucker. I'd like to see you carry this around for nine months. You're not man enough."

"True. I'm more than thankful the women get that job."

Lulu's eyes narrow. There's no love lost right now, and I need to get her out of here before she has that kid on my expensive vinyl dance floor.

"Sorry, Dom, Lulu's water broke. We need to get her to the hospital," I interrupt.

His gaze shoots to the floor and back to me. I nod, and he jumps back a step.

"It's not contagious." Lulu waddles out of the studio after Gia.

"Do you want me to go with you?" he asks, concern in his tone.

I almost laugh, but I hold it in. "If you want, but I can handle it. Is that for me?" I eye the bakery bag and iced coffee.

He holds them out. "You didn't eat this morning, and I know how you can be when there's a performance. One of these days, you're going to pass out."

I smile at him.

The door opens, and Lulu steps back in with Gia's hand in hers. "Hello! Let's go!" Then she looks at me and shakes her head. "Don't look at him like that." She steps farther in and plucks the bakery bag out of my hand. "I need this because I won't be able to eat once I get to the hospital." She opens the bag to inspect the contents and smiles. "Sorry, Val, it's your favorite chocolate coconut cupcake. I'll repay you."

"Cupcake!" Gia screams. "I want one."

"Ask the big guy. Who only brings one cupcake?"

Gia walks over to Dom, and he stares at me as if he's asking me what to say. I shrug.

"I know I'm pretty lax, but I'm like a leaking faucet over here," Lulu says.

"Oh, right." I take Gia's hand. "I'll take you for a treat after the hospital."

Gia throws her head back and her body goes limp. "He's ruining my life. First, my recital and now I can't get a cupcake."

I pull, but she digs her heels into the floor.

"Gia," Lulu says. "Let's go."

"I want a cupcake!"

I blow out a breath and stare at Dom. Why didn't he bring two?

Lulu hands the bag to her. "Here."

Now I've had it.

"No." I snatch it before Gia can and hand it back to Lulu. "You're eating the cupcake."

"Auntie Val!" Gia yells, and Dom rears back again.

"Gia, your mom is about to have a baby. You can eat something at Nonna's. If you're really good, I'll go to the cupcake shop and pick you up one after. That's the end of the discussion. Go outside with your mom. We're going to drop you off, then we're going to the hospital. I don't want to hear one more word from you."

Gia tries to intimidate me with mean-spirited eyes, but I stand my ground and she stomps out of the studio again.

"Okay, so I'm gonna tag you in for all mother duties for a bit." Lulu laughs and looks at Dom. "Is she this bossy in bed?" Without waiting for an answer, she walks out.

"Are you coming?" I ask.

Dom's face is white, but he surprises me when he says,

"You go to the hospital. I'll take Gia to Lulu's parent's. Same house?"

I nod. "Are you sure?"

"Yeah, then I'll meet you at the hospital after. What else do you need? Do you need clothes for tonight?"

I shake my head, a calmness coming over me. He's willing to put himself in an uncomfortable situation for me. *Oh, Dom, why can't we make this work?* "Thank you."

His hand is about to touch my cheek as his lips descend, but the door opens.

"*Hello*. Baby." Lulu points at her stomach and the door shuts again.

"Go," he whispers.

We walk out of my studio, and for the first time in a long time, it feels as though we're a united front, a team.

CHAPTER TWENTY-EIGHT

Dominic

Lulu is scary, but Gia is downright frightening.

She sits next to me in the taxi, seat-belted in, her feet hanging off the seat, still pushing her agenda. "We could go to the cupcake place now."

"No, we're going to your Nonna's place."

When I made the trek to Brooklyn to bring Val something, I'd hoped for a heavy make-out session in her office. Not to be escorting the daughter of the woman who hates me to her grandmother's house.

"What's your name again?" she asks, crossing her arms. Her pink-and-black dance outfit is cute, but she screams attitude, just like her mother did at her age.

"Dom."

"Dominic Mancini?"

I glance at her, away from my phone, where Val keeps sending apologetic text messages. "How do you know that?"

Her eyes narrow. "My mom and Auntie Val talk about you a lot."

"What do they say?" I tuck my phone away. Now I'm interested in what this little fireball has to say.

There's a bakery at the corner right before Gia's grandmother's house. They might not have cupcakes, but they have cookies. I lean forward and instruct the cab driver to stop one block up.

"You make Auntie Val cry. Why?"

Shit. My shoulders sag and I run a hand through my hair. "I don't know why she'd cry about me." I do actually, but it depends how recent we're talking.

"They were arguing about you. Right before the baby ruined my day."

"Was Val crying then?"

The taxi stops at the corner and Gia looks out the window. "This isn't Nonna's."

"There's a bakery. I'll buy you a cookie."

She slides out after me, and I pay the cab driver through the passenger window.

"Are you Italian?" she asks.

"Yeah."

"Why did you only buy one cupcake? Italians buy things in dozens, so everyone has one." She strolls into the bakery as though she owns the place and didn't just school me on Italian manners.

She's right though. I should've brought Val an entire dozen cupcakes. One thing is for certain—if I'd done that, I wouldn't be at a bakery with an eight-year-old right now.

We walk up to the cashier and she smiles at Gia. *Don't be fooled, woman.* "How can I help you?"

"A dozen cookies," Gia informs her with her face pressed to the glass.

The woman gives me a questioning look and I nod. I've learned my lesson.

I wait as Gia points out the cookies she wants, instructing the woman down to the specific cookie in the row of identical cookies. The girl explains that there's a mistake on one and the colors are prettier on another. She's so much like Lucia when she was younger, I feel as though I'm twenty-five years younger and it's her in front of me. Thank God that woman has mellowed over the years.

"Nonna is gonna love them." Gia beams at me as I pay for the cookies.

She grabs the bag and waves to a boy she must know from school. He's sitting with his mother at one of the small tables.

We walk down the block, past the houses of my child-hood friends. It's crazy how small town a borough of New York can feel, but some parts of Carroll Gardens make me feel so welcome, I wonder why I was so hellbent on getting the hell out of here.

"So, are you excited to have a baby brother or sister?" I ask Gia.

"Brother, and no."

"Why not? I love my brothers and my sister."

"Because he'll get all the attention. Like when my other brothers were born. No one will be at my recital."

We reach the house in question and I glance at her. "I'll come."

She stops at the bottom of the stairs to her grandparents' house. I remember hanging around these stairs when we were younger. Val was always over here. My buddy Pauly was head over heels for Lulu, and everyone knew I couldn't stay away from Val.

"Really?"

"Yeah." I shrug. I wasn't planning on staying, but what can it hurt? I understand why Gia might be acting out. Ma still tells the story about Enzo and me running away when Carm was born. It's like we knew what was coming.

"Oh yeah!" Her small hands dig into the plastic bag. "This is for you."

She hands me the smiley face cookie she picked out. It took the lady pointing to five different ones before Gia settled on this particular cookie, so I know I've been granted a rare honor in her world.

"Thank you."

She picks up the bag. "I don't care what my mommy says about you. You're okay in my book."

I chuckle, escorting her up the stairs. I can only imagine what she's overheard.

The door opens, and there stands Lulu's ma. If you put the three of them side by side, it'd look like one person's progression of age. Scary.

"Hi, Dominic," she says, staring at my cookie.

Lulu's ma has always liked me.

"Hi, Mrs. Milano." I kiss her cheeks and step back. "I assume you heard the news?"

"We did. We were going to sneak over there before the recital, sounds like we should have time. She's not dilated enough to push yet. Vin is stuck in traffic, and poor Val is having to deal with Lucia." She widens her eyes because we both know what her daughter can be like.

"*Nonno*, I got cookies," Gia screams into the house.

"Would you like me to keep Gia?" I ask. This is the polite Italian boy in me rearing his head. The one who has no experience with a child.

"Really?" Mrs. Milano's eyebrows raise.

NO. NO. NO.

I mentally calculate the distance to my mother's house. "Well... sure."

"You're a lifesaver. I'd hate for a grandchild to be born without any family there. I mean, Val is like family, but she's not blood." She squeezes my arm. "You're an angel." She turns her head. "MARIO, GET YOUR SHOES ON, DOM'S TAKING GIA!"

Mr. Milano saunters to the door, cookie crumbs on his extended stomach. "Dom!" His deep voice booms through the house and into the open air. "Gia was just sharing the cookies. Thank you."

I lower my head and offer my hand. "Congratulations on becoming a nonno again."

"What are you waiting for? Get your shoes." Mrs. Milano opens the closet door, pulls out her own shoes, and flings his to him. "Dom's going to watch Gia."

"Really?" He looks at me skeptically.

I'm with you, buddy.

"Oh wait. I have to get her outfit." Mrs. Milano runs up the stairs and comes down with the smallest rhinestoned leotard in a clear garment bag. I see a set of ballet shoes in one of the pockets of the bag, as well as a pair of light pink tights. She thrusts it at my chest. "Here. She needs to be there at five. Hair and makeup done."

"I'm sorry?"

"It's just a bun and some eyeliner. We may be there beforehand. Lulu's labors are fast. Just like mine."

"What's fast? Like, an hour?" I flip my wrist to glance at my watch. I've already had Gia for forty-five minutes. That suddenly feels like enough.

"Within twelve to eighteen hours."

"I give you credit, Dom." Mr. Milano pats my back as they file out the door.

"Oh wait." Mrs. Milano laughs. "Gia! You're going with Mr. Mancini."

"Yay!" She runs to the door, her bag of cookies swaying in her hand. She jumps off the first step. "Where are we going?"

"A salon?"

Mrs. Milano laughs. "Oh, don't stress. It doesn't need to be perfect."

I stand dumbfounded on the stairs while the Milanos walk down the sidewalk to wherever their car is parked.

Gia smiles up at me. "Where to?" She slides her small hand in mine, leading me down the stairs.

I glance at my watch again. It's only eleven-thirty in the morning. "You hungry? My ma is the best cook in Carroll Gardens."

She shrugs, her stomach probably full from all the cookies.

I bite into mine, the sugar the only positive thing about what just transpired. "Let's go."

We walk down the sidewalk toward my parents' place. We'll just consider this a little practice for Ma before she has any real grandchildren.

CHAPTER TWENTY-NINE

Valentina

"What?" I ask because surely all Lulu's screaming has damaged my eardrums.

Mrs. Milano grabs her daughter's hand. "Dom took Gia." She repeats herself as though it's every day a person leaves a small child in the care of a bachelor.

"And he was okay with that?"

"Delighted. His suggestion." She wipes the hair off Lulu's forehead. "Any word on Vin?"

"He's on his way," I answer because Lulu's breathing through a contraction. Her eyes are wide with questions about why Gia is with Dom. "I'll be right back."

I make my way over to the couch to grab my purse off of it.

"Ma! You left him with Gia?" I guess Lulu's contraction is finished.

"It's Dominic Mancini."

"Yeah, exactly," Lulu says.

"He's a good boy. Successful."

"And single! He doesn't know the first thing about kids."

"You worry too much. Gia's easy."

I cringe, wondering if Mrs. Milano really believes that's the truth.

"You let him bring her to us. I don't see the problem?" Mr. Milano decides to chime in.

"Because I was in labor and all he had to do was get her to you."

"He bought her cookies. A whole dozen," Mrs. Milano brags.

Once I'm in the hallway, I pull out my phone and lean back against the hospital wall.

"She told me she had to explain that Italians buy enough to share. That he only brought one cupcake to the dance studio, but she made sure he had enough cookies for everyone." Mr. Milano laughs.

I hold my phone close to my heart. How can a man I've known almost my entire life continue to surprise me? I dial Dom, and he answers on the first ring, the sound of blow dryers in the background.

"I'm sorry," I say.

He chuckles. "It's fine. I'm not gonna lie, I freaked out for a second."

I can only imagine. I'm surprised he's not at his ma's with her. "Where are you?"

"Well, I was told that her hair and makeup needs to be done for tonight, so I took her to a salon."

I smile, imagining him walking into a place filled with that much estrogen. Damn, all those women are probably wondering if he's single or not. "They were able to take you without an appointment?"

Why am I asking? Of course they took him. He's a gorgeous guy with a cute little girl.

"They fit us in. Just a bun is good, right?"

I laugh. "Yes. Perfect. Do you want me to meet you?"

"Nah, I have this handled. You should be there for Lucia."

Speaking of, she's screaming again.

"Thanks a lot, Dom." I lean back against the wall, my knees wanting to sink to the floor.

"You can thank me later," he says in a suggestive voice.

"I'm already imagining all the ways."

"Me too, and I shouldn't be having those thoughts with an eight-year-old nearby."

I chuckle. "Okay, I'll bring a bottle of alcohol as a thank you instead."

"Let's not get carried away." I can hear the smile in his voice, and a warm feeling spreads through my chest. "Go be with Lulu, I've got this handled."

Of course, what can he not handle?

"Okay. See you at five."

"I'll be there with the little maniac. I can't believe how much she's like Lulu."

I laugh. "I know. It's crazy."

"Bye, babe," he says, and the line clicks.

My mind travels to what a mini Dom would be like to raise. Lulu's screaming distracts me, which is a good thing, and I head into the room to see her parents on either side of her, *Maury Povich* playing on the TV bolted onto the wall in the corner of the room.

"Dom has Gia at a salon, getting ready for her performance."

Lulu breathes heavily a few times, grimacing, then falls back onto the bed. "She'll be the best-looking one tonight."

"Yeah, she will. But it's so sweet."

"It's good that the rest of the kids are already with Vinny's parents for a couple of weeks," Mrs. Milano says.

Lulu told me on the way over that Gia got to stick around because she's the oldest and could use some one-on-one attention before the baby was born.

A nurse comes in to check on Lulu, so Mr. Milano leaves the room.

Lulu stares at me for an uncomfortable minute while Mrs. Milano watches the *Maury Povich* show with fascination.

"What?" I ask.

"It's over, right?"

I shrug because I can't hold back my heart or the truth anymore. I can't even say I've fallen in love with Dom because I've loved him my entire life. These weeks we've spent together have only reminded me of all the reasons why. My marriage to Max never felt right from the get-go, and if not for Ryder, it never would've happened. But I can't regret my relationship with Max because Ryder is my whole life.

"What are you going to do about it?" Lulu asks.

"About what?" Mrs. Milano turns her attention from the TV for a minute.

"Val married Dom."

Mrs. Milano's eyes widen, and I want to smack Lulu. What is she thinking? "About time."

Lulu laughs. "He's an asshole, but I guess he's your asshole."

"Not yet. We're supposed to start the annulment procedures after Ryder gets back tomorrow."

"Come here." Lulu beckons me with her finger.

I walk toward her and stop at her bedside. She smacks the back of my head.

"Lu!"

"Did it knock any sense into you?"

I hold the back of my head. "What?"

"Fight for him. Stop letting him dictate what's going to happen. Put everything out there again and see what he says. Both of you need to stop playing games."

"Games are never good," Mrs. Milano chimes in, trying to stay in our conversation while at the same time trying to find out whether the brother or the husband is the real father of the child.

"What if he—"

"What if he doesn't?" Lulu says in a soft voice.

"You hate him."

"I do. Only because of the way he makes you feel. But I still trust him with my daughter. How does that add up?" Her eyebrows are perfectly arched. How the hell does she keep up everything while being pregnant? I was a mess with Ryder.

"What exactly are you saying?" I ask.

"I'm saying nothing other than you need to fight for what you want. As far as I know, you were a teenager the last time you laid your heart on the line with this man. Maybe it's time to do it again?"

"There you are." Vinny runs into the hospital room, and I slide over to let him at his wife. He kisses her forehead and looks at the monitor. "Are you okay?"

"Now that you're here, I am."

He rests his forehead on hers, and her arm wraps around him as though she needs him closer. Vinny and Lulu have been together since their senior year in high school and always wore their feelings on the outside for others to see.

Sure, Lulu can get a tad jealous at times, but they're the fairytale love story of Carroll Gardens, while Dom and I are the cautionary tale without a happy ending.

"Thanks for getting her here." He looks around and says a quick hello to his mother-in-law. "Where's Gia?"

"Dom Mancini has her," Lulu says.

"Really?"

"He's a good boy." Mrs. Milano stands by her choice to leave her with him.

Lulu and I laugh until another contraction takes over, and Vinny helps her breathe through it.

The nurse returns with the doctor. "Okay, we're going to check you out again, Lucia."

I move toward the head of the bed on the opposite side of Vinny, my head still swirling with thoughts about a future with Dom. It's something I've always wanted but never thought was a possibility. Was I wrong?

"Almost there. I'd say maybe another hour," the doctor says.

I glance at the clock. That would mean the baby is coming around three. Man, I was in labor with Ryder forever. "Maybe I should have Dom bring Gia here? She could wait in the waiting room until you deliver, then I can take her to the recital."

"That'd be great. She's already so disconnected from this baby. Maybe seeing him will spur that heart of hers to open for him." Lulu grabs my hand and gives me a smile before another contraction hits and she damn near breaks my fingers.

A part of me thinks she actually enjoys it.

AN HOUR LATER, Dom messages me to say he and Gia are in the waiting room.

Lulu is heavy in labor, so I excuse myself, letting Vinny and Mrs. Milano help Lulu through this. When I enter the waiting area, I find Gia asleep on Dom's lap. I stop before he sees me, his own eyes drifting closed. My heart flutters, and I take a minute to commit the image to memory.

Eventually, I sit in the chair next to them and lightly touch Dom's arm. He jolts, and a smile emerges when he sees me. My stomach flutters, and it's all I can do to not tell him how much I love him right now. That it's always been him.

"Tired?" I ask.

"Kids are exhausting."

I look at Gia with her hair in a bun and sparkles covering her dark strands. Her makeup is a little overdone, but she looks adorable. "I'll reimburse you for all this."

"My treat. Ma wasn't home."

I laugh and shake my head.

"Did you bet that I'd take her there?" he asks.

"No. I figured you might though."

He picks up a bag off the chair beside him, and I sneak a peek inside to see a box from the bakery by the Milanos' house.

"Cookie?" he asks.

"I heard something about her having to school you on Italian manners."

"Yeah. From now on, expect a dozen of everything."

Gia shifts in his lap.

"How long has she been out?"

"Since the taxi. I carried her up here."

I rub her back. "I bet a few ovaries exploded watching that scene."

"I do think I might be a natural at this parenting thing."

I kiss him on the lips. "I think so too." Although he has no idea what it's like to do it twenty-four hours a day on little-to-no sleep, but I'll keep that thought to myself. "Maybe you should have one and find out."

"It's impossible to have one by myself."

"You can afford a surrogate."

His hand runs along my thigh as he stares me dead in the eye. "If I have a kid, I'm doing it with my wife."

I swallow the lump in my throat. I'm not clear on whether he's implying me, since I'm technically his wife, or if he means it in more general terms. "I thought you were against marriage and kids?"

He shakes his head, his fingers pressing under my chin. Using a slight pull, he brings me into him. "Do you not pay attention to me? There's only one woman I want that with."

"Who?" I whisper.

"If you have to even ask, then I'm not doing a very good job here."

Is that a secret promise?

I press my mouth to his.

As our lips touch, Mr. Milano interrupts. "He's here!"

His voice stirs Gia, and her forehead hits mine because the three of us are so close.

"Ow," I say, holding my forehead.

"He's here?" Gia wiggles out of Dom's lap, running to her nonno.

"Yep. Do you want to meet him?" Mr. Milano asks.

"Is the Pope Catholic?" She walks right past him.

"Was that a change of attitude?" I ask Dom, assured he had something to do with it.

"We had a talk about how great siblings are."

I squeeze his thigh and rise to my feet, holding my hand out for him. "Ready to see the baby?"

"Not really, but I'm here."

We walk down the hall with his arm around my shoulders, like a real couple. It doesn't feel like a facade or as though he's acting.

A half hour later, I get Gia ready to go, and Mr. and Mrs. Milano say they'll meet us at the hall before the recital starts. Vinny says he'll make it over there too.

I turn to Dom while the three of us wait for the elevator. "Thanks a lot. I should be home around nine or ten."

He tilts his head at me.

"What? You're not coming?" Gia asks, displeasure clear in her tone.

"I'm coming," he says to her, then looks at me. "When we thought no one else was coming, I promised Gia I'd be at the recital."

Gia takes my hand then Dom's. The three of us walk into the elevator, Dom and me sharing a look over Gia's head. My heart unlocks the gilded cage around it, splaying the doors wide open. I'm ready to be honest with him about how I feel, though I can't help but worry that he'll end up breaking my heart again.

CHAPTER THIRTY

Dominic

"This will only take a minute," Val says as we step off the elevator. It's late and I can tell she's tired.

I lug the bag she meant to run over to her condo earlier today—before both our days went crazy—down the hall. "It's fine. I haven't been to your place in a while."

She inserts her key, and the door opens to a stale-smelling apartment. It's probably a good thing we came here tonight.

"You'll have to open your windows and light some candles tomorrow," I say.

She flicks on the lights, revealing her living space. Her place is so much homier than mine. There are purposeful accents to the dark gray and navy that swaths the space. She keeps it feminine with the addition of pinks and yellows and oranges. Pictures of her and Ryder, from a newborn to now, hang on the walls or are set in picture frames on tables, along with pieces of art she probably picked up at street fairs.

I forgot how much I loved her condo. Her view isn't as great as mine, but it's not much to complain about either. Her kitchen table has scratches and dents from the wear of a child. Most of all, I like that her condo looks lived in. Mine is more like the MET.

I take her duffle to her room and drop it on the bed, then I head back into the living room and sink into the couch that's lost a lot of bounce because it sees more wear than mine.

She opens the fridge and slams it shut. "I forgot to clean it out before I left." She rounds the sofa. "I did find these though." She cracks open two beers and hands one to me.

We clink the bottles together and each take a sip.

"We should've stayed here." I look around again, still in love with her place.

"You would've had to sleep in Ryder's bed." She cringes. "He's fifteen, you know, and from what I gather when I wash his sheets, there's a lot of spilled milk going on late at night."

I laugh and put my arm around her to pull her closer. "Yeah, I remember spilling a lot of milk in my bed when I was a teen. Usually when I was thinking of you."

My lips meet the top of her head. I can't lie, something has shifted between us since Luca's wedding. Sleeping together brought us closer, and I have no idea where her head is at. I'm scared shitless to have this conversation with her, but I guess I'm more afraid of walking away tomorrow and never having her in my life again, because I push the fear aside and barrel ahead.

"Can we talk?"

She draws back, sipping her beer. "Sure."

"We're supposed to call it quits tomorrow, right?" I ask.

She takes another sip of her beer and then peels away the label on the bottle.

I cover her hands with mine. "Val?"

"Yeah." Her voice cracks. I hope that's a sign to say she doesn't want it.

"Do you want the annulment?" Asking the question out loud feels like someone pointing a loaded gun to my head. I'm sweating along my hairline because this is where the bomb exploded last summer and it all went to shit. Putting myself out there again feels damn near impossible, but what are the chances of history repeating itself?

It was Max's weekend with Ryder. In the divorce, Val got the house in the Hamptons, and though I was never comfortable there, I went because when push came to shove, I always followed Val. It was either that or let my brothers know we were hooking up by bringing her back to the house we were all renting together.

I was in the kitchen, making breakfast. Pancakes with fresh blueberries that we'd picked up the day before at the farmer's market. Val was in bed still when I sneaked out to prepare my surprise. I was nervous as hell, but I'd waited patiently all weekend for that moment.

The doorbell rang, and for a moment, I feared it was Ryder, but why would he ring the doorbell? So I trudged along the hardwood floors, opening the door to find her ex-husband, Max.

"What are you doing here?" My eyes zoomed in on the giant bouquet of calla lilies in his hand.

He was close, but Val's favorite were actually madonna lilies. I'd spent an hour with a florist once, figuring out which ones she'd pointed to on a whim when we were walking through Central Park.

"I could ask you the same question. This was once my house." He stepped in without me giving him permission. It wasn't his house, but it wasn't mine either, so I didn't put up a fight.

"Was being the key to that sentence."

"Don't get too high and mighty. I spent my weekends here fucking her too," he sneered, looking around as though he did own the place.

This was why I'd been close to buying my own house in the Hamptons. I hated the idea of being anywhere Max had been. "Let's remember who had her first."

Max was just as threatened by me as I was by him. We'd both fallen in love with the same girl. "It's funny how you're always there for Val when I'm out of the picture. I think you're the sloppy seconds in this equation now."

My jaw clenched. "Why are you here?"

"Val doesn't need you messing with her head. We're a family. We share a son."

"Who said I'm messing with her head?"

"Come on. You think Val's enough for you to change? You're a bachelor. Always will be. You're not meant to settle down. Step aside and allow her to be happy again."

"What?" I laughed out loud, although it was hollow. "You're here to win her back?"

"Yeah." He nodded at the flowers. "Like I said, we're a family."

I looked at him, through him, to figure out if he really wanted to commit to Val again. He seemed earnest.

"You don't deserve her." But I knew I would set aside what I wanted so she could have what she'd always wanted—a family.

"Maybe, but that's her decision, isn't it?"

I stayed in the same spot, debating, then eventually nodded and held up my finger. "Give me a minute."

Surprisingly, he nodded and went out to the patio.

I walked into Val's bedroom and sat down next to her, running my hand along her forehead to pull back her dark hair. She opened her eyes right away, so I knew she'd heard the doorbell and had probably figured out who was here.

Our relationship had crossed a line. After she'd dumped me a few months before, citing her own confusion, I couldn't get her out of my mind. That had always been the case, but this time, it was different. So when I had the opportunity to spend my summer in the Hamptons, I jumped at the chance, knowing she spent most of the summer there too. Since the first weekend of the summer, we'd been hooking up—we never could resist one another—but in my mind, it was leading somewhere this time.

"Max is here," I said as nonchalantly as saying breakfast was ready, because if I was going to do this, I couldn't allow her to see any reason to hold out for me.

"I heard."

"I'm going to go."

"No." She gripped my hand as it slid along her leg over the sheet, and I allowed her to hold it.

"He wants to talk with you."

"So what? I don't want to talk to him."

I gave her the look—the one that said, 'I know you better than you know yourself.' Val had confessed to me that Ryder still held out hope his family would become one again, though they'd been divorced for a few years by that point. I knew that the weight of Ryder's hope that his parents would be together again was strong enough for her to give it a try with her ex. Even if that thought killed me.

"Think of Ryder," I said.

She tightened her hold on my hand. "What about us?"

I shrugged and looked out the window at the ocean, second-guessing what I was about to say. I pushed back nausea, knowing that in order to do what was best for her, I'd have to hurt her. Schooling any emotion that would reveal the lie I was about to tell her, I met her gaze. "We're just casual. We hook-up. This is your family we're talking about."

"That's all I am to you?" She released my hand. "I thought maybe—"

I shook my head before she had a chance to finish, reminding myself that this is what was right. Even if we stayed together, Val would always wonder what would've happened if she'd tried to put her family back together again, and I couldn't stand in the way of that. "Max will always be in your life. We knew that the day you found out you were pregnant."

"You honestly don't feel anything more?"

I should've known she wouldn't let go easily. She wanted me to say point-blank that what we had meant nothing.

"I told you, Val, I'm not a marriage kind of guy. I prefer casual and uncomplicated."

Her whole body sank into the bed, and the weight of all the Manhattan skyscrapers crumbled on top of me. How could I do this to her? My eyes flickered to a picture of Ryder when he was six, playing on the same beach we'd made love on last night. He was with Val but smiling at whoever was holding the camera—Max, I assumed.

"I'm sorry if you thought different," I said.

"Get out," she seethed through gritted teeth.

I rose from the bed, every footstep feeling as though I'd added another pound of cement to my shoes. After throwing on my T-shirt, I grabbed my bag, leaving behind any toiletries. If I didn't get out of there fast, I'd lose my nerve and beg her forgiveness.

Max saw me with my bag, and I wanted to punch the cocky grin off his face. Instead, I slid into the kitchen and grabbed the jewelry box off the breakfast tray I'd prepared. I looked at the diamond ring I'd designed for her, the large oval diamond in the center and the diamonds on the band glittering in the morning sun and shut the box before shoving it into my bag.

Without a glance back, I walked out of Val's house, leaving my entire heart inside.

I push back the memory because we're not there

anymore. I need to concentrate on the here and now, so I don't lose my nerve.

"What happened with you and Max last year?" The question slips out. Though I shouldn't care, I need to know.

She blinks. "What? Why?"

"Did you guys give it a shot?"

"We did. It was brief. Things were okay at first, but then Max's true colors came out again. We kept it on the downlow and didn't really go out in public so that Ryder wouldn't find out about it in case it didn't work out, thank goodness." She puts her beer on the table and faces me. She stares at me for a moment, and I realize that she's nervous.

"What's wrong?"

"I don't want the annulment."

A slow smile slips across my face. "Neither do I."

My hand slides to the back of her neck, and I bring her lips to mine. That's all I need right now. To know that just because Ryder is coming home, it doesn't mean we're over. I'll take that for now.

I get her on her back, and she splays opens her legs. "For old time's sake?" I nod at the couch, then my lips travel down her jaw and her throat, my hands unbuttoning her blouse.

"God yes." She opens her legs wider and her hands pull at my shirt.

I devour her under me, stripping us bare, needing to be skin to skin with her. Her arms tighten around my torso and I guide myself into her, sinking into her wetness and warmth. She's mine. She's finally truly mine.

"I love you," I murmur into her neck.

She freezes for a moment, her legs losing their pressure against my hips. She tightens them again, puts her hands on either side of my face, and maneuvers me so I'm staring into her eyes. "I love you... always have."

I crash my lips to hers, my hands greedy and my pace chaotic, but I can't get enough of her. I'm mid-thrust when the sound of a key entering the door makes me freeze. She pushes me off of her, but we're not fast enough.

"Mom!" Ryder screams, seeing the two of us naked on the couch.

"Great example, Val."

Max follows him in, and I grab the blanket from the back of the couch and toss it to her. The last person who will see her naked again is Max.

CHAPTER THIRTY-ONE

Valentina

"Max! What the hell are you doing here? Why wouldn't you call me?"

Dom tosses me a blanket, and I cover myself enough to slide on my clothes.

Ryder heads down the hall. "Hey, Dom. I'm out."

"Ryder," Dom says, putting on his own clothes.

"Surprise, surprise, I guess the whole Vegas wedding thing worked out for the two of you?" Max sits on a stool at the breakfast bar, facing us.

"I thought you were getting in tomorrow. What happened?" I wait for Dom to finish putting on his shirt.

"I had to come home early for work."

"And Ryder?"

"He was cool with it. He's kind of a mama's boy." He shrugs, looking at Dominic. "Funny, we're in very different places this time, huh?"

"Seems the same to me." Dom puts his hands into his pockets. "I was just inside your ex-wife before your surprise appearance."

I slap Dom in the stomach and glance down the hall.

"She was always willing to let you in more than me. That's why our marriage never worked. It's hard when there are three people involved."

"You'd know." Dom steps forward. "Don't blame me. I stepped away for thirteen years. You're the one who fucked it up."

Max slides off the stool, stepping up to Dom, but Dom is bigger in both height and weight. "You might not have physically been there, but you were always on her mind. Hell, half the time I'm surprised she wasn't screaming your name when she came."

"Stop it," I seethe under my breath. "The both of you. Ryder is down the hall."

Dom crosses his arms over his chest and pins Max with a stare.

"Well, your boy is back safe and sound. I told him I'll be at his game in two weeks. I have to go out of town for a story, so I'll let you know." I roll my eyes as he heads to the door. "Dom. Don't fuck it up again, you two."

Dom steps forward, but I grab his hand, keeping him at my side. Max leaves, and I glance down the hall for the fifth time since Ryder disappeared.

"I need to talk to him," I say, taking Dom's hands.

"I know. Call me after?" He releases my hands and presses his to my cheeks, tilting my face up. I nod. "And tomorrow, dinner at my parents' house. Bring Ryder."

I nod again. I hope Ryder wants to go.

"It's going to be hard to sleep without you." He kisses

me, his tongue sliding into my mouth and his arm falling around my waist and pulling me to him.

By the time he releases me, I'm gasping for breath, wishing we could do it all over again.

"Goodnight, Val." He kisses my forehead and steps back.

My hands want to reach out for him, but I let them fall to my sides. He has to leave, and I want to spend time with Ryder and feel him out on this whole situation.

When I shut the door behind him, hoping Max isn't lurking down the hallway and the two of them don't have words, I head to Ryder's room and knock on the door.

"Come in," he says in his tortured voice.

I open the door a crack and see him on the bed with his phone in his hands. "I'm so sorry." I sit down on his bed, embarrassment heating my cheeks.

He shrugs. "So you and Dom?"

I shift on the mattress. "Yes, but there's more I have to tell you."

"I know."

"You do?" I messed this up good. I should've known he'd find out. "You saw that blog?"

"Dad slipped." He shrugs like *what else did I expect.*

I tighten my fists. Asshole.

"Do I have to call him dad?" He looks at me with a smirk so similar to his father's, I'm surprised it makes me laugh.

"No."

He nudges me in the shoulder. "You could've told me. I'm almost sixteen, Mom. I'm over the idea of you and Dad getting back together. Besides, I like Dom. He's always been cool whenever I've seen him over the years."

"I know, but it was Vegas and I was..."

"Wasted?" He raises an eyebrow.

I push him in the shoulder. "I had a few drinks."

"It's okay. Nonna's talked about you and Dom before. He makes you happy."

Did I really raise my son to be so great?

"Well, she's always put him on a pedestal."

He shrugs. "I'm good with it, but I don't want to walk in on the two of you again. I'll be reliving that moment with my shrink twenty years from now."

I chuckle and squeeze his shoulder. "I'm sorry. I thought you'd be home tomorrow."

"But the couch? How can I sit there ever again? Just keep it in your bedroom."

I look at my fingers. "Can we not talk about that at all?"

"I'd prefer it that way."

I smile. "So tell me about Europe. What did you see? What country did you love the most?" I get comfortable on his bed, crossing my legs.

He glances at the door. "Did Dom leave?"

I nod.

"He didn't have to."

"It's fine. We'll see him tomorrow for Sunday dinner."

"So it's really happening, huh?"

"It appears so."

He nods a few times as though he's soaking in this new information. "Where are we going to live?"

"Let me handle all those details. I'll let you know as soon as we discuss it."

"I'd like to move to his place. It's probably fancier than ours. He has lots of money."

"Ryder!"

He laughs. "Spain. I loved Spain the most."

Ryder continues to tell me about his trip with his dad.

We chatted once a week while he was gone, but he never went into too much detail as to what they were doing. He tells me about all the countries they visited and how up until the last week, it was only the two of them, but then Max met someone. Ryder breezes by that fact as if it's meaningless. They didn't go to half the museums I would've taken him to, but that's Max. He likes to absorb the culture by submerging himself in it, and it appears Ryder likes that too.

We end up ordering a pizza, which Ryder says is what he missed the most. No one can make a pizza like New York can. I watch him eat, happy to have him home. Happy that he doesn't mind that Dom is technically his stepdad right now. Happy that everything in my life is even-keeled at the moment.

After dinner, I message Dom that I'll see him tomorrow. There's no more discussion about I love yous, and I figure that's a topic best left for when we discuss exactly where we're at. Saying we don't want an annulment doesn't mean we're ready to move in together and be a real family. When it comes to my relationship with Dom, I need to take things slow.

I RING THE MANCINIS' doorbell. Ryder's on his phone with his AirPods in. He doesn't notice how nervous I am with my sad excuse of a cheesecake that I bought.

Anna opens the door, wipes her hands on her apron, and opens her arms. "Valentina!"

The woman has a way of making people feel welcome.

I nudge Ryder, and he startles before taking out his

AirPods and shoving them into his pocket. He puts out his hand. "Hi."

Anna looks at me then at Ryder, laughing and shooing his hand away. "Come here." She envelops him in her small frame before he has a chance to realize what's happening. "Ryder, so happy to have you. Welcome. You've grown so much since the last time I saw you."

She releases him just as fast, and he stumbles for a second to find his footing. Ryder isn't used to a big family. Max's parents live in Texas and he rarely sees them, and though Ryder's close with my parents, there's no other family nearby.

"Hey." Dom comes out of the kitchen. He must've come from the gym because he's in track shorts and a T-shirt, freshly showered.

My breath hitches and Ryder glances over. Did he hear me?

Dom puts his hand out in front of Ryder. "Welcome, Ryder."

Ryder shakes his hand then busies himself with his phone.

Dom kisses me on the cheek. "I missed you like crazy," he whispers.

I bite my lip to calm myself.

"No phones," Anna says to Ryder.

Ryder looks at me like 'tell this lady she's crazy because I'm not spending an entire afternoon with your new husband and his family without using my phone as a distraction.'

"I have a job for you." Anna slides her arm through Ryder's and escorts him into the kitchen.

"He's good?" Dom asks, turning me around so I'm facing him, his hands locked behind my back.

I chuckle as I watch Anna pull his stiff frame into the kitchen. "Appears so."

"Good." He looks around, opens the door, and pulls me outside with him.

As he tucks us in the corner of the stairs, his lips land on mine and his fingers dip under the waist of my shorts in the back. My skin comes alive and I bring our kiss to a ravishing state.

"Jeez, get a room you two." Bella walks up with Carm, both of them laughing.

We unlock from one another, and I slyly wipe my mouth.

"Thanks for ruining the moment," Dom says, taking my hand and pulling me back into the house.

"I should check on Ryder."

"I heard your little guy is here." Bella hands Carm the wine they brought. I think they're the designated alcohol suppliers for Sunday night dinners. "I want to meet him."

"Come on. Anna has already put him to work."

"Poor guy." Bella follows me.

When we walk into the kitchen, Ryder looks at me from where he's rolling meatballs with plastic gloves on like he did the day I dropped him off at kindergarten.

"Wow, he's not so little. Damn." She washes her hands, puts on plastic gloves, and sits down next to him. "I'm Bella, Carm's girlfriend."

Ryder nods, still pleading with his eyes for me to save him.

I kiss the top of his head. He tries to dodge me, but I hold his head firm. "Thank you."

"Remember this when my birthday comes up next month," he says but continues to roll the meatballs.

"What do you do for fun?" Bella asks him.

Before he can answer, Annie barrels into the room and stops in her tracks. We share a look. Although I don't know her well, the smile on her face says she's happy Ryder's here because that means things are good with Dom and me.

"Hi, Ryder, I'm Annie." She smiles.

Ryder blows out a breath and glances at me again. He's done being the center of attention. I jab his side with my finger.

"Hi," he says as though Annie's the dentist.

"Are we making meatballs?"

She heads to the sink to wash her hands, but Anna turns around with her wooden spoon. "You're on sauce."

"Sauce?" Annie's eyes light up. She glances at Bella.

"Favorite," Bella mouths.

Annie shakes her head, but it's the truth.

"I've been teaching the girls to cook," Anna says with pride.

Dom and his brothers walk in, Enzo hugging and kissing his way around. He pats Ryder on the back. "I've heard great things about you on the football field."

"Really?" Ryder's eyes light up for the first time since we arrived.

"Yeah. I was a running back."

"Yeah, in about two thousand BC," Carm says.

"Want to go to the park and throw the football around?" Enzo asks.

Ryder looks at me. and I shrug. "Sure."

"Perfect." Enzo looks at Anna. "Ma?"

"Go." She waves him off. "The girls and I have it."

I smile as Ryder wastes no time taking off his plastic gloves and throwing them away.

"We'll be back." Dom kisses my cheek.

"Okay." I sit down in Ryder's empty seat.

The front door slams shut, and all eyes turn my way.

"So?" Annie says.

"So... we're not getting an annulment as of right now."

"Yay!" Bella screams, hugging me while trying not to get me dirty from the meat on her gloves.

"That's great," Annie says.

Anna looks at me and smiles contently with an expression that says, "See, I'm always right."

Blanca walks in. "What'd I miss?"

"The marriage is still on," Annie says.

Blanca drops her purse on a kitchen chair before washing her hands. "Well, duh."

"Yeah, but they were going to get it annulled since they were drunk and—" Bella notices Blanca's expression.

"What?" Blanca comes over with her paper towel, drying her hands with wide eyes.

"You didn't know?" Bella asks.

"No! Am I the only one?" She points at Anna's back as she pretends like she didn't know.

I nod. "We were drunk and were going to get it annulled, but now we're going to try to make it work."

Blanca plops down on a chair. "Why am I the last to know everything?"

We all share a laugh, but Blanca reminds me a lot of Gia with the cupcake thing.

CHAPTER THIRTY-TWO

Dominic

"You prick!" Blanca hits me square in the upper arm.

"What?" I hold it though she's not tough enough to hurt me.

"You never told me the marriage was a sham!"

I inhale and glance at Val setting the table. She shrugs and bites her lip. I nod to Blanca to head outside. She follows, and I sit on the ledge of my parents' small porch while she takes the swing.

"I'm sorry, but I liked that you thought it was real."

"Why?" she asks, pulling her legs up to her body.

I shrug. "It made me think we could make it. There's so much against us. So much past to overcome. I didn't deliberately leave you out."

She tilts her head. "Are you guys really going to make it work?"

I look at the street, dodging her question. After I left

Val's last night, I was able to think clearly. I want Val so badly it hurts, but so much of me still doubts we can work. Every time we're together and I feel like that wound has healed, something opens it back up like a scab that won't heal.

"We're going to try." I shrug.

"You don't sound like it."

I turn to her, crossing my arms. "What?"

"You told me to go with my gut and trust that I could change careers. You need to trust in what you and Val have."

I nod. She's naive and doesn't fully understand what a grownup relationship is like. She's been hopping between douche after douche for years. "I do trust in it."

She shrugs and stands from the swing. "It doesn't appear so from what you just told me." She walks toward the door. "And I'm sick of feeling left out of the Mancini sibling gang." She opens the door and slams it behind her.

She's right. We still treat her like the little baby, and it's about time we include her in our adult lives.

I push off the railing of the porch, but the door opens and out comes Val. She's wearing a short sundress, and I kind of want to thank her for giving me some great beat-off material for tonight. In my head, the dress is already a ball in the corner of my room.

"Hey, you. Ryder can't stop talking about playing with you guys." She slides her arms around my waist, resting her chin on my chest. "Thanks."

"He's a good kid." I lock my arms around her. "He's got a great mom. A sexy one. One I really wish I could have alone right now."

She lays her cheek on my chest and squeezes me. "We need to discuss some things."

I lead her to the swing and pat the seat, think better of it, then pat my lap.

She smiles and sits down, putting her arms around my neck. "So no annulment?"

I shake my head. "Nope."

"And living arrangements?"

I run my thumb along her hip. "You tell me what works."

"I'm not sure we should live together right now. Maybe just stay together when Ryder's with Max?"

She can't be saying no sex. I'll never survive. "I should go home to sleep then? Like that summer?"

She nods.

"So no living together?"

"Well..." Her smile dips. "I don't want to upheave Ryder's life should something happen."

"So you think something is going to happen?" I ask, a low-key panic creeping up my spine.

"No..."

I can't fault her for her doubts. I have them too. I'm so scared, but I'll never tell her that. "Okay, we can delay that. We'll date and go from there."

"I think that's best. You good with that?"

I give her a chaste kiss. "You call the shots."

She smiles, and I know I've said what she wants to hear. "The only thing I ask is that you be conscious of Ryder. I can see it on his face. He thinks you and your brothers are gods. Just—"

"You have no worries there. I understand you guys are a package deal."

She hugs me, and my face ends up in her tits. She's not making this easy. I suck lightly on her flesh and she doesn't pull away. I love that she wants sex as much as I do. My length grows hard underneath her and she grinds against it.

"Dinner!" Blanca screams out the door and shuts it.

"This is going to be hard." She kisses me then gets up off my lap.

I grab her hand and pull her back toward me, opening my legs for her to step between them. My hands slide up the backs of her thighs, dipping under the fabric of her dress. My fingers dive under her silk panties, grabbing her ass and pulling her toward me. "Can you sneak out tonight?"

"I'll try to figure out some excuse."

I run one finger along the edge of her panties, over her hip, until it graces her pussy. She sighs and her eyes flutter closed.

"What about now?"

She laughs, and I run my knuckle over her clit. "Dom."

"Are you wet for me?" I don't have to dip my finger under her panties to reveal the truth. She's wet, and now I'm hard as steel.

"You already know the answer to that."

"Yeah, I do."

"We're outside," she says, stopping my hand from continuing.

"Dinner!" Blanca screams and slams the door again.

Val steps back, my hands sliding off of her. "Trouble!" She points at me, but she's laughing.

I follow her into my parents' house, grabbing her at the waist to keep her back. We stumble in and my entire family, plus Ryder and her parents, are at the table. They all turn their heads in our direction.

"I have to use the facilities." I walk past them, doing my best to hide my hard-on, and leave Val to fend for herself.

After dinner, Val's parents ask Ryder if he wants to spend the night at their house since they've missed him. He doesn't seem thrilled, but Val must've done some convincing because he leaves with a smile. Which means I get to take my wife home and fuck her properly.

My wife. For the first time I feel a sense of peace when I think of Valentina that way because we're no longer playing house.

We leave my parents' house shortly after because I'm not a dumbass. No teenager tonight means running around naked in my condo until tomorrow.

CHAPTER THIRTY-THREE

Valentina

I click off the morning show after watching Max's announcement that he's engaged. I've yet to meet her—though Ryder did when they were in Europe—but to Max, if he's happy, then everyone else should be too.

It's been two weeks since Ryder returned, and his first football game of the season is tonight. He drops his backpack on the floor, shovels a few spoonfuls of cereal into his mouth, and heads for the door.

"Ryder!"

He sighs, kisses my cheek, then heads back to the door.

"I'll see you at the field tonight. Dom is coming too. Maybe we can all have dinner after?"

"Uh, maybe. The guys said something about doing something."

"Well, I can see why 'something' would interfere with dinner."

He laughs and shuts the door behind him but opens it back up right away. "Tell Dom he can come out and have breakfast now. I'm gone."

My mouth drops open, and I hear Ryder laugh all the way to the elevator.

Dom opens the bedroom door, wearing his wrinkled shirt and slacks, his suit jacket over his arm. "Gotta love sneaking around."

"Well, Ryder just called us out."

He laughs. "Smart kid." He pulls something out of his pocket and twirls my ring on the tip of his pointer finger. "How come you haven't been wearing the rock?"

"Snooping?" I ask, taking it from him.

Truth is, I'm not sure where we stand. Yes, we're married, but he gave me that ring when it was fake. Putting it on now feels weird.

"You know I like to smell your panties." He laughs.

I shake my head as he pours himself a cup of coffee. We've been doing the sneaking around thing since Ryder returned, and although it started off as thrilling, I'm over it.

"So... why haven't you been wearing the ring?" he asks again.

"I don't know. You always hated it, and we're still sneaking around about sleeping together. It feels weird if I wear it."

"Okay," he says with a shrug.

His answer upsets me. Shouldn't he be convincing me to wear it? That he wants me to wear it?

He grabs an apple and bites it. "I gotta get to the office. Ash keeps calling me out every time I'm late. I need to show her who's the boss."

That'll never happen. Ash owns Dom. He wouldn't survive without her.

"Yeah, you show her, big guy."

He shakes his head, coming to my side, and puts his hand on the counter behind me. "Seven tonight, right?"

"Yep. You have the address?"

He kisses my lips. "I won't be late."

"You better not be. And be civil when you see Max."

He mocks offense. "When am I not?"

"Oh, I don't know... every time you run into him."

He laughs. "I'll be on my best behavior." He kisses me again, and I really wish we could head down the hall to my bedroom.

Once Dom pulls away, I say, "He just got engaged."

"Really?" His eyebrows just about hit his hairline.

"Yeah."

"And you're okay with that?" He studies me for a second, so I wrap both arms around his neck.

"Yes," I draw my answer out. Will he ever believe me?

"Good. See you tonight, wife." He presses his body to mine, pushing me back into the counter. Our hands cling to one another and his tongue dives into my mouth.

I trail my hand down his chest and below his belly button. "You should just be late."

He chuckles and steps back. "Believe me, I could stay in bed with you all day, but then we'd be poor."

He walks out of my condo and I touch my lips, remembering the feel of him.

It isn't until ten minutes later, after I clean up the kitchen from breakfast, that I notice the ring is gone. He took it? Why would he do that?

Because he doesn't want you to wear it, dumbass. I push that nasty thought out of my head and get ready for the day.

———

FALL IS APPROACHING and we're experiencing colder than normal temperatures. I sit in the stands of the football field with a blanket over my lap. Ryder's team is warming up while the cheerleaders practice on the sidelines. All of it brings a sense of nostalgia. How many times did I sit in the stands and watch Dom play while Lulu cheered?

I'd watch as the girls waited outside the school for the players to come out of the locker room. I lingered too and watched Dom thank all the girls for coming. He'd always give me a hug and thank me for showing up. Sometimes we'd go to a party together, just to separate once we were there, or if they'd lost, we'd drive somewhere and talk or make out. Our on-and-off-again relationship always made me feel as though Dom kept me in his back pocket.

"Hey." Max approaches rubbing his palms together and takes the seat next to me.

I move my purse to the other side to save a spot for Dom. This should be interesting, but the two of them will have to learn to coexist at some point. "Hi."

"It's so damn cold." He clenches his fists and blows onto them.

"Uh-huh." I glance at the gate where people are coming in. Still no Dom.

"Did you hear the news?" Max asks.

I shift to look at him. "I did."

"And?"

"Congratulations?"

"Thanks." The corners of his smile almost reach his earlobes.

"She's young."

"That's what's so great about her."

I roll my eyes. I won't say that I give them a year. They might not even see the wedding. But I can't say much when

I'm married to a man I'm sneaking in and out of my bedroom.

"Ryder told me how Dom and his brothers have helped him out these past couple Sundays. I wish I could be there, but I was stuck in bum-fuck nowhere for the show."

Max can't show Ryder anything because he ran cross country in high school, but I'm not going to call him out on his shit. Knowing him, he was holed up in the hotel room his work was paying for with his new fiancée.

"I'm glad things seem to be working out for you two."

"Okay." I shrug.

"I mean it. I know he makes you happy."

I look at him and narrow my eyes. "Why do I feel like you're only doing this now because you have a fiancée?"

He shrugs, clearly unembarrassed. "Truce?" He puts his hand out between us.

With Ryder getting older, I don't have to worry so much about a woman taking my spot as his mother. He can handle himself. His reaction to Dom and me has been so mature, but I don't want him thinking women are interchangeable either.

Keeping my son's best interests in mind, I shake his hand.

"Good."

I nod, looking at the gate again.

"Where is the prince anyway?"

"On his way." I wonder if it's a lie though, because Dom hasn't messaged me at all today. If I add up everything, I'm afraid he's high-tailing it out of my life again. He took the ring, he refused the sex I offered this morning, he's late for the game, and he hasn't called.

But I try to push those fears out of my head, because

this isn't the old Dom and Val. This is the new, improved version. I know he'll show.

––––––––––

HE DIDN'T SHOW.

I had to stand there like an idiot without Dom, making the excuse that he shot me a text and was stuck at work.

Ryder decides he's going out with his friends after. "Do you mind if I spend the night at Dad's?"

His friends already trying to pull him away, saying they gotta go.

"Sure." I know better than to give him a hug before he takes off, so I nod and smile.

Max tells him not to be too late and to remember his curfew.

On my way to the car, I pull out my phone to text Dom again, but there's already a message waiting for me.

Dom: *Tonight's a bust. Sorry. Work.*

I don't even bother responding. This is the Dom from years before. The one who consistently put work first and treated me like an afterthought.

"You wanna go get coffee?" Max asks, pulling me back to the present.

"No. But thank you."

"Gonna go track him down?" Max stuffs his hands into his jacket, rocking back on his heels.

"I'm going to surprise him at work and fuck him on his desk. Do you want more details?"

His perma-smile erases off his face, and I flag down a taxi.

"Bye, Max. Let's keep this cordial relationship going. Next time bring the fiancée." I get in, not at all amused by him.

The taxi ride takes longer because it's Friday night and everyone and their mother comes into the city. I slide out once we reach Dom's office building. I have no idea if I can get up there. Security might be gone for the day, which means I'd have to have a key. The last time I came and surprised him after hours, I got lucky and someone was leaving. Hopefully it's the same this time around.

I get into the lobby and see a man sitting behind the security desk. Score.

"Hi." I smack on my friendliest and most flirtatious voice. I know it's wrong, but if I want to get up there, I have no choice. I glance at his name tag. "Mick. I need a big favor."

"I'm sure you do." He doesn't smile, but he doesn't turn me away either. I'd say he's in his mid-fifties and looks fitter than me. If I made a run for the elevators, he'd probably catch me.

"My husband is upstairs working late, and I really want to surprise him."

"Are you on the list?"

I frown. "The list?"

"Of approved guests. If he's here and you're on his list, you can go up. What's his name?"

"Dominic Mancini," I say although I'm certain I'm not on his list. He wouldn't add me.

"And you're?"

"Valentina," I say. "Or Val."

He clicks the mouse and reads the computer screen in front of him. "There you are, under wife." He looks at my left hand. "I thought you were lying, what with no ring. I'd be awfully upset with my wife if she didn't wear my ring. ID please." He holds out his hand.

It takes me a moment before I dig inside my purse for ID. "Our marriage is new, so I haven't changed my name yet."

Am I even going to change my name? There're so many decisions to be made.

He hands me back my ID and picks up the phone and listens, then he hangs up. He writes up a tag and hands it to me. "He's not answering, but that's common at this hour. I assume you know the way?"

"I do."

"Here you go, Valentina Mancini."

I smile sweetly because the man is doing me a favor. "Thanks, Mick."

When I get into the elevator, I think about what Mick said. He's right. We're totally doing this half-assed. If we're going to stay married, we need to be married. I need to decide on the name. I need to wear the ring. We need to move in together. We're being idiots about all of this. Both of us are still too scared to jump right in.

The elevator doors open at his floor, and the hallway is dark with the exception of a few lights. I swear everyone at this company works crazy hours. Ash's desk is all closed up, a picture of her and Molly near her keyboard. Dom's office door is open with his desk lamp on, so I assume he's here somewhere. I sit down to wait. When he doesn't come after a few minutes, I wonder if he's already left.

I figure I'll be cute and leave him some little notes to find at random times, so he knows I'm thinking about him.

His desk is spotless. Who doesn't have a pen holder or a pack of Post-it notes on their desk? I open the drawer on the left, finding the Post-it notes but no pens. I open the other drawer and spot a row of pens, highlighters, and pencils in separate compartments. I shake my head. He'll never be able to live with Ryder and me.

Beside the pens is something black and silky with a note attached. I pull it out. Written in girly script handwriting on the note attached to the black silk thong is, "You know where to find me."

I drop them and plop down in the chair.

Okay, think rationally, Val.

I pull out my phone and text him only to get a reply that confirms my suspicions.

Dom: *I'm heading home.*

Fucking liar. I snag the panties and shove them in my purse. All the convincing I did on the way up. How fucking stupid am I? Always Dom's little puppet.

CHAPTER THIRTY-FOUR

Dominic

I pour myself a double scotch and stare out the window of my penthouse.

I was happier before I got tangled in Valentina's web again. Wasn't I? All these doubts about whether she loves me as much as I love her are still swirling around my head, making me question everything that's happened over the past few months.

My condo door opens, and I turn around to find Val. Her eyes rage with fire, but they're red-rimmed and it causes a stabbing pain in my chest.

"How was work?" She drops her bag on the floor.

"Fine."

"Fine?" She crosses her arms and pins me with a stare.

"Yeah. Fine."

"Showered and changed already?"

I can't help but feel like this is an interrogation. "It was a long day and I needed to clear my head."

"Or clean off the smell?"

"What?" I walk toward her.

"Put on a shirt. I can't think with you looking like that."

"I'm not doing anything until you explain to me why you've been crying and what has you so riled up."

She plops down on the couch and tosses a pair of panties onto the coffee table. Panties that look similar to the pair Nell put in my desk only weeks ago that I threw away. Tell me that woman isn't up to her old tricks again.

I squeeze my eyes shut. "Where did you—"

"Are they hers?"

"Yes, probably but—"

"Were you with her tonight?"

My eyes snap open. "No." I sit next to her. "I told you I stopped that when you entered my life again. She left those in there on her own accord."

"It's coincidental, right? That you didn't show up tonight. Said you had to work late. I find a pair of panties in your drawer with a note from the woman you used to fuck saying that you know where to find her. Tell me how this doesn't add up to what it's equated to in my head." She heads into the kitchen.

"It might look that way, but that's not what happened tonight." I follow her, my temper simmering.

She grabs a glass and pours herself a triple scotch. She's going to spit it out. She's not a fan of hard alcohol.

"Then enlighten me. Why was work so much more important than Ryder and me tonight?" She sips it then turns and spits it into the sink.

I shake my head and grab a bottle of white wine from

the fridge, but she snatches the bottle from my hand and pours it down her throat without a glass.

"Well, if you must know, I was running late, but I got to the field right before kickoff."

The bottle drops from her mouth, hanging from her hand at her side.

"I searched the bleachers and there you were—all cozy with your ex."

"We were talking. I told you he got engaged."

"You were sharing a blanket and laughing at whatever stupid thing he said."

"So you left?" she asks.

"I didn't like it."

"That's so juvenile. What are you, a jealous sixteen-year-old?"

I down the rest of my drink and grab the bottle of scotch. "I don't trust him."

"You don't trust *me*."

"And you don't trust me." If I haven't convinced her over the past couple of months how much she means to me, I don't know how I ever could.

"I—"

"What? You found a pair of panties from a woman who's trying to get me to sleep with her. There's no proof I was sleeping with her. I told you I was at work because I was embarrassed by how it cut me to the quick, watching you with him. He's stolen you from me twice now. Who's to say he won't do it again?"

Her shoulders slump and she steps back. "He didn't steal me from you. You pushed me away and then I got pregnant."

"I told you not to marry him. That you didn't need him." My eyes narrow at her.

"And who was going to help me? You? Mister 'I'm not ready yet but give me a few years to conquer the world and then we can be a couple'? I was young, with a shattered career, and pregnant. My parents were embarrassed enough as it was. Could you imagine what it would do to them if I hadn't married him?"

"Look at what it did to us." I pour scotch into my glass then down a healthy amount, desperate for anything to relieve this clawing pain in my chest. We're right back where we always are. "All that has nothing to do with the fact that you thought I was fucking around on you. I told you I didn't want the annulment. I've been honest about my feelings for you."

"You took the ring with you this morning. You didn't call me all day. You haven't repeated the 'I love you' since the night Ryder returned. You didn't even take me on the counter this morning when I offered myself to you."

I run a hand through my hair and take another swig of scotch. It's time to lay everything out for her. "I didn't call you because in order to leave early, I had to work every minute of the day. I didn't want to disappoint you. I worked all day with a half-hard dick because I didn't sleep with you this morning only because again, I had work to finish so I could be there for you tonight. I'm scared to tell you how much I love you because I don't want to scare you away and because I'm pretty sure I care more than you do. And lastly, I took the ring because I bought you that ring last summer. I was going to ask you to be my wife that morning when Max showed up!"

She's silent, wrapping her brain about everything I just said. "But you said you hated the ring. You asked me to take it off before we had sex. I figured—"

"Because I only ever wanted you to wear it when it was

real. When I had the jeweler design the ring, it was meant to symbolize that we'd finally live our lives together. I knew you'd have to have the ring for my cousin's wedding, but I hated looking at it knowing that it wasn't a promise of our future, it was a promise of our end."

"Dom," she sighs and steps forward, but I put up my hand.

"Don't."

She stops, tears in her eyes. "All we do is hurt one another. I hurt you."

"I'm fine. I'll be fine."

"We'll figure this out." She touches my hand, but I pull back.

"No, we won't. Neither one of us will trust the other long term."

"That's not true. I had no idea you were going to propose. I was mad that you didn't fight for me. Why didn't you fight for me then?"

I stare at her. "Because you had a family. And a son who deserved to have his parents back together if it was possible. I couldn't take that away from Ryder."

"But you have to know it's always been you, Dom. Always."

I press my hand to her cheek. "And it's always been you, but we're no good for one another. Our love was tainted from the moment I let you go, and you ran into Max's arms. I don't see how we can ever get back there."

"Isn't it worth a try?" she says, stepping closer, a lone tear running down her cheek.

"I'm not sure anymore."

She inhales a deep breath, steps away from my touch, and turns on her heels. Grabbing her purse, she pulls out a stack of papers and tosses them on the breakfast island before swinging the purse over her shoulder. "Fine, have it your way... again."

I have no fight left in me to stop her, so I let her leave and slam the door, acting as her final goodbye. I walk right by the annulment papers. Go figure she had another set printed and ready to go at a moment's notice. She wants me to fight for her? Yeah, well, she should try the same sometime.

CHAPTER THIRTY-FIVE

Valentina

"Congratulations!" I said, coming up to Dom at the small graduation party his parents were having for him. "You're a college graduate."

"For about a millisecond until my job starts, and then there's graduate school in the fall."

"Always a man with a plan." I smiled at him. We'd been on and off all through college. I figured graduation was a good time for us to figure out a way to be together permanently.

"Without a plan, we'll be poor."

Dom talked about our future a lot. How we'd get married at thirty, kids at thirty-two, once my dancing career was drying up. We'd stay in Manhattan and raise our kids in the city. Close enough to both sets of grandparents that we could visit, but far enough away to have our own lives. But as much as he liked to boost me up with hopes of a future, he was always quick to take away that hope with details of whatever his next plan was.

"What do you want to do?" I ask.

"Let's go eat. I have something to talk to you about."

"What about the party?" I asked.

He shrugged. "I've said hello to everyone. No one will notice if we slip out for a bit."

We headed to the diner we often went to pig out after finals or on our rare nights out. He slid in across from me and we each ordered fries and shakes, his strawberry and mine chocolate.

"Just spit it out." I wasn't going to play his game of waiting until the end of the night when he'd drop something huge on me then go home.

"Graduate school is intense. I barely had time to see you during undergraduate. Not to mention my job. We have a plan and I think we should put us on pause until I finish. Without you as a distraction, I'll take an extra course load and graduate sooner than—"

"And then what? You tell me you have to work a few years? By pushing your life off, you're pushing mine too. I don't understand why we can't be together while you accomplish everything you want to."

"Because I'd rather be with you than study. It's distracting. Only because you're so hot." He smirked, but I didn't return his smile.

"And what if I find someone else?"

He leaned back, a perplexed look on his face. He hadn't thought about that. Should I join the nunnery while he became the success he wanted to? "Do you want to find someone else?"

"No. But I'm sick of spending Friday and Saturday nights watching you study or saying you have a paper due and we'll have to postpone whatever plans. I've been out with Lulu and Vinny more than you recently."

He sighed and mulled over my words. I thought he was changing his mind. That he'd pick up his head, grab my hand, and say I was right. He was being stupid. How could he decide to put me on a shelf until the perfect moment arrived?

But he didn't. "I know we're sacrificing a lot, but the payoff will be worth it. I promise." He reached for my hand, but I slid it off the table and tucked it in my lap. "Don't do this, Val."

"Why is being successful so important to you?"

He blew out a breath. We each thanked the waitress when she set our fries and milkshakes in front of us.

"Well?" I prodded.

"I don't know. It just is. I want to have money. Look how hard our parents work for almost nothing. I want to have savings and not sit with my wife at the dining room table, wondering how we're going to pay for the air conditioning that just quit. I want to look my kids in the eye and say I've got you covered for college. I want to be able to travel with my family and spoil my wife like she should be."

His reasons held weight. I'd seen my parents struggle for years. Witnessed Ma's tears because she couldn't afford to go visit her family in Italy. I understood the reasons for him wanting to be financially secure. But I didn't understand why we couldn't do it together.

"If you love me, why are you so willing to set me aside and chance losing me?"

He took a straw out of the holder and put it in my milkshake. I wanted to stab him with it. Tell him not to do nice things for me when he was in the process of breaking my heart.

"Because I trust that you love me as much as I love you. I trust that we're meant to be together. Forever."

I smiled because he'd been so forthcoming with his feelings. Sometimes he was better at it than me. But I was bitter and mad that he'd risk losing me and our future over money. Money couldn't buy happiness.

"Have it your way, Dom." I picked up my milkshake and poured it into his lap. "Have a nice life."

I walked out of the diner. He didn't chase me, and I didn't stop to second-guess myself. I didn't see him until six months later when I had to tell him I was pregnant with Ryder after spending one night with Max.

I slid out of the taxi with my arms wrapped around myself, the anger from that moment resurfacing. In my condo, I sit on the couch and tell myself that this is for the best. Dom doesn't cherish anything but the numbers in his bank account. That sweet kid who promised me the moon and stars is now a bitter man who holds grudges for the consequences of his own decisions.

CHAPTER THIRTY-SIX

Dominic

Two weeks later and I'd like to say my life is better than it was with Val in it, but it's not. Thoughts of her consume me, but that's no surprise. She's not been mine more than she's been mine over the years. I should be used to it by now.

"The final paperwork is here." Ash sets the envelope on my desk. "You're officially single again."

"Thanks." I nod toward my inbox, not taking my fingers off the keys.

"Can I just say—"

"No. I know you're Team Val."

"But—"

I stop and lean back in my chair. "It's over. We're not good for one another."

"Are you sure about that? Because you're always the happiest when she's in your life."

"And look at me when she runs out of my life."

Ash sighs. "The two of you need a big long talk."

"We had one of those and now we have these." I pick up the envelope and drop it into the trash basket.

"Hey, Ash!" Carm bursts into my office with Enzo right behind him. Carm gives Ash a quick hug. "I'm assuming the dickhead here has time for us?"

"He has all the time you want." Ash smiles and leaves, waving to Enzo.

My brothers each take a chair.

"You didn't rock, paper, scissors on who was going to talk to me, did you?" I eye Enzo since he always loses.

"We figured this would take both of us," Enzo says.

"You're being a jackass," Carm says.

"You don't have to concern yourself with it." I glance at the clock. "It's Thursday. Why aren't you at the Trading Post?"

"We came to pick you up and we might hijack the taxi to take us to Val's."

"I invited Blanca." I stand, grabbing my jacket, and put it on.

"You what? Why?" Carm says with a look of horror.

"Because she's a Mancini and she's old enough to be at our Thursday lunches." I open my office door and signal for them to leave.

"I can't talk about Bella and me screwing in front of Blanca, and I sure as hell don't want to hear about her sex life."

"Good, then I did us all a favor," I say and follow them out the door.

"Relax. It's Blanca. It's only fair," Enzo says.

Twenty minutes later, we're at the restaurant. Blanca's already arrived and has her drink. She's not at our usual table, but that's okay. We can fill her in on what we usually do.

"I thought you assholes stood me up. Like some lame initiation thing," she says.

"Sorry." I slide into the booth next to her. "They tried to ambush me at my office."

She raises her hand for a high five, which Carm and Enzo return. "Seriously, you need to clear up this thing with Val. She's miserable."

I spin in Blanca's direction. "You saw her?"

She points at me. "See? That right there. That face says you need to stop this charade and just figure it out. You're perfect together."

"You lied?" Enzo asks, smirking.

Blanca shrugs and nods.

Enzo high-fives her. "Well played."

The waitress comes over and we all order.

As soon as she's stepped away from the table, Blanca starts in on me again. "Seriously though, you love her. Why are you doing this to yourself and her?"

"I feel like I'm on repeat. We're not good together." I push a hand through my hair, sick of this line of conversation.

"Give it another try," Carm says.

"I fuck it up with her every time. I stupidly let her go when we were young and lived thirteen years without her. Just when I had her back, I let her go again to give her a second chance with her ex. And this time…"

"*You're* letting her go. It's on you. You're not fighting to keep her. For someone so smart, how do you not learn from your mistakes?" Blanca throws her hands into the air, apparently exasperated.

The boys let her take the lead, which makes me wonder if they actually did the rock, paper, scissors thing.

"It's too late," I grumble, looking around for the waitress and wondering where my drink is.

"I get it. It's scary to put yourself out there. And I've never met anyone worth it but look at these two." She motions to Carm and Enzo. "Look how happy they are."

They both put on exaggerated grins.

"I'm happy."

"You're not happy," all three say in unison.

"You were when you were with Val." Blanca pulls out her phone and her thumbs run over the screen until she thrusts it in my direction. "Look at these fools in love."

I stare at a picture from Luca's wedding. Val in my arms, smiling, and the two of us looking at one another. I was happy. Happy to have her back in my arms where I always thought she belonged.

"Cut the bullshit and go get her back," Carm says.

"She'll never take me. I accused her of wanting Max back. I didn't show up at Ryder's game. She doesn't think I believe in us."

"Funny you should mention Ryder." Blanca looks away from the table.

All three of them get up and head over to the bar. Ryder turns around on a bar stool then makes his way over and sits down across from me.

"Shit, my siblings schooled me."

He nods. "They did."

"Does your mom know you're here?"

He shakes his head.

"You shouldn't be involved in this."

"I reached out to Blanca on Instagram." He stares at the table for a minute then looks at me. "I get that I have no idea what your history is with my mom. I know there's something, because my parents fought about you a lot. My mom has a shoebox on the top shelf of her closet, filled with pictures of the two of you. She has letters and notes that you guys wrote to each other in high school. There was a time I wished my parents could stay married, but not now. They're not the ones who should be together. That's you and her. If it's about me, I'm going to college in two years."

"It's not you," I say.

He nods. "Then what is it?"

I lean back in the booth. "Like you said, it's complicated."

Staring at the kid who unknowingly changed your life's course is hard. Because of Ryder, Val married Max and our future separated into two paths. But I recognize that I'm the one who set her on that course in the first place.

"When we were playing football, you told me that to be a good running back, I can't be afraid. I needed to trust my instincts. Trust my coaching. Trust myself. I know you're going to say I'm young, but why don't you trust yourself? Because if after all these years my mom is still the one you want to be with, why don't you trust yourself that it's the right decision?"

Shit. I inhale and exhale. He's right. I don't trust myself to make her happy because I'm the reason she went into Max's arms in the first place. I'm the reason she lost her dance career and fell into motherhood at such a young age. The reason she lived with a cheating husband and wasn't happy. I know she'd never change anything—because she has Ryder—but we both suffered through those years.

"You're right. You're totally right."

"Really?" he asks, looking surprised.

Blanca comes over and presses her hand on Ryder's

shoulder. I have a feeling she coached him on what to say. Good thing my sister is smarter than me.

"Did you guys rock, paper, scissors to see who was going to deliver the speech?"

Blanca laughs and looks at our brothers. "Hell no. I volunteered. That's the difference between the Mancini men and the Mancini women."

"So what are you going to do?" Ryder asks.

My mind is going crazy. Could Val and I actually have our forever? "I'm gonna win her back and make sure I never lose her again."

"There you go, big bro." Blanca high-fives me. "What are you waiting for? You need a big plan."

"Help me?"

"What are sisters for?" She waves me up, and the two of us leave the restaurant with Ryder.

"Whoa, what about us?" Carm asks from behind us. "You can't just toss us aside."

"Great, I'll cover the bill for all the shit we're not eating," Enzo says.

I hail a taxi, trying to figure out how to convince Val to take one last chance on me. On us.

CHAPTER THIRTY-SEVEN

Valentina

I hate Sundays now, and I'm not sure my parents are big fans of them either. We sit at the table for four in my parents' house. Ryder's been acting strange for the past three days. Asking me questions about my dance schedule when he never cared before. I think he's worried about me. I try to mask my sadness around him, but I know I wear it like a layer of foundation.

It reminds me a lot of the aftermath of telling Dom I was pregnant. I was miserable but trying for the sake of everyone around me to pretend that everything was all right. I was excited to be carrying a new life inside me after the shock wore off, but I wasn't doing it with the man I'd always imagined I would be.

I felt like I was going to throw up the closer I came to Dom's apartment door. I'd been avoiding his calls for weeks now—ever since I'd found out I was pregnant.

I'm not sure what was going to be worse, telling him or telling my parents.

No, we weren't together, and I technically had nothing to feel guilty about but knowing that and feeling it were two different things. It hadn't been my intention to sleep with Max the night we met but I'd still been rebounding from my break-up with Dom after he told me that he wanted to set our relationship aside for grad school. Lucia took me out to get drunk and I had, so with a little encouragement from her I'd thrown caution to the wind when Max wanted to take me home. I was determined to prove to myself that I could move on from Dom by sleeping with someone else.

Sober me hated what I'd done when I crawled out of his bed the next day.

But I never really thought that Dom and I were done after our last break-up. That was what we did. Broke up and got back together.

At that moment I knew that would be the end of us.

With a deep voice and the small amount of lunch I'd been able to keep down swirling in my stomach I knocked on his door and held my breath.

He looked surprised to see me when he opened the door and I couldn't help but think how good he looked in his jogging pants, bare feet and t-shirt. "Val." He exhaled a big breath and drew me into a hug. "I've been calling your parents for a couple of weeks trying to get a hold of you. Didn't you get my messages?" He pulls away and holds me by my shoulders at arm's length.

I nodded. "I did. I had some things to figure out before I talked with you." A crease formed between his eyebrows. "Can I come in?"

"Yeah, of course." He stepped back to let me pass him and I walked into the small apartment he was renting close to Columbia. "I actually have some-thing I need to say to you."

I turned around and faced him once I'd reached his living room and I knew. I knew from the expres-sion on his face that he was going to apologize and ask if I wanted to get back together.

And under any other circumstances the answer would've been yes.

Instead the knowledge that we would never be what we once were tore at my insides until I felt like I was drowning in my own blood. My throat constricted and my eyes watered until they overflowed.

Dom frowned. "What's wrong? I know what I said about us not being together—"

I placed my hand over his mouth and savored what would probably be our last physical contact. Because once Dom heard what I had to say I knew he'd never feel the same way about me.

My stomach revolted and I placed a hand over it, very near to where new life was growing inside me.

"I need to tell you what I came here to say before you say anything further." I let my hand drop and went to sit on his couch. It was cheap student *version of furniture, but I had no doubts that one day it'd be replaced with something worth envying.*

He came to sit beside me, and I looked at him one last time, committing his face and the way he looked at me to memory.

"What's going on Val?"

With a deep breath I dove in. "A couple of months ago I went out with Lulu to try and get you off my mind. I was still pining away for you and not understanding why you pushed me away and Lulu was sick of it, so we decided the best way to get over you would be to go out and have some fun. With a little liquid courage I went home with someone that night."

I watched as his face twisted into anger and I fisted my hands in my lap.

His jaw was clenched, and it was clear he was trying to reign himself in. "I could've lived without you telling me that."

I knew I had to barrel forward, or I'd never get the words out. "But I have to tell you. And the reason is... "

Time seemed to slow, and I became aware of everything around me in that second. The way his nostrils flared in anticipation of whatever I was going to say, how the sunlight through the window hit the edge of the coffee table and reflected up onto his chest, and the ticking sound of the clock in the background.

"I'm pregnant."

He stared at me unblinking for a second before he shot up off of the couch and roared, "You're what?"

I looked down to my hands, unable to stand the raw pain that was radiating out of him. When I finally had the courage to look back up the betrayal I saw there was almost my undoing. But I had no choice but to be strong. This baby didn't ask to be born and I was going to do my best to give him or her the best life I could.

When I'd met Max and went home with him I wasn't intending for it to be anything other than that. Even when he'd given me his number the next day I had never planned to use it. But he'd stepped up when I'd told him I was pregnant and was in agreement with me that we had to find a way to make it work.

Borrowing all the courage I had inside I looked up at Dom and steeled myself. "I'm pregnant and the father and I are going to be married."

His jaw hung open, but he said nothing.

"I wanted you to hear it from me and not someone else. I haven't even told my parents yet, but I'm going to after I leave here." I stood from the couch.

My movement seemed to pull Dom from his stupor, and he reached out and held me by the shoulders. "You can't marry him. You don't have to marry him. I'll find a way to take care of you."

I wasn't able to help the tear that slipped from my eye. There was nothing I'd love more than to let Dom do what he'd offered.

"This baby deserves to have both parents in its life. I have to try to make it work for the baby's sake."

"No, you don't." His fingertips pressed harder into my skin.

I looked at him with a sad smile. "You could never raise another man's baby, Dominic. I think we both know that. Eventually it would come between us."

I had no doubt that he would try, but Dom was a proud man, and at some point the fact that I'd gone and gotten pregnant by another man would eat away at the foundation of our relationship until there was nothing to salvage.

He stared at me hard. "Don't do this, Valentina. We can figure out a way to make it work. Don't commit your life to someone else. The two of us were supposed to end up together. I'd give you a beautiful life."

I choked back a sob. "I'm sorry. I can't. I have to go."

I raced out of the apartment and down the stairs, not willing to wait for the elevator in case Dom would try to come after me.

He didn't.

"We were wondering if you could help us with something," ma says.

Ma's voice drags me from my thoughts of the past. She sounds hesitant, so I put down my silverware. "What is it?"

"Now that you're not married to Dominic anymore and the two of you are well and truly over, we need to get a loan."

"A loan? Why, and what does that have to do with Dom?" I ask, glancing at Ryder, but he's on his phone. Figures.

"Oh, we figured he told you." Ma seems genuinely surprised that I don't know what she's talking about.

I tilt my head. "Told me what?"

"Do you remember back when the store wasn't doing well? Anna suggested that we meet with Dom. Said he might have some contacts or some advice to offer us about getting a loan to get us through the tough times."

My forehead crinkles. "When was this?"

Ma looks at my dad. "Maybe ten years ago?"

"Okay. And?"

"We met with Dom and he ended up giving us the loan."

"I'm sorry?"

Ma looks at my dad again, seeming unsure if she should continue.

Oh, she's continuing.

"He told us that a bank would charge us a high-interest rate and make paying it back difficult. He gave us the money interest-free and he's been letting us pay him back slowly as we can afford it. But now that you two have been married and divorced—or annulled, I guess—it doesn't seem right."

I'm speechless. Why would Dom do that for my parents? I've heard the rumors of Anna sending Dom to people to offer advice. Surely he's not the funder of all the businesses his ma sends his way. Some people swear at him and others swear by him. It's a fine line when dealing with money.

"How much do you still owe?" I ask.

My dad shrugs. "I think around ten thousand now."

"Jesus, how much did you take?"

Ma's cheeks redden, and she draws back.

"I'm sorry," I say. "I didn't mean to yell. How much was Dom willing to loan you?"

"Around twenty-five thousand. The economy was so bad. It took a long time to recover—"

"It's okay, Ma. I understand. But I'm your daughter. We could have helped you. I was married to Max then, and we were doing okay."

She waves me off. "You two were having your own problems. We didn't want a loan to your parents to be the cause of a fight. And Dom suggested it. We were only looking for advice."

I nod and remain silent, a tear slipping from my eye.

Ma's hand lands on mine with a squeeze. "What happened between you two anyway?"

"Nothing. We just broke up." I swipe the tear away.

Ryder touches my arm. "Don't cry."

"I'm fine. Honestly. It's all for the best." I stand and clear my plate, picking up Ryder's as well.

"Sweetie, we haven't eaten yet." Ma stops me before I head to the kitchen.

"Oh." I glance at our full plates. "Sorry." I put the plates back down. "I'm just going to go to the bathroom. I'll be right back."

They let me go, sharing a look of 'what are we supposed to do?'

There's nothing for them to do. I miss Dom so much my entire body aches. I barely get out of bed every morning. If it wasn't for Ryder, I wouldn't. I put up a front every time he's around. I've thrown away more wine bottles in the last two weeks than my entire life and I feel as though I'm hiding an alcohol problem.

My parents' doorbell rings, and I use Kleenex to wipe my tears. No need for anyone else to see how upset I am.

Walking out of the bathroom and down the hall, I stop when I see Annie, Bella, and Lulu at the door. Little Gia is at Lulu's side and baby Anthony is strapped to her chest in one of those wrap concoctions.

"What? What are you guys doing here?" I ask.

"Sorry for interrupting your dinner," Annie says.

"We're not sorry. Sit down." Lulu points at the couch. "This is ridiculous. I've had it and I'm about to call us *ex*-best friends if you continue to hide shit from me."

Gia crosses her arms and nods.

Seriously?

"Blanca reached out to Lulu. Turns out she didn't know that you and Dom had filed your papers and broken up." Bella purses her lips as though she wants to say whoopsie.

"Lulu, just stop. We're over for good. You should be happy."

Lulu digs in her purse and pulls out a twenty. "Ryder, take your grandparents down to that new gelato place. We need to have a talk with your mom, and you three don't need to hear what I'm about to say."

"What about Gia?" Annie asks, concern marring her smooth forehead.

"Oh, she's fine. She's heard it all before."

Annie and Bella share a look.

Ryder plucks the money out of Lulu's hand, and surprisingly, my parents follow him out the door.

Gia sits on the chair across from me, her feet not touching the floor, while Lulu continues to stand so that she's lording over me. "Okay, this bull—crap that's going on between the two of you is over. I know Dom has pushed you away. And I know he's mad that you got pregnant. The two of you love one another and I'm through with all this 'it's complicated' and 'it just didn't work out' and 'it's not meant to be' stuff." She distorts her voice as though she's an actor in an animated movie. "You two belong together. He made a mistake by letting you go so young. He knows it. You know it. You married Max when you shouldn't have. He knows it. You know it. You had your reasons. Own the decision. Last year, you gave your marriage one final attempt. It hurt Dom so much because he fell in love with you. He knows it and you know it. Own it and, for the sake of all of us, move on. Be together. Leave the past behind."

"Lulu—"

"No!" She raises her hand. "You're not talking. I am."

Gia high-fives her mom, nodding.

"I think she understands," Bella says.

At least someone here is on my side.

"No, she doesn't. An excuse will come out any second." Lulu turns back to me. "You have one chance. One final chance to make your dream of a future with you and Dom happen. It's all in your hands at this point. Gia."

Gia stands as if on cue, opens the front door, and comes in with a box she can barely hold. Bella helps her, and they plop it on my parents' coffee table.

"What is this?" I ask.

"Just remember what I said. This is your final chance. If you can't forgive him and yourself for everything and move on, then don't open that box. If you think you can, open it and do something with it. Erase the past with the future, Val."

Lulu sits next to me on the couch, and Gia kneels at my feet. Annie and Bella each slide closer.

"Open it." Annie nudges me.

I pull off the lid with Gia's help. Two envelopes lay on top of pink tissue paper. Dom's handwriting is on each and he's labeled them number one and number two.

I look around at everyone in the room. "What did he do?"

"We're going to wait outside." Annie squeezes my shoulder and rises.

Lulu signals for Gia to get up, and they all go outside.

I sit back on my parents' couch, sliding my finger along the seam of the first envelope.

Valentina,

I took us for granted. I took you for granted. My love for you is all-consuming. Whether we're together or apart, you're always the first thing on my mind when I wake up and the last thing I think of when I go to bed.

I don't want to rehash our past in this letter, but I do need you to know that I'm sorry. I should've seen how loving you was more important than any dollar I made. I've felt so much resentment all these years that I lost sight of the future we could still have.

I'm done convincing that sixteen-year-old boy inside me to shut up. To not let you know how much I love you. How when you walk in a room, my body relaxes and peace washes over me. That when you smile at me, I can't help but need to get you to do it more. When we kiss, it's never enough, whether it's a short kiss hello or a lingering kiss goodbye. You're the first and only girl I've ever loved, and I want you to be my last. That decision is up to you.

Open envelope number two if you think you might be willing to give this ex-husband another chance.

Love always,
Dominic

I GRAB a Kleenex from the side table and pat my eyes, dropping letter one onto the table and opening letter two.

Inside are two tickets to Vegas with a Post-it note attached.

Marry me?
The right way this time.
One ticket is for you and one is for Ryder.
If your answer is yes, open the box and make sure you pack this.

I drop the tickets and tear open the tissue paper. What lies inside the box is a stunning candlelight gown with beading that will show off my lithe figure. I stand and hold it up to myself. He has great taste.

"Girls!" I yell, and the front door opens.

"Oh, it's gorgeous." Bella's mouth drops as she stares at it. "So what's your answer?"

"It better be yes!" Lulu says, rocking the baby and patting his bum.

I nod, unable to form the words. All of them run toward me, jumping up and down.

"Okay, but you're going to have to say it at the altar too." Lulu laughs.

"Let's get her to the airport," Annie says.

"Where's Ryder?" I ask, scrambling to get all my stuff.

"He has a cab and is ready to go," Lulu says.

"Wait. Did you *all* know?"

"Of course we did. Do you think I'd let you be ambushed? Hello... best friend card." Lulu rolls her eyes.

Before I know it, we're all leaving the house to head to the airport.

"Wait. My parents." I stop before I get inside the cab.

"They're fine. You'll see them when you get back. I'll fill them in," Lulu says.

TWO HOURS LATER, I'm at the airport with the carry-on Ryder packed for me trailing behind me. Good luck to me.

Ryder's beside me and delaying us, still trying to decide what meal he wants to bring on the flight.

"We're going to miss our flight," I say.

I have no idea whether Dom is waiting for me in Vegas or what he has planned. I'd hoped he'd be at the terminal, but he wasn't, and when I called him, he didn't pick up. I'm still crossing my fingers that he's on the plane because I want to kiss and hug him and tell him how sorry I am too.

"We have five minutes." Ryder spares me half a glance and continues to stroll through the store. "C'mon. You're going to have to pick something on the plane."

He says nothing, and we end up at our gate as the employee is getting ready to close the door to the jetway.

"See!" I run, flagging her down. "We're here!"

She stops and smiles, holding out her hand. I give our boarding passes, relieved when she lets us pass. We rush down the jetway. God, if Dom is on this plane, he probably thinks I'm not coming.

"Ryder," I say through gritted teeth.

"I'm coming."

As I step through the door to the plane and into the aisle, I see Dom sitting in a first class seat with a sea of empty chairs behind him. The curtain has already been drawn between first class and economy. Relief causes my body to sag, and I smile at the man I love.

"Have fun, you two." Ryder slides by me down the aisle, bumping me until I fall into Dom's lap.

"Just where I want you," Dom says.

"I'm so sorry," I say, but he puts his finger to my lips.

"None of that. Just answer my question. That's all I want." He opens his palm and there lies the ring. The one he had designed for me. The one I thought was a loaner. The one that was always meant to be mine. "Marry me?"

"Yes! Of course!" I smash my lips to his before he has a chance to put it on my finger, then pull back for a second. "Third time's a charm, right?"

He grins and leans in to meet my lips again.

When our kiss comes to a close, he says, "God, I missed you. Never again."

"Champagne?" The flight attendant brings over a tray with two glasses.

We both look at one another and laugh. "No."

She looks confused, but then the curtain opens and my parents and Dom's parents and Enzo and Annie and Bella and Carm and Blanca and Lulu and Vinny all emerge. I don't see Gia or baby Anthony, so I'll have to get those details from her later.

"We'll take some," Carm says, signaling to our families to move into first class.

"This time we do it right?" I ask Dom, repeating his words from the letter.

"Can I slide this on now?" He holds up the ring.

I hold out my left hand.

"Okay, everyone to their seats. We need to prepare for takeoff," the flight attendant says, trying to get my family in order.

I cringe because it's like herding cats.

"Once this goes on, it never comes off. Deal?" Dom says.

"Deal."

He slides it on my finger, kisses me, and his lips trail

down my jaw. "Seeing it on your finger for real this time... let's just say we'll be joining the mile-high club."

"Sounds good to me." I smile so wide my cheeks hurt. I sit down in my seat and get buckled in.

He leans over and kisses me slowly. "I love you."

"Forever."

EPILOGUE

Dominic

A year or so later...

"It's so hot, can you please turn up the air conditioning again?" Val sits on the sofa, her hands on her bulging belly.

"I'm out." Ryder walks out of his bedroom in a parka and sweatpants. Right before he's about to go out the door, he strips down to a T-shirt and athletic shorts.

"Wait. Hug before you leave." Val puts out her arms.

Ryder looks at me like *she's kidding, right?*

I raise my hands in a *just make it fast* motion.

He runs over, pats her on the back, kisses her cheek, and runs to the door.

"Have fun at your father's."

"Yep. Bye, Dom. Hope you got the mink blanket for tonight." He laughs and leaves the condo.

I don't adjust the air conditioning again because she's six months pregnant, not nine. But I'll give her that it's hotter than hell in New York right now since we're in the middle of the worst heatwave in years.

Things are great with us. We're happy, and that's all that matters. I spend fewer hours at the office than I used to. Less being an eight in the morning to six at night workday. But when I have the choice between spending time with Val or my computer, she wins every time.

Mama is beyond excited about her first grandchild. I might've been a late starter, but I got the job done before any of my siblings.

Before I have a chance to sit down with my wife, another knock sounds on the door. The worst part about us being pregnant and married and having everyone know it is that I have to share her with all our family.

"It's Blanca," Val says. "She just texted me she was here."

"Okay, thanks."

I'm not even in the loop with my own sister anymore.

I open the door, and Blanca steps in and wraps her arms around herself.

"It's freezing in here. You have icicles on your eyebrows." She points, and I feel my face because she could legitimately be telling the truth. She hits me in the stomach and steps past me. "I'm kidding. You and Ryder need to stop giving her hell."

Blanca makes her way over to the couch and curls up beside Val, pulling a blanket over her.

"I love you, Blanc, but you gotta get away from me with that blanket. You and your brother, I swear."

"Be careful, she punched me when I tried to cuddle last night." I sit in the chair across from them, propping my feet up on the table.

Val narrows her eyes at me, but I challenge her right

back until we both laugh. Blanca slides over to the other end of the couch.

"How's the job?" I ask. My little sis got a job at a small magazine. I'm proud of her, and she seems to love it.

"It's good. I'm enjoying it."

"Any cute boys work there?" Val asks with a smile. After Blanca played such a major role in us getting together, Val wants to help her find someone. Unfortunately, we don't know anyone her age.

"Well..."

"Oh spill." Val turns on the couch to face her. "I'm over Netflix. I've watched everything. I want some real gossip."

"It's just this guy I work with."

"And?" Val prods.

I roll my eyes. I don't really want to hear all the details. "Office romance isn't a good way to start, Blanc. Tell me he isn't your boss?"

"No, it's not that cliché."

"But it's a little cliché?" Val asks, and I watch her mind whirling.

Blanca shrugs. "Kind of."

"An office romance! Are you guys pinned against one another?" Val asks.

Blanca chuckles. "No."

"Oh! Oh! Are you *his* boss?" Val raises her hand as if we're in a game show.

I roll my eyes again.

"Nope." Blanca shakes her head.

"What about... is he an ex?" Val asks.

Blanca's smile falls. "Sort of?"

"Is he an ex of one of your friends?" I ask.

Blanca's face drains of color, and she nods.

"Dom! You can't opt out of playing and then steal the

winning answer. I was playing!" Val crosses her arms over her tummy that holds my son or daughter.

"Sorry," I mumble.

And then Blanca buries her head in a pillow and cries. Val looks at me and I widen my eyes. This is her territory. I do the business advice. She's the relationship advice go-to.

She slides closer to Blanca and wraps her arm around her shoulders. "Like how close of a friend?"

"My best friend. One of my roommates."

Val shoots me a look over Blanca's head, and I don't need to be a relationship expert to know that a friend's ex is a no-fly zone.

The End

COCKAMAMIE UNICORN RAMBLINGS

For all of you who read our ramblings in the back of Dirty Flirty Enemy you understand now why we told you Dom and Val were going to pull at your heartstrings.

We love to write tropes that we haven't written before and we decided early on that we wanted an impromptu Vegas wedding in one of the books in this series, hence... Wild Steamy Hook-up. We loved the idea of an opening scene where our hero was hung over and finds out he married someone. So, we had this storyline decided upon before we knew anything else about the series.

We strive to make every hero we write different. Sometimes we plan them out and other times they show up on the page that way. Rayne remembers telling Piper, "Dom is really quiet. He's kind of just there as the older brother." That's when we decided that Dom's Vegas bride had to be tied to a second chance romance trope. He just wasn't the type who would marry a stranger, no matter how many drinks were involved. Carm maybe, but not Dom.

Dom and Val's story was different than any other book we've written as Piper Rayne, but we enjoyed writing a more twisted journey toward a happily ever after. It was fun exploring how mistakes, misconceptions and fear can keep you away from the love of your life. Especially when we get to wrap it all up with a shiny bow at the end. These two probably weren't our funniest couple ever, but that just wasn't their journey. At least we could always count on Carm and the addition of Lulu and Gia to bring in some humor.

And yes Blanca will get her own happily ever after some time in 2020 so we don't have to say goodbye to these Mancini boys just yet!

We can't give you all these books without our awesome team!

Wander Aguiar for an amazing photo
    Travis S for modeling being our muse for Dom (newbie).
    Shari Ryan from Mad Hat Covers
    Cassie from Joy Editing
    Ellie from Love N Books
    Shawna from Behind the Writer
    Dani Sanchez and the Wildfire Marketing gang
    All the bloggers who carve out time to read and review our books.
    All our early ARC readers
    And of course, all our unicorns who stick with us on this journey. <3

ABOUT THE AUTHOR

Piper Rayne, or Piper and Rayne, whichever you prefer because we're not one author, we're two. Yep, you get two USA Today Bestselling authors for the price of one. Our goal is to bring you romance stories that have "Heart-warming Humor With a Side of Sizzle" (okay...you caught us, that's our tagline). A little about us... We both have kindle's full of one-clickable books. We're both married to husbands who drive us to drink. We're both chauffeurs to our kids. Most of all, we love hot heroes and quirky heroines that make us laugh, and we hope you do, too.

www.piperrayne.com
Amazon
Goodreads
Facebook
Instagram
Pinterest
Bookbub

ALSO BY PIPER RAYNE

White Collar Brothers

Sexy Filthy Boss

Dirty Flirty Enemy

Wild Steamy Hook-up

The Rooftop Crew

My Bestie's Ex

A Royal Mistake

The Rival Roomies

Our Star-Crossed Kiss

The Do-Over

A Co-Workers Crush

Hockey Hotties

My Lucky #13

The Trouble with #9

Faking it with #41

Sneaking around with #34

Second Shot with #76

Offside with #55

Kingsmen Football Stars

You had your chance, Lee Burrows

You can't kiss the Nanny, Brady Banks

Over my Brother's Dead Body, Chase Andrews

The Baileys

Lessons from a One-Night Stand

Advice from a Jilted Bride

Birth of a Baby Daddy

Operation Bailey Wedding (Novella)

Falling for My Brother's Best Friend

Demise of a Self-Centered Playboy

Confessions of a Naughty Nanny

Operation Bailey Babies (Novella)

Secrets of the World's Worst Matchmaker

Winning My Best Friend's Girl

Rules for Dating your Ex

Operation Bailey Birthday (Novella)

The Greenes

My Beautiful Neighbor

My Almost Ex

My Vegas Groom

The Greene Family Summer Bash

My Sister's Flirty Friend

My Unexpected Surprise

My Famous Frenemy

The Greene Family Vacation

My Scorned Best Friend

Blue Collar Brothers

Flirting with Fire

Crushing on the Cop

Engaged to the EMT

Made in United States
North Haven, CT
20 July 2023

39317670R00178